Praise for #1 *New York Times* bestselling author

NORA ROBERTS

"America's favorite writer."

—*New Yorker*

"When Roberts puts her expert fingers on the pulse of romance, legions of fans feel the heartbeat."

—*Publishers Weekly*

"Nora Roberts is among the best."

—*Washington Post*

"Roberts' bestselling novels are some of the best in the romance genre."

—*USA TODAY*

"Roberts' style has a fresh, contemporary snap."

—*Kirkus Reviews*

"You can't bottle wish fulfillment, but Nora Roberts certainly knows how to put it on the page."

—*New York Times*

NORA ROBERTS

SUMMER COVE

Includes *Impulse* & *The Name of the Game*

Silhouette Books

SILHOUETTE™

Recycling programs
for this product may
not exist in your area.

Summer Cove

ISBN-13: 978-1-335-23086-7

Copyright © 2022 by Harlequin Enterprises ULC

Impulse
First published in 1989. This edition published in 2022.
Copyright © 1989 by Nora Roberts

The Name of the Game
First published in 1988. This edition published in 2022.
Copyright © 1988 by Nora Roberts

For questions and comments about the quality of this book, please contact us
at CustomerService@Harlequin.com.

Silhouette
22 Adelaide St. West, 41st Floor
Toronto, Ontario M5H 4E3, Canada
www.Harlequin.com

Printed in U.S.A.

CONTENTS

IMPULSE

CHAPTER ONE

She knew it was crazy. That was what she liked best about it. It was crazy, ridiculous, impractical and totally out of character. And she was having the time of her life. From the balcony of her hotel suite Rebecca could see the sweep of the beach, the glorious blue of the Ionian Sea, blushed now with streaks of rose from the setting sun.

Corfu. Even the name sounded mysterious, exciting, glamorous. And she was here, really here. Practical, steady-as-a-rock Rebecca Malone, who had never traveled more than five hundred miles from Philadelphia, was in Greece. Not just in Greece, she thought with a grin, but on the exotic island of Corfu, in one of the most exclusive resorts in Europe.

First-class, she thought as she leaned out to let the sweet breeze ruffle over her face. As long as it lasted, she was going first-class.

Her boss had thought she was suffering from temporary insanity. Edwin McDowell of McDowell, Jableki and Kline was never going to understand why a promising young CPA would resign from her position with one of the top accounting firms in Philadelphia. She'd made a good salary, she'd enjoyed excellent benefits, and she'd even had a small window in her office.

Friends and associates had wondered if she'd suffered a breakdown. After all, it wasn't normal, and it certainly wasn't Rebecca's style to quit a solid, well-paying job without the promise of a better one.

But she'd given her two weeks' notice, cleared out her desk and had cheerfully walked out into the world of the unemployed.

When she'd sold her condo and then in one frantic week, auctioned off every possession she owned—every stick of furniture, every pot and pan and appliance—they'd been certain she'd gone over the edge.

Rebecca had never felt saner.

She owned nothing that didn't fit in a suitcase. She no longer had any tax-deferred investments or retirement plans. She'd cashed in her certificates of deposit, and the home entertainment center she'd thought she couldn't live without was now gracing someone else's home.

It had been more than six weeks since she'd even looked at an adding machine.

For the first—and perhaps the only—time in her life, she was totally free. There were no responsibilities, no pressures, no hurried gulps of cold coffee. She hadn't packed an alarm clock. She no longer owned one. Crazy? No. Rebecca shook her head and laughed into the breeze. For as long as it lasted, she was going to grab life with both hands and see what it had to offer.

Aunt Jeannie's death had been her turning point. It had come so suddenly, so unexpectedly, leaving Rebecca without any family. Aunt Jeannie had worked hard for most of her sixty-five years, always punctual, always responsible. Her position as head librarian had been her whole life. She'd never missed a day, never failed to do her duty. Her bills had been paid on time. Her promises had always been kept.

More than once Rebecca had been told she took after her mother's older sister. She was twenty-four, but she was—had been—as solid and sturdy as her maiden aunt. Two months into retirement, two months after dear Aunt Jeannie began to make plans to travel, to enjoy the rewards she'd worked so hard to earn, she was gone.

After Rebecca's grief had come the anger, then the frustration, then slowly, the realization that she was traveling the same straight road. She worked, she slept, she fixed well-balanced meals that she ate alone. She had a small circle of friends who knew she could be counted on in a crisis. Rebecca would always find the best and most practical answer. Rebecca would never drop her own problems in your lap—because she didn't have any. Rebecca, bless her, was a port in any storm.

She hated it, and she'd begun to hate herself. She had to do something.

And she was doing it.

It wasn't running away as much as it was breaking free. All her life she'd done what was expected of her and tried to make as few waves as possible while doing it. All through school a crushing shyness had kept her more comfortable with her books than with other teenagers. In college a need to succeed and justify her aunt's faith had locked her tightly into her studies.

She had always been good with figures—logical, thorough, patient. It had been easy, perhaps too easy, to pour herself into that one area, because there, and really only there, had she felt confident.

Now she was going to discover Rebecca Malone. In the weeks or months of freedom she had, she wanted to learn everything there was to know about the woman within. Perhaps there wasn't a butterfly inside the cocoon she'd wrapped herself in so comfortably, but whatever she found—whoever she found—Rebecca hoped she would enjoy her, like her, perhaps even respect her.

When the money ran out, she'd get another job and go back to being plain, practical Rebecca. Until that time she was rich, rootless and ready for surprises.

She was also hungry.

Stephen saw her the moment she entered the restaurant. It wasn't that she was particularly striking. Beautiful women passed through the world every day and they usually warranted a glance. But there was something about the way this one walked, as if she were ready for anything, even looking forward to it. He stopped, and because business was slow at this hour he took a second, longer look.

She was tall for a woman, and more angular than slender. Her skin was pale, and that made him think she had only just arrived at the resort or was shy of the sun. The white sundress that left her shoulders and back bare accented the lack of color and gave dramatic contrast to her short cap of raven hair.

She paused, then seemed to take a deep breath. Stephen could almost hear her satisfied sigh. Then she smiled at the headwaiter, and followed him to her table, tossing her head back, so that her hair, which she wore arrow-straight, swung away from her chin.

A nice face, Stephen concluded. Bright, intelligent, eager. Especially the eyes. They were pale, an almost translucent gray. But there was nothing pale in their expression. She smiled at the waiter again, then laughed and looked around the restaurant. She looked as if she'd never been happier in her life.

She saw him. When Rebecca's gaze first skimmed over the man leaning against the bar, her automatic shyness kicked in and had her looking away. Attractive men had stared at her before—though it wasn't exactly a daily event. She'd never been able to handle it with the aplomb—or even cynicism—of most of her contemporaries. To cover her momentary embarrassment, she lifted her menu.

He hadn't meant to linger more than a few moments longer, but the impulse came suddenly. Stephen flicked a hand at the waiter and had him scurrying over, nodding quickly at Stephen's murmured request and hurrying off. When he returned it was to deliver a bottle of champagne to Rebecca's table.

"Compliments of Mr. Nickodemus."

"Oh." Rebecca followed the waiter's gaze over to the man by the bar. "Well, I—" She brought herself up short before she could stammer. A sophisticated woman wouldn't stutter over a gift of champagne, she reminded herself. She'd accept it graciously, with dignity. And maybe—if she wasn't a complete fool—she'd relax enough to flirt with the man who offered it.

Stephen watched the expressions pass across her face. Fascinating, he mused, and realized that the vague boredom he'd been feeling had vanished. When she lifted her head and smiled at him, he had no idea that her heart was pounding. He saw only a casual invitation, and he answered it.

He wasn't just attractive, Rebecca realized as he crossed to her table. He was gorgeous. Eye-popping, mouth-dropping gorgeous. She had an image of Apollo and ancient Greek warriors. Thick blond hair streaked by the sun fell over the collar of his shirt. Smooth, bronzed skin was marred—and somehow enhanced— by a faint scar under his jawline. A strong jaw, she thought. A strong face, with the darkest, deepest blue eyes she'd ever seen.

"Good evening, I'm Stephen Nickodemus." His voice wasn't accented, it was rounded, rich. He might have come from anywhere. Perhaps it was that, more than anything else, that intrigued her.

Lecturing herself on poise and image, she lifted her hand. "Hello. I'm Rebecca, Rebecca Malone." She felt a quick flutter when he brushed his lips over her knuckles. Feeling foolish, she drew her hand away and balled it in her lap. "Thank you for the champagne."

"It seemed to suit your mood." He studied her, wondering why he was getting such a mix of signals. "You are by yourself?"

"Yes." Perhaps it was a mistake to admit it, but if she was going to live life to the fullest she had to take some risks. The restaurant wasn't crowded, but they were hardly alone. Take the plunge, she told herself, and tried another smile. "The least I can do is offer you a glass."

Stephen took the seat across from her, brushing the waiter aside to pour the wine himself. "You are American?"

"It shows."

"No. Actually, I thought you were French until you spoke."

"Did you?" That pleased her. "I've just come from Paris." She had to force herself not to touch her hair. She'd had it cut, with trepidation and delight, in a French salon.

Stephen touched his glass to hers. Her eyes bubbled with life as cheerfully as the wine. "Business?"

"No, just pleasure." What a marvelous word, she thought. *Pleasure.* "It's a wonderful city."

"Yes. Do you go often?"

Rebecca smiled into her glass. "Not often enough. Do you?"

"From time to time."

She nearly sighed at that. Imagine anyone speaking of going to Paris "from time to time." "I nearly stayed longer, but I'd promised myself Greece."

So she was alone, restless, and on the move. Perhaps that was why she had appealed to him, because he was, too. "Is Corfu your first stop?"

"Yes." She sipped at her drink. A part of her still believed it was all a dream. Greece, champagne, the man. "It's beautiful. Much more beautiful than I imagined it could be."

"It's your first trip, then?" He couldn't have said why that pleased him. "How long do you stay?"

"As long as I like." She grinned, savoring the feeling of freedom. "And you?"

He lifted his glass. "Longer, I think, than I had planned." When the waiter appeared at his side, Stephen handed over the menu, then spoke to him in soft, quick Greek. "If you don't object, I'd like to guide you through your first meal on the island."

The old Rebecca would have been too nervous to sit through a meal with a stranger. The new Rebecca took a second, deeper sip of champagne. "I'd love it. Thank you."

It was easy. Easy to sit, to laugh, to sample new and exotic tastes. She forgot that he was a stranger, forgot that the world she was living in now was only temporary. They didn't speak of anything important—only of Paris, and the weather, and the wine. Still, she was sure it was the most interesting conversation of her life. He looked at her when he spoke to her, looked at her as though he were delighted to spend an hour talking of nothing. The last man she'd had dinner with had wanted her to give him a discount when she did his taxes.

Stephen wasn't asking her for anything more than her company for dinner. When he looked at her it seemed unlikely that he'd care if she knew how to fill out Schedule C.

When he suggested a walk along the beach, she

agreed without a qualm. What better way to end an evening than a walk in the moonlight?

"I was looking out at this from my window just before dinner." Rebecca stepped out of her shoes, then dangled them from her fingers as she walked. "I didn't think it could look more beautiful than it did at sunset."

"The sea changes, like a woman, in the light." He paused to touch a flame to the end of a slim cigar. "So men are drawn to her."

"Are you? Drawn to the sea?"

"I've spent my time on her. I fished in these waters as a boy."

She'd learned at dinner that he'd grown up traveling the islands with his father. "It must have been exciting, moving from place to place, seeing new things almost every day."

He shrugged. He'd never been sure whether the restlessness had been born in him or had been a product of his upbringing. "It had its moments."

"I love to travel." Laughing, she tossed her shoes aside, then stepped into the surf. The champagne was making her head swim and the moonlight felt as soft as rain. "I adore it." She laughed again when the spray washed up to dampen her skirts. The Ionian Sea. She was standing in it. "On a night like this I think I'll never go home."

She looked so vibrant, so alive, standing in the surf with her white skirts billowing. "Where's home?"

She glanced over her shoulder. The flirtatious look was totally unplanned and completely devastating. "I haven't decided. I want to swim." On impulse, she dived into the surf.

Stephen's heart stopped when she disappeared. He'd already kicked off his shoes and started forward when she rose up again. For a second time, his heart stopped.

She was laughing, her face lifted to the moonlight. Water cascaded from her hair, from her skin. The drops that clung to her were the only jewels she wore. Beautiful? No, she wasn't beautiful. She was electric.

"It's wonderful. Cool and soft and wonderful."

With a shake of his head, he stepped in far enough to take her hand and pull her toward shore. She was a little mad, perhaps, but engagingly so. "Are you always so impulsive?"

"I'm working on it. Aren't you?" She combed her hand through her dripping hair. "Or do you always send champagne to strange women?"

"Either way I answer that could be trouble. Here." He shrugged out of his jacket and draped it over her shoulders. Unframed, washed clean, her face glowed in the moonlight. There was a graceful kind of strength in it, to the sweep of cheekbone, the slightly pointed chin. Delicate—except for the eyes. One look there showed power, a power that was still. "You're irresistible, Rebecca."

She stared at him, confused all over again, as he gathered the neck of the jacket close around her throat. "I'm wet," she managed.

"And beautiful." With his hands still on the jacket, he brought her toward him. "And fascinating."

That made her laugh again. "I don't think so, but thanks. I'm glad you sent me the champagne and guided me through my first meal." Her nerves began to jangle. His eyes stayed on hers, journeying only once to her mouth, which was still damp from the sea. Their bodies were close, close enough to brush. Rebecca began to shiver, and she knew it had nothing to do with wet clothes and the breeze.

"I should go in...change my dress."

There was something about her. The impulsiveness, the easy flirtatiousness, hid an unmistakable innocence that baffled and attracted him. Whatever it was, he wanted more.

"I'll see you again."

"Yes." She prayed for her heartbeat to slow. "It's not a very big island."

He smiled at that, slowly. She felt, with a mixture of relief and regret, the relaxation of his hands. "Tomorrow. I have business early. I'll be done by eleven, if that suits you. I'll show you Corfu."

"All right." Better judgment and nerves be damned. She wanted to go with him. "I'll meet you in the lobby." Carefully, because she suddenly wasn't sure she could manage it, she stepped back. Moonlight silhouetted him against the sea. "Good night, Stephen."

She forgot to be sophisticated and dashed toward the hotel.

He watched her go. She puzzled him, puzzled him as no woman had since he'd been a boy and too young to understand that a woman was not meant to be understood. And he wanted her. That wasn't new, but the desire had come with surprising speed and surprising force.

Rebecca Malone might have started out as an impulse, but she was now a mystery. One he intended to solve. With a little laugh, he bent to scoop up the shoes she'd forgotten. He hadn't felt quite so alive in months.

CHAPTER
TWO

Stephen wasn't the kind of man who rearranged his schedule to spend the day with a woman. Especially a woman he barely knew. He was a wealthy man, but he was also a busy man, driven by both pride and ambition to maintain a high level of involvement in all his projects. He shouldered responsibility well and had learned to enjoy the benefits of hard work and dedication.

His time on Corfu wasn't free—or rather hadn't been planned as free. Mixing business and pleasure wasn't his style. He pursued both, separately, with utter concentration. Yet he found himself juggling appointments, meetings, conference calls, in order to have the afternoon open for Rebecca.

He supposed any man would want to get to know a woman who flirted easily over a champagne flute one moment and dived fully dressed into the sea the next.

"I've postponed your meeting with Theoharis until five-thirty this evening." Stephen's secretary scribbled on a notepad she had resting on her lap. "He will meet you for early cocktails in the suite. I've arranged for hors d'oeuvres and a bottle of ouzo."

"Always efficient, Elana."

She smiled and tucked a fall of dark hair behind her ear. "I try."

When Stephen rose to pace to the window, she folded her hands and waited. She had worked for him for five years, she admired his energy and his business acumen, and—fortunately for both of them—had long since gotten over an early crush. There was often speculation about their personal relationship, but though he could be friendly—even kind when it suited him—with Stephen, business was business.

"Contact Mithos in Athens. Have him telex that report by the end of the day. And I want to hear from Lereau by five, Paris time."

"Shall I call and give him a nudge?"

"If you think it's necessary." Restless, he dug his hands in his pockets. Where had this sudden discontent come from? he wondered. He was wealthy, successful, and free, as always, to move from place to place. As he stared out at the sea, he remembered the scent of Rebecca's skin. "Send flowers to Rebecca Malone's suite. Wildflowers, nothing formal. This afternoon."

Elana made a note, hoping she'd get a look at this Rebecca Malone before long. She had already heard through the grapevine that Stephen had had dinner with an American woman. "And the card?"

He wasn't a man for poetry. "Just my name."

"Anything else?"

"Yes." He turned and offered her a half smile. "Take some time off. Go to the beach."

Pad in hand, she rose. "I'll be sure to work it in. Enjoy your afternoon, Stephen."

He intended to. As she left him, Stephen glanced at his watch. It was fifteen minutes before eleven. There was work he could do to fill in the time, a quick call that could be made. Instead, he picked up Rebecca's shoes.

After three tries, Rebecca settled on an outfit. She didn't have an abundance of clothes, because she'd preferred to spend her funds on travel. But she had splurged here and there on her route through Europe. No tidy CPA suits, she thought as she tied a vivid fuchsia sash at the waist of her sapphire-colored cotton pants. No sensible shoes or pastel blouses. The last shock of color came from a primrose-hued blouse cut generously to layer over a skinny tank top in the same shade as the slacks.

The combination delighted her, if only because her firm had preferred quiet colors and clean lines.

She had no idea where she was going, and she didn't care.

It was a beautiful day, even though she'd awoken with a dull headache from the champagne, and the disorientation that went with it. A light, early breakfast on her terrace and a quick dip in the sea had cleared both away. She still had trouble believing that she could lounge through a morning as she pleased—and that she'd spent the evening with a man she'd just met.

Aunt Jeannie would have tut-tutted and reminded her of the dangers of being a woman alone. Some of her friends would have been shocked, others envious. But they would all have been astonished that steady Rebecca had strolled in the moonlight with a gorgeous man with a scar on his jawline and eyes like velvet.

If she hadn't had his jacket as proof, she might have thought she'd dreamed it. There had never been anything wrong with her imagination—just the application of it. Often she'd pictured herself in an exotic place with an exotic man, with moonlight and music. Imagined herself, she remembered. And then she'd turned on her calculator and gotten down to business.

But she hadn't dreamed this. She could still remember the giddy, half-terrified feeling that had swarmed through her when he'd gathered her close. When his mouth had been only an inch from hers and the sea and the champagne had roared in her head.

What if he had kissed her? What tastes would she have found? Rich, strong ones, she mused, almost able to savor them as she traced a fingertip over her lips. After just one evening she was absolutely certain there would be nothing lukewarm about Stephen Nickodemus. She wasn't nearly so certain about Rebecca.

She probably would have fumbled and blushed and stammered. With a shake of her head, she pulled a brush through her hair. Exciting men didn't tumble all over themselves to kiss neat, practical-minded women.

But he'd asked to see her again.

Rebecca wasn't certain whether she was disappointed or relieved that he hadn't pressed his advantage and kissed her. She'd been kissed before, held before, of course. But she had a feeling—a very definite feeling—that it wouldn't be the same with Stephen. He might make her want more, offer more, than she had with any other man.

Crossing bridges too soon, she decided as she checked the contents of her big straw bag. She wasn't going to have an affair with him, or with anyone. Even the new, improved Rebecca Malone wasn't the type for a casual affair. But maybe— She caught her lower lip between her teeth. If the time was right she might have a romance she'd remember long after she left Greece.

For now, she was ready, but it was much too early to go down. It would hardly make her look like a well-traveled woman of the world if she popped down to the lobby and paced for ten minutes. This was her fantasy, after all. She didn't want him to think she was inexperienced and overeager.

Only the knock on the door prevented her from changing her mind about her outfit one more time.

"Hello." Stephen studied her for a moment, unsmiling. He'd nearly been certain he'd exaggerated, but she was just as vibrant, just as exciting, in the morning as she had been in the moonlight. He held out her shoes. "I thought you might need these."

She laughed, remembering her impulsive dunk in the sea. "I didn't realize I'd left them on the beach. Come in a minute." With a neatness ingrained in her from childhood, she turned to take them to the bedroom closet. "I'm ready to go if you are."

Stephen lifted a brow. He preferred promptness, but he never expected it in anyone but a business associate. "I've got a Jeep waiting. Some of the roads are rough."

"Sounds great." Rebecca came out again, carrying her bag and a flat-brimmed straw hat. She handed Stephen his jacket, neatly folded. "I forgot to give this back to you last night." Should she offer to have it cleaned? she wondered when he only continued to look at her. Fiddling with the strap of her bag, she decided against it. "Does taking pictures bother you?"

"No, why?"

"Good, because I take lots of them. I can't seem to stop myself."

She wasn't kidding. As Stephen drove up into the hills, she took shots of everything. Sheep, tomato plants, olive groves and straggly sage. He stopped so that she could walk out near the edge of a cliff and look down at a small village huddled near the sea.

She wouldn't be able to capture it on film; she wasn't clever enough. But she knew she'd never forget that light, so pure, so clear, or the contrast between the orange tiled roofs and the low white-washed walls and the deep, dangerous blue of the water that flung itself against the weathered rock that rose into harsh crags. A stork, legs tucked, glided over the water, where fishing boats bobbed.

There were nets drying on the beach and children playing. Flowers bloomed and tangled where the wind had planted them, more spectacular than any planned arrangement could ever be.

"It's beautiful." Her throat tightened with emotion, and with a longing she couldn't have defined. "So calm. You imagine women baking black bread and the men coming home smelling of fish and the sea. It looks as though it hasn't changed in a hundred years."

"Very little." He glanced down himself, surprised and more than a little pleased that she would be touched by something so simple. "We cling to antiquity."

"I haven't seen the Acropolis yet, but I don't think it could be any more spectacular than this." She lifted her face, delighted by the way the wind whipped at it. Here, high above the sea, she absorbed everything—the salty, rough-edged bite of the wind, the clarity of color and sound, and the man beside her. Letting her camera dangle from its strap, she turned to him. "I haven't thanked you for taking the time to show me all of this."

He took her hand, not to raise it to his lips, just to hold it. It was a link he hadn't known he wanted. "I'm enjoying seeing the familiar through someone else's eyes. Your eyes."

Suddenly the edge of the cliff seemed too close, the sun too hot. Could he do that just by touching her? With an effort, Rebecca smiled, keeping her voice light. "If you ever come to Philadelphia, I'll do the same for you."

It was odd. She'd looked almost frightened for a moment. Fragile and frightened. Stephen had always carefully avoided women who were easily bruised. "I'll consider that a promise."

They continued to drive, over roads that jarred and climbed and twisted. She saw her first of the *agrimi*, the wild goat of Greece, and the rocky pastures dotted with sturdy sheep. And everywhere, rich and defiant, was the intense color of flowers.

He didn't complain when she asked him to stop so that she could snap pictures of tiny blue star blossoms that pushed their way through cracks in the rock. He listened to her delight as she framed a thick, thorny stem topped with a ragged yellow flower. It made him realize, and regret, that it had been years since he'd taken the time to look closely at the small, vital things that grew around him.

He looked now at Rebecca standing in the sunlight, her hat fluttering around her face and her laugh dancing on the air.

Often the road clung to cliffs that plunged dizzily into the sea. Rebecca, who was too timid to fight rush-hour traffic, found it exhilarating.

She felt almost like another person. She *was* another person, she thought, laughing as she held on to her hat to keep the wind from snatching it away.

"I love it!" she shouted over the wind and the noise of the engine. "It's wild and old and incredible. Like no place I've ever been."

Still laughing, she lifted her camera and snapped his picture as he drove. He wore sunglasses with amber lenses and had a cigar clamped between his teeth. The wind blew through his hair and chased the smoke behind them. He stopped the Jeep, took the camera and snapped a picture of her in turn.

"Hungry?"

She dragged her tousled hair back from her face. "Starving."

He leaned over to open her door. A current passed

through her, sharp and electric, strong enough to make him pause with his arm across her body and his face close to hers. It was there again, he thought as he waited and watched. The awareness, ripe and seductive. And the innocence, as alluring as it was contradictory. In a test—a test for both of them—he lifted a hand to stroke her cheek. It was as soft as her scent.

"Are you afraid of me, Rebecca?"

"No." That was true; she was nearly sure of it. "Should I be?"

He didn't smile. Through the amber lenses she saw that his eyes were very intense. "I'm not entirely sure." When he pulled away he heard her release an unsteady breath. He wasn't feeling completely steady himself. "We'll have to walk a little first."

Confused, her mind churning, she stepped out onto the dirt path. A woman on a simple date didn't tremble every time a man got close, Rebecca told herself as Stephen lifted the picnic basket out of the back. She was behaving like a teenager, not a grown woman.

Troubled by his own thoughts, Stephen stopped beside her. He hesitated, then held out a hand. It felt good, simply good, when she put hers in it.

They walked through an olive grove in a companionable silence while the sun streamed down on dusty leaves and rocky ground. There was no sound of the sea here, but when the wind was right she could hear the screech of a gull far away. The island was small, but here it seemed uninhabited.

"I haven't had a picnic in years." Rebecca spread the cloth. "And never in an olive grove." She glanced around, wanting to remember every leaf and pebble. "Are we trespassing?"

"No." Stephen took a bottle of white wine from the basket. Rebecca left him to it and started rummaging in search of food.

"Do you know the owner?"

"I'm the owner." He drew the cork with a gentle pop.

"Oh." She looked around again. It should have occurred to her that he would own something impressive, different, exciting. "It sounds romantic. Owning an olive grove."

He lifted a brow. He owned a number of them, but he had never thought of them as romantic. They were simply profitable. He offered her a glass, then tapped it with his own. "To romance, then."

She swept down her lashes, battling shyness. To Stephen, the gesture was only provocative. "I hope you're hungry," she began, knowing she was talking too fast. "It all looks wonderful." She took a quick sip of wine to ease her dry throat, then set it aside to finish unpacking the basket.

There were sweet black olives as big as a man's thumb, and there was a huge slab of sharp cheese. There were cold lamb and hunks of bread, and fruit so fresh it could have been just plucked from the stem.

Gradually she began to relax again.

"You've told me very little about yourself." Stephen topped off her wine and watched her bite into a ripe red plum. "I know little more than that you come from Philadelphia and enjoy traveling."

What could she tell him? A man like him was bound to be bored with the life story of the painfully ordinary Rebecca Malone. Lies had never come easily to her, so she skirted between fact and fiction. "There's little more. I grew up in Philadelphia. I lost both of my parents when I was a teenager, and I lived with my aunt Jeannie. She was very dear, and she made the loss bearable."

"It's painful." He flicked his lighter at the end of a cigar, remembering not only the pain, but also the fury he had felt when his father had died and left him orphaned at sixteen. "It steals childhood."

"Yes." So he understood that. It made her feel close to him, close and comfortable. "Maybe that's why I like to travel. Every time you see a new place you can be a child again."

"So you don't look for roots?"

She glanced at him then. He was leaning back against the trunk of a tree, smoking lazily, watching carefully. "I don't know what I'm looking for."

"Is there a man?"

She moved her shoulders, determined not to be embarrassed. "No."

He took her hand, drawing her closer. "No one?"

"No, I..." She wasn't certain what she would have said, but could say nothing at all when he turned her palm upward and pressed his lips to its center. She felt the fire burst there, in her hand, then race everywhere.

"You're very responsive, Rebecca." He lowered her hand but kept it in his. He could feel the heat, but he wasn't sure whether it had sprung to her skin or to his own. "If there's no one, the men in your Philadelphia must be very slow."

"I've been too...busy."

His lips curved at that. There was a tremor in her voice, and there was passion in her eyes. "Busy?"

"Yes." Afraid she'd make a fool of herself, she drew her hand back. "This was wonderful." Trying to calm herself, she pushed a hand through her hair. "You know what I need?"

"No. Tell me."

"Another picture." She sprang to her feet and, steadier, grinned. "A memento of my first picnic in an olive grove. Let's see...you can stand right over there. The sun's good in front of that tree, and I should be able to frame in that section of the grove."

Amused, Stephen tapped out his cigar. "How much more film do you have?"

"This is the last roll—but I have scads back at the hotel." She flicked him a quick laughing glance. "I warned you."

"So you did." Competent hands, he thought as he watched her focus and adjust. He hadn't realized he could be as attracted to competence as he was to beauty. She mumbled to herself, tossing her head back so that her hair swung, then settled. His stomach tightened without warning.

Good God, he wanted her. She'd done nothing to make him burn and strain this way. He couldn't accuse her of taunting or teasing, and yet...he felt taunted. He felt teased. For the first time in his life he felt totally seduced by a woman who had done nothing more than give him a few smiles and a little companionship.

Even now she was chattering away as she secured her camera to the limb of a tree. Talking easily, as though they were just friends, as though she felt nothing more than a light, unimportant affection. But he'd seen it. Stephen felt his blood heat as he remembered the quick flash of arousal he'd seen on her face. He'd see it again. And more.

"I'm going to set the timer," Rebecca went on, blissfully unaware of Stephen's thoughts. "All you have to do is stand there. Once I get this damn thing set, I'm going to run over so it'll take one of both—There." She interrupted herself, crossed her fingers and ran to Stephen's side in a dash. "Unless I messed up, it'll snap all by itself in—"

The rest of the words slid down her throat as he crushed her against him and captured her mouth.

CHAPTER
THREE

Heat. Light. Speed. Rebecca felt them, felt each separate, distinct sensation. Urgency. Demand. Impatience. She tasted them, as clearly as wild honey, on his lips. Though she'd never experienced it, she had known exactly what it would be like to be with him, mouth to mouth and need to need.

In an instant the world had narrowed from what could be seen and understood to a pure, seamless blanket of emotion. It cloaked her, not softly, not in comfort, but tightly, hotly, irresistibly. Caught between fear and delight, she lifted a hand to his cheek.

God, she was sweet. Even as he dragged her closer,

aroused by the simplicity of her acceptance, he was struck by—disarmed by—her sweetness. There had been a hesitation, almost too brief to be measured, before her lips had parted beneath his. Parted, invited, accepted.

There was a sigh, so soft it could barely be heard, as she stroked her hands up his back to his shoulders. Curious, simple, generous. A man could drown in such sweetness, fall prisoner to such pliancy. And be saved by it. Beneath the patterned shade of the olive tree, she gave him more than passion. She gave him hope.

Charmed, he murmured some careless Greek phrase lovers might exchange. The words meant nothing to her, but the sound of them on the still air, the feel of them stroking across her lips…seduction. Glorious seduction.

Pleasure burst in her blood, in her head, in her heart, thousands of tiny bubbles of it, until she was straining against him.

The quiet explosion rocked him. It tightened his chest, fuddled his mind. She fitted into his arms as if she'd been born for him. As if, somehow, they had known each other before, loved before, hungered before. Something seemed to erupt between them, something molten, powerful, dangerous. But it wasn't new. It was ancient, a whispering echo of ageless passions.

She began to tremble. How could this be so right, so familiar? It wasn't possible to feel safe and threatened at the same time. But she did. She clung to him while a dim, floating image danced through her head. She had kissed him before. Just like this. As her mind spun, she heard her own mindless murmurs answer his. As freely, as inescapably as the sun poured light, response flowed from her. She couldn't stop it. Frightened by her sudden loss of control, she struggled against him, against herself.

He slipped his hands up to her shoulders, but not to free her, to look at her. To look at how their coming together had changed her. It had changed him. Passion had made her eyes heavy, seductive. Fear had clouded them. Her lips were full, softened and parted by his. Her breath shivered through them. Under his hands he could feel the heat of her skin and the quick, involuntary trembling of her muscles.

No pretense here, he decided as he studied her. He was holding both innocence and delight in his hands.

"Stephen, I—"

"Again."

Then his face filled her vision and she was lost.

Differently. Should she have known that one man could hold one woman in so many different ways? That one man could kiss one woman with such stunning variety? There was gentleness now, as familiar and as novel as the urgency. His lips persuaded rather than demanded. They savored instead of devouring. Her surrender came as quietly, and as unmistakably, as her earlier passion. The trembling stopped; the fear vanished. With a complete trust that surprised them both, she leaned against him, giving.

More aroused by her serenity than by the storm that had come before, Stephen pulled back. He had to, or what had begun would finish without either of them saying a word. As he swore and pulled out a cigar, Rebecca placed a hand on the olive tree for support.

Moments, she thought. It had been only moments,

and yet she felt as though years had passed, racing backward or forward, perhaps spinning in circles. In a place like this, with a man like this, what difference did it make what year it was? What century?

Half-terrified, she lifted a hand to her lips. Despite her fear, they curved under her touch. She could still taste him. Still feel him. And nothing, nothing, would ever be quite the same again.

He stared out at the rough and dusty land he'd known as a boy, and beyond, to the stark, tumbling rocks where he and other wild things had climbed.

What was he doing with her? Furious with himself, he drew on the cigar. What was he feeling? It was new, and far from comfortable. And it was comfort he preferred, he reminded himself. Comfort and freedom. Bringing himself under control, he turned to her again, determined to treat what had happened as a man should—lightly.

She just stood there, with the sun and the shade falling over her. There was neither recrimination nor invitation in her eyes. She didn't flinch or step forward, but merely stood, watching him with the faintest of smiles, as if… As if, Stephen realized, she knew what questions he was asking himself—and the answers.

"It grows late."

She felt the ache and fought not to let it show on her face. "I guess you're right." She dragged a hand through her hair—it was the first sign of her agitation—then walked over to pick up her camera. "I should have a picture to remember all this by," she said, forcing brightness into her voice. Her breath caught when his fingers closed over her arm and whirled her around.

"Who are you?" he demanded. "What are you?"

"I don't know what you mean." The emotion burst out before she could stop it. "I don't know what you want."

With one jerk he had her tumbling against him. "You know what I want."

Her heart was in her throat, beating wildly. She found it strange that it was not fear but desire that she felt. She hadn't known she was capable of feeling a need that was so unreasonable, so reckless. It was almost purifying to experience it, and to see it mirrored in his eyes.

"It takes more than one afternoon." Didn't it? Her voice rose as she tried to convince herself. "It takes more than a picnic and a walk in the moonlight for me."

"One moment the temptress, the next the outraged innocent. Do you do it to intrigue me, Rebecca?" She shook her head, and his fingers tightened. "It works," he murmured. "You've hardly been out of my mind since I first saw you. I want to make love with you, here, in the sun."

Color flooded her face, not because she was embarrassed, but because she could imagine it, perfectly. And then what? Carefully she leveled her breathing. Whatever impulses she had followed, whatever bridges she had burned, she still needed answers.

"No." It cost her to go against her own needs and say it. "Not when I'm unsure and you're angry." She took a deep breath and kept her eyes on him. "You're hurting me, Stephen. I don't think you mean to."

Slowly he released her arm. He was angry, furious, but not at her refusal. The anger stemmed from the need she pulled from him, a need that had come too fast and too strong for him to channel. "We'll go back."

Rebecca merely nodded, then knelt to gather the remains of the picnic.

He was a busy man, much too busy to brood about a woman he barely knew and didn't understand at all. That was what Stephen told himself. He had reports to read, calls to make and paperwork—which he had both a talent and a distaste for—to deal with. A couple of simple kisses weren't enough to take a man's mind off his work.

But there hadn't been anything simple about them. Disgusted, Stephen pushed away from his desk and wandered to the terrace doors. He'd left them open because the breeze, and the fragrances it brought, helped him forget he was obligated to be inside.

For days he'd worked his way through his responsibilities, trying to ignore the nagging itch at the back of his mind—the itch that was Rebecca. There was no reason for him to stay on Corfu. He could have handled his business in Athens, or Crete, or in London, for that matter. Still, he'd made no plans to leave, though he'd also made no attempt to approach her.

She…concerned him, he decided. To be drawn to an attractive woman was as natural as breathing. To have the attraction cause discomfort, confusion, even annoyance was anything but natural. A taste of her hadn't been enough. Yet he hesitated.

She was…mysterious. Perhaps that was why he couldn't push her from his mind. On the surface she appeared to be an attractive, free-spirited woman who grabbed life with both hands. Yet there were undercurrents. The hints of innocence, of shyness. The sweetness. The complexity of her kept him wondering, thinking, imagining.

Perhaps that was her trick. Women had them...were entitled to them. It was a waste of time to begrudge them their illusions and their feminine magic. More than a waste of time, it was foolish, when a man could enjoy the benefits. But there was more, and somehow less, to Rebecca than innate feminine magic.

When he had kissed her, though it had been the first time, it had been like coming back to a lover, to a love, after a painful separation. When his lips had found hers, something had filled him. A heat, an impatience, a knowledge.

He knew her, knew more than her name and her background and the color of her eyes. He knew all of her. Yet he knew nothing.

Fantasies, he told himself. He didn't have time for them. Leaning a hip against the railing, he lit a cigar and watched the sea.

As always, it pulled at him, bringing back memories of a childhood that had been careless and too short. There were times, rare times, when he allowed himself to regret. Times when the sun was a white flash of heat and the water was blue and endless. His father had taught him a great deal. How to fish, how to see both beauty and excitement in new places, how to drink like a man.

Fifteen years, Stephen thought, a smile ghosting around his mouth. He still missed him, missed the companionship, the robust laughter. They had been friends, as well as parent and child, with a bond as easy, and as strong, as any Stephen had ever known. But his father had died as he would have wanted to, at sea and in his prime.

He would have taken one look at Rebecca, rolled his eyes, kissed his fingers and urged his son to enjoy. But Stephen wasn't the boy he had once been. He was more cautious, more aware of consequences. If a man dived into the sea, he should know the depth and the currents.

Then he saw her, coming from the sea. Water ran down her body, glistening in the strong sun, sparkling against skin that had warmed in the last few days to a dusky gold. As he looked, as he wanted, he felt his muscles clench, one by one, shoulders, stomach, thighs. Without his being aware, his fingers tightened, snapping the cigar in two. He hadn't known that desire could arouse a reaction so akin to anger.

She stopped, and though he knew she was unaware of him, she might easily have been posing. To taunt, to tease, to invite. As drops of water slid down her, she stretched, lifting her face skyward. Her skimpy suit rested low over her boyish hips, shifted enticingly over the subtle curve of her breasts. At that moment, she was totally absorbed in her own pleasure and as unselfconscious as any young animal standing in the sun. Nothing had ever been so alluring.

Then, slowly, seductively, she combed her fingers through her hair, smiling, as if she enjoyed the wet, silky feel of it. Watching her, he felt the air back up and clog in his lungs. He could have murdered her for it, for making him want so unreasonably what he did not yet understand.

She plucked a long, mannish T-shirt from a straw bag and, after tugging it on, strolled barefoot into the hotel.

He stood there, waiting for the need to pass. But it built, layered with an ache that infuriated him and a longing that baffled him.

He should ignore her. Instinct warned him that if he didn't his life would never be the same. She was nothing more than a distraction, a momentary impulse he should resist. He should turn away, go back to work. He had commitments, obligations, and no time to waste on fantasies. With an oath, he tossed the broken cigar over the rail.

There were times, he thought, when a man had to trust in fate and dive in.

CHAPTER FOUR

Rebecca had hardly shut the door behind her before she turned back to answer the knock. The sun and the water had left her pleasantly tired, but all thoughts of a lazy catnap vanished when she saw Stephen.

He looked wonderful. Cool, a little windblown, intense. For days she'd wondered about him, wondered and wished. She felt her pulse skip and her lips curve just at the sight of him. With an effort, she kept her voice breezy.

"Hello. I wasn't sure you were still on the island."

It wasn't really a lie, she told herself. An offhand

inquiry had assured her that Mr. Nickodemus hadn't checked out, but she hadn't actually seen him.

"I saw you come up from the beach."

"Oh." Unconsciously she tugged at the hem of her cover-up. To Stephen the small gesture was one more contradictory signal. "I can't seem to get enough of the sun and the sea. Would you like to come in?"

By way of an answer he stepped through and shut the door behind him. It made a very quiet, a very final sound. Rebecca's carefully built poise began to crumble. "I never thanked you for the flowers." She made a gesture indicating the vase near the window, then brought her hands back together and linked them in front of her. "They're still beautiful. I…I thought I might run into you, in the dining room, on the beach, or…" Her words trailed off when he lifted a hand to her hair.

"I've been busy." He watched her eyes, eyes that were as clear as rainwater, blur at the slight touch. "Business."

It was ridiculous, she knew, but she wasn't at all sure she could speak. "If you have to work, I doubt you could pick a more beautiful place."

He stepped closer. She smelled of the water and the sun. "You're enjoying the resort, and the island."

Her hand was in his now, caught lightly. It took only that to make her knees weak. "Yes, very much."

"Perhaps you'd like to see it from a different perspective." Deliberately, wanting to test them both, he lifted her hand to his lips. He grazed her knuckles—it was barely a whisper of contact—and felt the jolt. She felt it, and he could see that she did, so it couldn't just be his imagination. "Spend the day with me tomorrow on my boat."

"What?"

He smiled, delighted with her response. "Will you come with me?"

Anywhere. Astonished, she stepped back. "I haven't any plans."

"Good." He closed the distance between them again. Her hands fluttered up in flustered defense, then settled again when he made no attempt to touch her. "Then I'll make them for you. I'll come for you in the morning. Nine?"

A boat. He'd said something about a boat. Rebecca drew in a deep breath and tried to pull herself together. This wasn't like her—going off into daydreams, feeling weak-kneed, being flooded with waves of desire. And it felt wonderful.

"I'd like that." She gave him what she hoped was an easy woman-of-the-world smile.

"Until tomorrow, then." He started for the door, then turned, a hand on the knob. "Rebecca, don't forget your camera."

She waited until he'd closed the door before she spun in three quick circles.

When Stephen had said "boat," Rebecca had pictured a trim little cabin cruiser. Instead, she stepped onto the glossy mahogany deck of a streamlined hundred-foot yacht.

"You could live on this," Rebecca said, then wished she'd bitten her tongue. But he only laughed.

"I often do."

"Welcome aboard, sir," a white-uniformed man with a British accent said.

"Grady. This is my guest, Miss Malone."

"Ma'am." Grady's cool British reserve didn't flicker for an instant, but Rebecca felt herself being summed up.

"Cast off when you're ready." Stephen took Rebecca's arm. "Would you like a tour?"

"Yes." A yacht. She was on a yacht. It took all her willpower to keep her camera in the bag. "I'd love to see it all."

He took her below, through four elegantly appointed cabins. Her comment about living on board had been said impulsively, but she could see now that it could be done easily, even luxuriously.

Above there was a large glassed-in cabin in which one could stretch out comfortably, out of the sun, and watch the sea, whatever the weather. She had known that there were people who lived like this. Part of her job had been to research and calculate so that those who did paid the government as little as possible. But to be there, to see it, to be surrounded by it, was entirely different from adding figures on paper.

There was a masculine feel to the cabin, to the entire boat—leather, wood, muted colors. There were shelves filled with books and a fully stocked bar, as well as a stereo system.

"All the comforts of home," Rebecca murmured, but she'd noted that there were doors and panels that could be secured in case of rough weather. What would it be like to ride out a storm at sea, to watch the rain lash the windows and feel the deck heave?

She gave a quick gasp when she felt the floor move. Stephen took her arm again to steady her.

"We're under way." Curious, he turned her to face him. "Are you afraid of boats?"

"No." She could hardly admit that the biggest one she'd been on before this had been a two-passenger canoe at summer camp. "It just startled me." Under way, she thought as she prayed that her system would settle. It was such an exciting, adventurous word. "Can we go out on deck? I'd like to watch."

It was exciting. She felt it the moment the wind hit her face and rushed through her hair. At the rail, she leaned out, delighted to see the island shrink and the sea spread. Because she couldn't resist and he didn't laugh at her, she took half a dozen pictures as the boat sped away from land.

"It's better than flying," she decided. "You feel a part of it. Look." With a laugh, she pointed. "The birds are chasing us."

Stephen didn't bother to glance at the gulls that wheeled and called above the boat's wake. He preferred to watch the delight and excitement bloom on her face. "Do you always enjoy so completely?"

"Yes." She tossed her hair away from her face, only to have the wind rush it back again. With another laugh, she stretched back from the railing, her face lifted to the sun. "Oh, yes."

Irresistible. With his hands at her waist, he spun her toward him. It was like holding a live wire. The shock rippled from her to him, then back again. "Everything?" His fingers spread over her back and, with the slightest pressure, moved her forward until their thighs met.

"I don't know." Instinctively she braced her hands on his shoulders. "I haven't tried everything." But she wanted to. Held close, with the sound of the water and the wind, she wanted to. Without giving a thought to self-preservation, she leaned toward him.

He swore, lightly, under his breath. Rebecca jolted back as if he had shouted at her. Stephen caught her hand as he nodded to the steward, who had just approached with drinks. "Thank you, Victor. Just leave everything." His voice was smooth enough, but Rebecca felt the tension in his hand as he led her to a chair.

He probably thought she was a fool, she decided. All but tumbling into his arms every time he touched her. He was obviously a man of the world—and a kind man, she added as she sipped her mimosa. Not all powerful men spoke kindly to those who worked for them. Her lips curved, a little wryly, as she sipped again. She knew that firsthand.

His body was in turmoil. Stephen couldn't remember, even in his youth, having had a woman affect him so irrationally. He knew how to persuade, how to seduce—and always with finesse. But whenever he was around this woman for more than five minutes he felt like a stallion being spurred and curbed at the same time.

And he was fascinated. Fascinated by the ease with which she went into his arms, by the trust he saw when he looked down into her eyes. As he had in the olive grove, he found himself believing he'd looked into those eyes, those rainwater-clear eyes, a hundred times before.

Still churning, he took out a cigar. The thought was fanciful, but his desire was very real. If there couldn't be finesse, perhaps there could be candor.

"I want you, Rebecca."

She felt her heart stop, then start up again with slow, dull throbs. Carefully she took another sip, then cleared her throat. "I know." It amazed her, flattered her, terrified her.

She seemed so cool. He envied her. "Will you come with me, to my cabin?"

She looked at him then. Her heart and her head were giving very different answers. It sounded so easy, so... natural. If there was a man she could give herself to, wholly, he was with her now. Complications, what complications there were, were her own.

But no matter how far she had run from Philadelphia and her own strict upbringing, there were still lines she couldn't cross.

"I can't."

"Can't?" He lit his cigar, astonished that they were discussing making love as though it were as casual a choice as what dinner entrée to chose. "Or won't?"

She drew a breath. Her palms were damp on the glass, and she set it down. "Can't. I want to." Her eyes, huge and lake-pale, clung to his. "I very much want to, but..."

"But?"

"I know so little about you." She picked up her glass again because her empty hands tended to twist together. "Hardly more than your name, that you own an olive grove and like the sea. It's not enough."

"Then I'll tell you more."

She relaxed enough to smile. "I don't know what to ask."

He leaned back in his chair, the tension dissolving as quickly as it had built. She could do that to him with nothing more than a smile. He knew no one who could excite and solace with so little effort.

"Do you believe in fate, Rebecca? In something unexpected, even unlooked-for, often a small thing that completely and irrevocably changes one's life?"

She thought of her aunt's death and her own uncharacteristic decisions. "Yes. Yes, I do."

"Good." His gaze skimmed over her face, quickly, then more leisurely. "I'd nearly forgotten that I believe it, too. Then I saw you, sitting alone."

There were ways and ways to seduce, she was discovering. A look, a tone, could be every bit as devastating as a caress. She wanted him more in that moment than she had ever known she could want anything. To give herself time, and distance, she rose and walked to the rail.

Even her silence aroused him. She had said she knew too little about him. He knew even less of her. And he didn't care. It was dangerous, possibly even destructive, but he didn't care. As he watched her with the wind billowing her shirt and her hair he realized that he didn't give a damn about where she had come from, where she had been, what she had done.

When lightning strikes, it destroys, though it blazes with power. Rising, he went to her and stood, as she did, facing the sea.

"When I was young, very young," he began, "there was another moment that changed things. My father was a man for the water. He lived for it. Died for it." When he went on it was almost as if he were speaking to himself now, remembering. Rebecca turned her head to look at him. "I was ten or eleven. Everything was going well, the nets were full. My father and I were walking along the beach. He stopped, dipped his hand into the water, made a fist and opened it. 'You can't hold it,' he said to me. 'No matter how you try or how you love or how you sweat.' Then he dug into the sand. It was wet and clung together in his hand. 'But this,' he said, 'a man can hold.' We never spoke of it again. When my time came, I turned my back on the sea and held the land."

"It was right for you."

"Yes." He lifted a hand to catch at the ends of her hair. "It was right. Such big, quiet eyes you have, Rebecca," he murmured. "Have they seen enough, I wonder, to know what's right for you?"

"I guess I've been a little slow in starting to look." Her blood was pounding thickly. She would have stepped back, but he shifted so that she was trapped between him and the rail.

"You tremble when I touch you." He slid his hands up her arms, then down until their hands locked. "Have you any idea how exciting that is?"

Her chest tightened, diminishing her air even as the muscles in her legs went limp. "Stephen, I meant it when I said…" He brushed his lips gently over her temple. "I can't. I need to…" He feathered a kiss along her jawline, softly. "To think."

He felt her fingers go lax in his. She was suddenly fragile, outrageously vulnerable, irresistibly tempting. "When I kissed you the first time I gave you no choice." His lips trailed over her face, light as a whisper, circling, teasing, avoiding her mouth. "You have one now."

He was hardly touching her. A breath, a whisper, a mere promise of a touch. The slow, subtle passage of his lips over her skin couldn't have been called a kiss, could never have been called a demand. She had only to push away to end the torment. And the glory.

A choice? Had he told her she had a choice? "No, I don't," she murmured as she turned to find his lips with hers.

No choice, no past, no future. Only now. She felt the present, with all its needs and hungers, well up inside her. The kiss was instantly hot, instantly desperate. His heart pounded fast and hard against hers, thunderous now, as he twisted a hand in her hair to pull her head back. To plunder. No one had ever taken her like this. No one had ever warned her that a touch of violence could be so exciting. Her gasp of surprise turned into a moan of pleasure as his tongue skimmed over hers.

He thought of lightning bolts again, thought of that flash of power and light. She was electric in his arms, sparking, sizzling. Her scent, as soft, as seductive, as a whisper, clouded his mind, even as the taste of her heightened his appetite.

She was all woman, she was every woman, and yet she was like no other. He could hear each quick catch of her breath above the roar of the motor. With her name on his lips, he pressed them to the vulnerable line of her throat, where the skin was heated from the sun and as delicate as water.

She might have slid bonelessly to the deck if his body hadn't pressed hers so firmly against the rail. In wonder, in panic, she felt his muscles turn to iron wherever they touched her. Never before had she felt so fragile, so at the mercy of her own desires. The sea was as calm as glass, but she felt herself tossed, tumbled, wrecked.

With a sigh that was almost a sob, she wrapped her arms around him.

It was the defenselessness of the gesture that pulled him back from the edge. He must have been mad. For a moment he'd been close, much too close, to dragging her down to the deck without a thought to her wishes or to the consequences. With his eyes closed, he held her, feeling the erratic beat of her heart, hearing her shallow, shuddering breath.

Perhaps he was still mad, Stephen thought. Even as the ragged edges of desire eased, something deeper and far more dangerous bloomed.

He wanted her, in a way no man could safely want a woman. Forever.

Fate, he thought again as he stroked her hair. It seemed he was falling in love whether he wished it or not. A few hours with her and he felt more than he had ever imagined he could feel.

There had been a few times in his life when he had seen and desired on instinct alone. What he had seen and desired, he had taken. Just as he would take her. But when he took, he meant to keep.

Carefully he stepped back. "Maybe neither of us has a choice." He dipped his hands into his pockets. "And if I touch you again, here, now, I won't give you one."

Unable to pretend, knowing they were shaking, she pushed her hands through her hair. She didn't bother to disguise the tremor in her voice. She wouldn't have known how. "I won't want one." She saw his eyes darken quickly, dangerously, but she didn't know his hands were balled into fists, straining.

"You make it difficult for me."

A long, shuddering breath escaped her. No one had ever wanted her this way. Probably no one ever would again. "I'm sorry. I don't mean to."

"No." Deliberately he relaxed his hands. "I don't think you do. That's one of the things about you I find most intriguing. I will have you, Rebecca." He saw something flicker in her eyes.... Excitement? Panic? A combination of the two, perhaps. "Because I'm sure of it, because I know you're sure of it, I'll do my best to give you a little more time."

Her natural humor worked through the sliver of unease she felt. "I'm not sure whether I should thank you politely or run like hell."

He grinned, surprising himself, then flicked a finger down her cheek. "I wouldn't advise running, *matia mou*. I'd only catch you."

She was sure of that, too. One look at his face, even with the smile that softened it, and she knew. Kind, yes, but with a steely underlying ruthlessness. "Then I'll go with the thank-you."

"You're welcome." Patience, he realized, would have to be developed. And quickly. "Would you like to swim? There's a bay. We're nearly there."

The water might, just might, cool her off. "I'd love it."

CHAPTER FIVE

The water was cool and mirror-clear. Rebecca lowered herself into it with a sigh of pure pleasure. Back in Philadelphia she would have been at her desk, calculator clicking, the jacket of her neat business suit carefully smoothed over the back of her chair. Her figures would always tally, her forms would always be properly filed.

The dependable, efficient Miss Malone.

Instead, she was swimming in a crystal-clear bay, letting the water cool and the sun heat. Ledgers and accounts were worlds away. Here, as close as a handspan, was a man who was teaching her everything she would ever want to know about needs, desires, and the fragility of the heart.

He couldn't know it, she thought. She doubted she'd ever have the courage to tell him that he was the only one who had ever made her tremble and burn. A man as physically aware as he would only be uncomfortable knowing he held an inexperienced woman in his arms.

The water lapped around her with a sound as quiet as her own sigh. But he didn't know, because when she was in his arms she didn't feel awkward and inexperienced. She felt beautiful, desirable and reckless.

With a laugh, Rebecca dipped under the surface to let the water, and the freedom, surround her. Who would have believed it?

"Does it always take so little to make you laugh?"

Rebecca ran a hand over her slicked-back hair. Stephen was treading water beside her, smoothly, hardly making a ripple. His skin was dark gold, glistening-wet. His hair was streaked by the sun and dampened by the water, which was almost exactly the color of his eyes. She had to suppress an urge to just reach out and touch.

"A secluded inlet, a beautiful sky, an interesting man." With another sigh, she kicked her legs up so that she could float. "It doesn't seem like so little to me." She studied the vague outline of the mountains, far out of reach. "I promised myself that no matter where I went, what I did, I'd never take anything for granted again."

There was something in the way she said it, some hint of sadness, that pulled at him. The urge to comfort wasn't completely foreign in him, but he hadn't had much practice at it. "Was there a man who hurt you?"

Her lips curved at that, but he couldn't know that she

was laughing at herself. Naturally, she'd dated. They had been polite, cautious evenings, usually with little interest on either side. She'd been dull, or at least she had never worked up the nerve to spread her wings. Once or twice, when she'd felt a tug, she'd been too shy, too much the efficient Rebecca Malone, to do anything about it.

With him, everything was different. Because she loved him. She didn't know how, she didn't know why, but she loved him as much as any woman could love any man.

"No. There's no one." She closed her eyes, trusting the water to carry her. "When my parents died, it hurt. It hurt so badly that I suppose I pulled back from life. I thought it was important that I be a responsible adult, even though I wasn't nearly an adult yet."

Strange that she hadn't thought of it quite that way until she'd stopped being obsessively responsible. Stranger still was how easy it was to tell him what she'd never even acknowledged herself.

"My aunt Jeannie was kind and considerate and loving, but she'd forgotten what it was like to be a young girl. Suddenly I realized I'd missed being young, lazy, foolish, all the things everyone's entitled to be at least once. I decided to make up for it."

Her hair was spread out and drifting on the water. Her eyes were closed, and her face was sheened with water. Not beautiful, Stephen told himself. She was too angular for real beauty. But she was fascinating… in looks, in philosophy…more, in the open-armed way she embraced whatever crossed her path.

He found himself looking around the inlet as he

hadn't bothered to look at anything in years. He could see the sun dancing on the surface, could see the ripples spreading and growing from the quiet motion of their bodies. Farther away was the narrow curving strip of white beach, deserted now, but for a few birds fluttering over the sand. It was quiet, almost unnaturally quiet, the only sound the soft, monotonous slap of water against sand. And he was relaxed, totally, mind and body. Perhaps he, too, had forgotten what it was like to be young and foolish.

On impulse he put a hand on her shoulder and pushed her under.

She came up sputtering, dragging wet hair out of her eyes. He grinned at her and calmly continued to tread water. "It was too easy."

She tilted her head, considering him and the distance between them. Challenge leaped into her eyes, sparked with amusement. "It won't be the next time."

His grin only widened. When he moved, he moved fast, streaking under and across the water like an eel. Rebecca had time for a quick squeal. Dragging in a deep breath, she kicked out. He caught her ankle, but she was ready. Unresisting, she let him pull her under. Then, instead of fighting her way back to the surface, she wrapped her arms around him and sent them both rolling in an underwater wrestling match. They were still tangled, her arms around him, her hands hooked over his shoulders, when they surfaced.

"We're even." She gasped for air and shook the water out of her eyes.

"How do you figure?"

"If we'd had a mat I'd have pinned you. Want to go for two out of three?"

"I might." He felt her legs tangle with his as she kicked out lazily. "But for now I prefer this."

He was going to kiss her again. She saw it in his eyes, felt it in the slight tensing of the arm that locked them torso to torso. She wasn't sure she was ready. More, she was afraid she was much too ready.

"Stephen?"

"Hmm?" His lips were a breath away from hers. Then he found himself underwater again, his arms empty. He should have been furious. He nearly was when he pushed to surface. She was shoulder-deep in the water, a few feet away. Her laughter rolled over him, young, delighted, unapologetic.

"It was too easy." She managed a startled "whoops" when he struck out after her. She might have made it— she had enough of a lead—but he swam as though he'd been born in the water. Still, she was agile, and she almost managed to dodge him, but her laughter betrayed her. She gulped in water, choked, then found herself hauled up into his arms in thigh-deep water.

"I like to win." Deciding it was useless to struggle, she pressed a hand to her heart and gasped for air. "It's a personality flaw. Sometimes I cheat at canasta."

"Canasta?" The last thing he could picture the slim, sexy bundle in his arms doing was spending a quiet evening playing cards.

"I can't help myself." Still breathless, she laid her head on his shoulder. "No willpower."

"I find myself having the same problem." With a

careless toss, he sent her flying through the air. She hit the water bottom first.

"I guess I deserved that." She struggled to her feet, water raining off her. "I have to sit." Wading through the water, she headed for the gentle slope of beach. She lay, half in and half out of the water, not caring that the sand would cling to her hair and skin. When he dropped down beside her, she reached out a hand for his. "I don't know when I've had a nicer day."

He looked down to where her fingers linked with his. The gesture had been so easy, so natural. He wondered how it could both comfort and arouse. "It's hardly over."

"It seems like it could last forever." She wanted it to go on and on. Blue skies and easy laughter. Cool water and endless hours. There had been a time, not so long before, when the days had dragged into nights and the nights into days. "Did you ever want to run away?"

With her hand still in his, he lay back to watch a few scattered rags of clouds drift. How long had it been, he wondered, since he'd really watched the sky? "To where?"

"Anywhere. Away from the way things are, away from what you're afraid they'll always be." She closed her eyes and could see herself brewing that first cup of coffee at exactly 7:15, opening the first file at precisely 9:01. "To drop out of sight," she murmured, "and pop up somewhere else, anywhere else, as someone completely different."

"You can't change who you are."

"Oh, but you can." Her tone suddenly urgent, she rose on her elbow. "Sometimes you have to."

He reached up to touch the ends of her hair. "What are you running from?"

"Everything. I'm a coward."

He looked into her eyes. They were so clear, so full of enthusiasm. "I don't think so."

"But you don't know me." A flicker of regret, then uncertainty, ran across her face. "I'm not sure I want you to."

"Don't I?" His fingers tightened on her hair, keeping her still. "There are people and circumstances that don't take months or years before they're understood. I look at you and something fits into place, Rebecca. I don't know why, but it is. I know you." He tugged her down for the lightest, the briefest, of kisses. "And I like what I see."

"Do you?" She smiled. "Really?"

"Do you imagine I spend the day with a woman only because I want to sleep with her?" She shrugged, and though her blush was very faint, he noticed it and was amused by it. How many women, he wondered, could kiss a man into oblivion, then blush? "Being with you, Rebecca, is a difficult pleasure."

She chuckled and began to draw circles in the wet sand. What would he say, what would he think, if he knew what she was? Or, more accurately, what she wasn't? It didn't matter, she told herself. She couldn't let it spoil what there was between them.

"I think that's the most wonderful compliment I've ever had."

"Where have you been?" he murmured.

When she moved restlessly, he held her still. "Don't. I'm not going to touch you. Not yet."

"That's not the problem." With her eyes closed, she tilted her chin up and let the sun beat down on her face. "The problem is, I want you to touch me, so much it frightens me." Taking her time, she sat up, gathering her courage. She wanted to be honest, and she hoped she wouldn't sound like a fool. "Stephen, I don't sleep around. I need you to understand, because this is all happening so quickly. But it's not casual."

He lifted a hand to her chin and turned her to face him. His eyes were as blue as the water, and, to her, as unfathomable. "No, it's not." He made the decision quickly, though he had been turning the idea over in his mind all day. "I have to go to Athens tomorrow. Come with me, Rebecca."

"Athens?" she managed, staring at him.

"Business. A day, two at the most. I'd like you with me." And he was afraid, more than he cared to admit, that when he returned she might be gone.

"I…" What should she say? What was right?

"You told me you'd planned to go." He'd push if necessary. Now that the idea had taken root, Stephen had no intention of going anywhere without her.

"Yes, but I wouldn't want to be in the way while you're working."

"You'll be in my way whether you're here or there."

Her head came up at that, and the look she gave him was both shy and stunning. He stifled the need to take her again, to roll until she was beneath him on the sand. He'd said he'd give her time. Perhaps what he'd really meant was that he needed time himself.

"You'll have your own suite. No strings, Rebecca. Just your company."

"A day or two," she murmured.

"It's a simple matter to have your room held for you here for your return."

Her return. Not his. If he left Corfu tomorrow she would probably never see him again. He was offering her another day, perhaps two. Never take anything for granted, she remembered. Never again.

Athens, she thought. It was true that she had planned to see it before she left Greece. But she would have gone alone. A few days before, that had been what she thought she wanted. The adventure of seeing new places, new people, on her own. Now the thought of going with him, of having him beside her when she first caught sight of the Acropolis, of having him want her with him, changed everything.

"I'd love to go with you." She rose quickly and dived into the water. She was in over her head.

CHAPTER SIX

Athens was neither East nor West. It was spitted meat and spices roasting. It was tall buildings and modern shops. It was narrow, unpaved streets and clamorous bazaars. It had been the scene of revolution and brutality. It was ancient and civilized and passionate.

Rebecca quite simply fell in love at first sight.

She'd been seduced by Paris and charmed by London, but in Athens she lost her heart. She wanted to see everything at once, from sunrise to moonlight, and the heat-drenched afternoon between.

All that first morning, while Stephen was immersed in business meetings, she wandered. The hotel he'd chosen was lovely, but she was drawn to the streets and the people. Somehow she didn't feel like a visitor here. She felt like someone who had returned home after a long, long journey. Athens was waiting for her, ready to welcome her back.

Incredible. All her life she had accepted the parameters set for her. Now she was touring Old Athens, with its clicking worry beads and its open-fronted shops, where she could buy cheap plaster copies of monuments or elegant antiques.

She passed tavernas, but she was too excited to be tempted by the rich smells of coffee and baking. She heard the clear notes of a flute as she looked up and saw the Acropolis.

There was only one approach. Though it was still early, other tourists were making their way toward the ruins in twos and in groups. Rebecca let her camera hang by its strap. Despite the chattering around her, she felt alone, but beautifully so.

She would never be able to explain what it felt like to stand in the morning sun and look at something that had been built for the gods—something that had endured war and weather and time. It had been a place of worship. Even now, after centuries had passed, Rebecca felt the spiritual pull. Perhaps the goddess Athena, with her gleaming helmet and spear, still visited there.

Rebecca had been disappointed that Stephen couldn't join her on her first morning in Athens. Now she was glad to be alone—to sit and absorb and imagine without having to explain her thoughts.

How could she, after having seen so much, go back to so little? Sighing, she wandered through the temples.

It wasn't just the awe she felt here, or the excitement she had felt in London and Paris, that had changed her. It was Stephen and everything she'd felt, everything she'd wanted, since she'd met him.

Perhaps she would go back to Philadelphia, but she would never be the same person. Once you fell in love, completely, totally in love, nothing was ever the same.

She wished it could be simple, the way she imagined it was simple for so many other women. An attractive man, a physical tug. But with Stephen, as with Athens, she'd lost her heart. However implausible it seemed, she had recognized the man, as well as the city, as being part of her, as being for her. Desire, when tangled up with love, could never be simple.

But how could you be sure you were in love when it had never happened to you before? If she were home, at least she would have a friend to talk to. With a little laugh, Rebecca walked out into the sunlight. How many times had she been on the receiving end of a long, scattered conversation from a friend who had fallen in love—or thought she had. The excitement, the unhappiness, the thrills. Sometimes she'd been envious, and sometimes she'd been grateful not to have the complication in her own life. But always, always, she'd offered calm, practical, even soothing advice.

Oddly enough, she didn't seem to be able to do the same for herself.

All she could think of was the way her heart pounded when he touched her, how excitement, panic and anticipation fluttered through her every time he looked at her. When she was with him, her feelings and fantasies seemed reasonable. When she was with him, she could believe in fate, in the matching of soul to soul.

It wasn't enough. At least that was what she would have told another woman. Attraction and passion weren't enough. Yet there was no explaining, even to herself, the sense of rightness she experienced whenever she was with him. If she were a fanciful person she would say it was as though she'd been waiting for him, waiting for the time and the place for him to come to her.

It sounded simple—if fate could be considered simple. Yet beneath all the pleasure and that sense of reunion was guilt. She couldn't shake it, and she knew she wouldn't be able to ignore it much longer. She wasn't the woman she had let him believe her to be. She wasn't the well-traveled at-loose-ends free spirit she pretended to be. No matter how many ties she'd cut, she was still Rebecca Malone. How would he feel about her once he knew how limited and dull her life had been?

How and when was she going to tell him?

A few more days, she promised herself as she began the walk back. It was selfish, perhaps it was even dangerous, but she wanted just a few more days.

It was midafternoon before she returned to the hotel. Ignoring the fact that she might be considered overeager, she went straight to Stephen's suite. She couldn't wait to see him, to tell him everything she'd seen, to show him everything she'd bought. Her easy smile faded a bit when his secretary Elana opened the door.

"Miss Malone." Gracious and self-confident, Elana

waved her in. "Please sit down. I'll let Stephen know you're here."

"I don't want to interrupt." Rebecca shifted her bags, feeling gauche and foolish.

"Not at all. Have you just come in?"

"Yes, I…" For the first time, Rebecca noticed that her skin was damp and her hair tousled. In contrast, Elana was cool and perfectly groomed. "I really should go."

"Please." Elana urged Rebecca to a chair. "Let me get you a drink." With a half smile, Elana began to pour a tall glass of iced juice. She had expected Stephen's mystery lady to be smooth, controlled and stunning. It pleased her a great deal to find Rebecca wide-eyed, a little unsure, and clearly a great deal in love.

"Did you enjoy your morning?"

"Yes, very much." She accepted the glass and tried to relax. Jealousy, she realized, feeling herself flush at the realization. She couldn't remember ever having experienced the sensation before. Who wouldn't be jealous? she asked herself as she watched Elana walk to the phone. The Greek woman was gorgeous, self-contained, coolly efficient. Above all, she had a relationship with Stephen that Rebecca knew nothing about. How long has she known him? Rebecca wondered. And how well?

"Stephen's just finishing up some business," Elana said as she hung up the phone. With easy, economical moves, she poured herself a drink, then walked to the chair facing Rebecca. "What do you think of Athens?"

"I love it." Rebecca wished she'd taken the time to brush her hair and freshen her makeup. Lecturing herself, she sipped at her juice. "I'm not sure what I expected, but it's everything and more."

"Europeans see it as the East, Orientals see it as the West." Elana crossed her legs and settled back. It surprised her to realize that she was prepared to like Rebecca Malone. "What Athens is is Greek—and, more particularly, Athenian." She paused, studying Rebecca over the rim of her glass. "People often view Stephen in much the same way, and what he is is Stephen."

"How long have you worked for him?"

"Five years."

"You must know him well."

"Better than some. He's a demanding and generous employer and an interesting man. Fortunately, I like to travel and I enjoy my work."

Rebecca rubbed at a spot of dust on her slacks. "It never occurred to me that farming required so much traveling. I never realized how much was involved in growing olives."

Elana's brows rose in obvious surprise, but she continued smoothly when Rebecca glanced back at her. "Whatever Stephen does, he does thoroughly." She smiled to herself, satisfied. She hadn't been certain until now whether the American woman was attracted to Stephen or to his position. "Has Stephen explained to you about the dinner party this evening?"

"He said something about a small party here at the hotel. A business dinner."

"Men take these things more lightly than women." Feeling friendlier, Elena offered her first genuine smile. "It will be small, but quite extravagant." She watched as Rebecca automatically lifted a hand to her hair. "If you need anything—a dress, a salon—the hotel can accommodate you."

Rebecca thought of the casual sportswear she'd tossed into her bag before the impulsive trip to Athens. "I need everything."

With a quick, understanding laugh, Elana rose. "I'll make some calls for you."

"Thank you, but I don't want to interfere with your work."

"Seeing that you're comfortable is part of my work." They both glanced over when the door opened. "Stephen. You see, she hasn't run away." Taking her glass and her pad, she left them alone.

"You were gone a long time." He hated the fact that he'd begun to watch the clock and worry. He'd imagined her hurt or abducted. He'd begun to wonder if she would disappear from his life as quickly as she'd appeared in it. Now she was here, her eyes alive with pleasure, her clothes rumpled and her hair windblown.

"I guess I got caught up exploring." She started to rise, but before she could gain her feet he was pulling her out of the chair, seeking, finding her mouth with his.

His desperation whipped through her. His hunger incited her own. Without thought, without hesitation, she clung to him, answering, accepting. Already seduced, she murmured something, an incoherent sound that caught in her throat.

Good God, he thought, it wasn't possible, it wasn't sane, to want like this. Throughout the morning while all the facts and figures and demands of business had been hammering at him, he'd thought of her, of holding her, of tasting her, of being with her. When she had stayed away for so long he'd begun to imagine, then to fear, what his life would be like without her.

It wasn't going to happen. He scraped his teeth over her bottom lip, and she gasped and opened for him. He wouldn't let it happen. Where she came from, where she intended to go, no longer mattered. She belonged to him now. And, though he'd only begun to deal with it, he belonged to her.

But he needed some sanity, some logic. Fighting himself, Stephen drew her away from him. Her eyes remained closed, and her lips remained parted. A soft, sultry sound escaped them as her lashes fluttered upward.

"I…" She took a deep breath and let it out slowly. "I should go sightseeing more often."

Gradually he realized how hard his fingers were pressing into her arms. As if he were afraid she would slip away. Cursing himself, he relaxed. "I would have preferred to go with you."

"I understand you're busy. I'd have bored you silly, poking into every shop and staring at every column."

"No." If there was one thing he was certain of, it was that she would never bore him. "I'd like to have seen your first impression of Athens."

"It was like coming home," she told him, then hurried on because it sounded foolish. "I couldn't get enough." Laughing at herself, she gestured toward her bags. "Obviously. It's so different from anywhere I've ever been. At the Acropolis I couldn't even take any pictures, because I knew they couldn't capture the feeling. Then I walked along the streets and saw old men with *kom—konbou—*" She fumbled over the Greek and finally made a helpless gesture.

"Kombouloi," he murmured. "Worry beads."

"Yes, and I imagined how they might sit in those shadowy doorways watching the tourists go by, day after day, year after year." She sat, pleased to share her impressions with him. "I saw a shop with all these costumes, lots of tinsel, and some really dreadful plaster copies of the monuments."

He grinned and sat beside her. "How many did you buy?"

"Three or four." She bent down to rattle through her bags. "I bought you a present."

"A plaster statue of Athena?"

She glanced up, eyes laughing. "Almost. Then I found this tiny antique shop in the old section. It was all dim and dusty and irresistible. The owner had a handful of English phrases, and I had my phrase book. After we'd confused each other completely, I bought this."

She drew out an S-shaped porcelain pipe decorated with paintings of the wild mountain goats of Greece. Attached to it was a long wooden stem, as smooth as glass, tipped by a tarnished brass mouthpiece.

"I remembered the goats we'd seen on Corfu," she explained as Stephen examined it. "I thought you might like it, though I've never seen you smoke a pipe."

With a quiet laugh, he looked back at her, balancing the gift in both hands. "No, I don't—at least not of this nature."

"Well, it's more ornamental than functional, I suppose. The man couldn't tell me much about it—at least not that I could understand." She reached out to run a finger along the edge of the bowl. "I've never seen anything like it."

"I'm relieved to hear it." When she sent him a puzzled look, he leaned over to brush her lips with his. "*Matia mou,* this is a hashish pipe."

"A hashish pipe?" She stared, first in shock, then in fascination. "Really? I mean, did people actually use it?"

"Undoubtedly. Quite a number, I'd say, since it's at least a hundred and fifty years old."

"Imagine that." She pouted, imagining dark, smoky dens. "I guess it's not a very appropriate souvenir."

"On the contrary, whenever I see it I'll think of you."

She glanced up quickly, unsure, but the amusement in his eyes had her smiling again. "I should have bought you the plaster statue of Athena."

Taking her hands, he drew her to her feet. "I'm flattered that you bought me anything." She felt the subtle change as his fingers tightened on hers. "I want time with you, Rebecca. Hours of it. Days. There's too much I need to know." When she lowered her gaze, he caught her chin. "What are those secrets of yours?"

"Nothing that would interest you."

"You're wrong. Tomorrow I intend to find out all there is to know." He saw the quick flicker of unease in her eyes. Other men, he thought with an uncomfortable surge of jealousy. The hell with them. "No more evasions. I want you, all of you. Do you understand?"

"Yes, but—"

"Tomorrow." He cut her off, suddenly, completely, frustratingly Greek. "I have business that can't be avoided now. I'll come for you at seven."

"All right."

Tomorrow was years away, she told herself. She had time to decide what she would say, how she would say it. Before tomorrow came tonight. She would be everything she'd ever wanted to be, everything he wanted her to be.

"I'd better go." Before he could touch her again, she bent to gather her bags. "Stephen…" She paused at the door and turned to look at him as he stood in the middle of the room, comfortable with the wealth that surrounded him, confident with who and what he was. "You might be disappointed when you find out."

She left quickly, leaving him frowning after her.

CHAPTER SEVEN

She was as nervous as a cat. Every time she looked in the mirror Rebecca wondered who the woman was who was staring back at her. It wasn't a stranger, but it was a very, very different Rebecca Malone.

Was it just the different hairstyle, poufed and frizzed and swept around her face? Could it be the dress, the glittery spill of aquamarine that left her arms and shoulders bare? No, it was more than that. More than makeup and clever stylists and glamorous clothes. It was in her eyes. How could she help but see it? How could anyone? The woman who looked back from the mirror was a woman in love.

What was she going to do about it? What could she do? she asked herself. She was still practical enough to accept that some things could never be changed. But was she bold enough, or strong enough, to take what she wanted and live with the consequences?

When she heard the knock on the door, Rebecca took a deep breath and picked up the useless compact-size evening bag she'd bought just that afternoon. It was all happening so fast. When she'd come back from Stephen's suite there had been a detailed message from Elana listing appointments—for a massage, a facial, hairstyling—along with the name of the manager of the hotel's most exclusive boutique. She hadn't had time to think, even for a minute, about her evening with Stephen. Or about any tomorrows.

Perhaps that was best, she decided as she pulled open the door. It was best not to think, not to analyze. It was best to accept and to act.

She looked like a siren, some disciple of Circe, with her windswept hair and a dress the color of seductive seas. Had he told himself she wasn't beautiful? Had he believed it? At that moment he was certain he'd never seen, never would see, a more exciting woman.

"You're amazing, Rebecca." He took her hand and drew her to him so that they stood in the doorway together. On the threshold.

"Why? Because I'm on time?"

"Because you're never what I expect." He brought her hand to his lips. "And always what I want."

Because she was speechless, she was glad when he closed the door at her back and led her to the elevators. He looked different from the man she had first met, the one who dressed with such casual elegance. Tonight there was a formality about him, and the sophistication she had sensed earlier was abundantly apparent in the ease with which he wore the black dinner jacket.

"The way you look," he told her, "it seems a shame to waste the evening on a business dinner."

"I'm looking forward to meeting some of your friends."

"Associates," he said with an odd smile. "When you've been poor—and don't intend to be poor again—you rarely make friends in business."

She frowned. This was a side of him, the business side, that she didn't know. Would he be ruthless? She looked at him, saw it, and accepted it. Yes, a man like Stephen would always be ruthless with what belonged to him. "But enemies?"

"The same rule, in business, applies to friends and enemies. My father taught me more than fishing, Rebecca. He also taught me that to succeed, to attain, you must learn not only how to trust, but how far."

"I've never been poor, but I imagine it's frightening."

"Strengthening." He took her hand again when the elevator doors opened. "We have different backgrounds, Rebecca, but, fortunately, we've come to the same place."

He had no idea *how* different. Trust. He had spoken of trust. She discovered she wanted to tell him, tell him everything. Tell him that she knew nothing of elegant parties and glamorous lifestyles. She was a fraud, and when he found out he might laugh at her and brush her aside. But she wanted him to know.

"Stephen, I want to—"

"Stephen. Once more you outdo us all in your choice of women."

"Dimitri."

Rebecca stopped, caught on the brink of confession. The man who faced her was classically handsome. His silver mane contrasted with bronzed skin lined by a half century of sun. He wore a mustache that swept majestically over gleaming teeth.

"It was kind of you to invite us here this evening, but it would be kinder still to introduce me to your lovely companion."

"Rebecca Malone, Dimitri Petropolis."

A diamond glittered on the hand he lifted to clasp Rebecca's. The hand itself was hard as rock. "A pleasure. Athens is already abuzz with talk of the woman who arrived with Stephen."

Certain he was joking, she smiled. "Then Athens must be in desperate need of news."

His eyes widened for a moment, then creased at the corners when he laughed. "I have no doubt you will provide an abundance of it."

Stephen slipped a hand under Rebecca's elbow. The look he sent Dimitri was very quick and very clear. They had competed over land, but there would be no competition over Rebecca.

"If you'll excuse us a moment, Dimitri, I'd like to get Rebecca some champagne."

"Of course." Amused—and challenged—Dimitri brushed at his mustache as he watched them walk away.

Rebecca had no way of knowing that to Stephen a small dinner party meant a hundred people. She sipped her first glass of wine, hoping she wouldn't embarrass them both by being foolishly shy and tongue-tied. In the past, whenever she had found herself in a crowd, she had always looked for the nearest corner to fade into. Not tonight, she promised herself, straightening her shoulders.

There were dozens of names to remember, but she filed them away as easily as she had always filed numbers. In the hour before dinner, while the guests mixed and mingled, she found herself at ease. The stomach flutters and hot blushes she'd often experienced at parties and functions simply didn't happen.

Perhaps she was the new Rebecca Malone after all.

She heard business discussed here and there. Most of it seemed to be hotel and resort business—talk of remodeling and expansions, mergers and takeovers. She found it odd that so many of the guests were in that trade, rather than prosperous farmers or olive growers.

Stephen came up behind her and murmured in her ear, "You look pleased with yourself."

"I am." He couldn't know that she was pleased to find herself at ease and comfortable in a party of strangers. "So many interesting people."

"Interesting." He brushed a finger over her wispy bangs. "I thought you might find it dull."

"Not at all." She took a last sip of champagne, then set the glass aside. Instantly a waiter was at her side, offering another. Stephen watched her smile her thanks.

"So you enjoy parties?"

"Sometimes. I'm enjoying this one, and having a chance to meet your associates."

Stephen glanced over her shoulder, summing up the

looks and quiet murmurs. "They'll be talking about you for weeks to come."

She only laughed, turning in a slow circle. Around her was the flash of jewels and the gleam of gold. The sleek and the prosperous, the rich and the successful. It pleased her that she'd found more to talk about than tax shelters.

"I can't imagine they have so little on their minds. This is such a gorgeous room."

She looked around the huge ballroom, with its cream-and-rose walls, its glittering chandeliers and its gleaming floors. There were alcoves for cozy love seats and tall, thriving ornamental trees in huge copper pots. The tables, arranged to give a sense of intimacy, were already set with ivory cloths and slender tapers.

"It's really a beautiful hotel," she continued. "Everything about it runs so smoothly." She smiled up at him. "I'm torn between the resort in Corfu and this."

"Thank you." When she gave him a blank look, he tipped up her chin with his finger. "They're mine."

"Your what?"

"My hotels," he said simply, then led her to a table.

She spoke all through dinner, though for the first fifteen minutes she had no idea what she said. There were eight at Stephen's table, including Dimitri, who had shifted name cards so that he could sit beside her. She toyed with her seafood appetizer, chatted and wondered if she could have made a bigger fool out of herself.

He wasn't simply prosperous. He wasn't simply well-off. There was enough accountant left in Rebecca to understand that when a man owned what Stephen owned he was far, far more than comfortable.

What would he think of her when he found out what she was? Trust? How could she ever expect him to trust her now? She swallowed without tasting and managed to smile. Would he think she was a gold digger, that she had set herself up to run into him?

No, that was ridiculous.

She forced herself to look over and saw that Stephen was watching her steadily. She picked up her fork with one hand and balled up the napkin in her lap with the other.

Why couldn't he be ordinary? she wondered. Someone vacationing, someone working at the resort? Why had she fallen in love with someone so far out of her reach?

"Have you left us?"

Rebecca jerked herself back to see Dimitri smiling at her. Flushing, she noticed that the next course had been served while she'd been daydreaming. "I'm sorry." With an effort she began to toy with the *salata Athenas*.

"A beautiful woman need never apologize for being lost in her own thoughts." He patted her hand, then let his fingers linger. He caught Stephen's dark look and smiled. If he didn't like the boy so much, he thought, he wouldn't get nearly so much pleasure from irritating him. "Tell me, how did you meet Stephen?"

"We met in Corfu." She thought of that first meal they had shared…quiet, relaxed, alone.

"Ah, soft nights and sunny days. You are vacationing?"

"Yes." Rebecca put more effort into her smile. If she stared into her salad she would only embarrass herself, and Stephen. "He was kind enough to show me some of the island."

"He knows it well, and many of the other islands of our country. There's something of the gypsy in him."

She had sensed that. Hadn't that been part of the attraction? Hadn't Rebecca just discovered the gypsy in herself? "Have you know him long?"

"We have a long-standing business relationship. Friendly rivals, you might say. When Stephen was hardly more than a boy he accumulated an impressive amount of land." He gestured expansively. "As you can see, he used it wisely. I believe he has two hotels in your country."

"Two? More?" Rebecca picked up her glass and took a long swallow of wine.

"So you see, I had wondered if you had met in America and were old friends."

"No." Rebecca nodded weakly as the waiter removed the salad and replaced it with moussaka. "We only just met a few days ago."

"As always, Stephen moves quickly and stylishly." Dimitri took her hand again, more than a little amused by the frown he saw deepening in Stephen's eyes. "Where is it in America you are from?"

"Philadelphia." Relax, she ordered herself. Relax and enjoy. "That's in the Northeast."

It infuriated Stephen to watch her flirting so easily, so effectively, with another man. She sat through course after course, barely eating, all the while gifting Dimitri with her shy smiles. Not once did she draw away when the older man touched her hand or leaned close. From where he sat, Stephen could catch a trace of her scent, soft, subtle, maddening. He could hear her quiet laugh when Dimitri murmured something in her ear.

Then she was standing with him, her hand caught in his, as he led her to the dance floor.

Stephen sat there, battling back a jealousy he despised, and watched them move together to music made for lovers. Under the lights her dress clung, then swayed, then shifted. Her face was close, too damn close, to Dimitri's. He knew what it was like to hold her like that, to breathe in the scent of her skin and her hair. He knew what it was to feel her body brush against his, to feel the life, the passion, bubbling. He knew what it was to see her eyes blur, her lips part, to hear that quiet sigh.

He had often put his stamp on land, but never on a woman. He didn't believe in it. But only a fool sat idly by and allowed another man to enjoy what was his. With a muttered oath, Stephen rose, strode out onto the dance floor and laid a hand on Dimitri's shoulder.

"Ah, well." The older man gave a regretful sigh and stepped aside. "Until later."

Before she could respond, Rebecca was caught against Stephen. With a sigh of her own, she relaxed and matched her steps to his. Maybe it was like a dream, she told herself as she closed her eyes and let the music fill her head. But she was going to enjoy every moment until it was time to wake up.

She seemed to melt against him. Her fingers moved lightly through his hair as she rested her cheek against his. Was this the way she'd danced with Dimitri? Stephen wondered, then cursed himself. He was being a fool, but he couldn't seem to stop himself. Then again, he'd had to fight for everything else in his life. Why should his woman be any different?

He wanted to drag her off then and there, away from everyone, and find some dark, quiet place to love her.

"You're enjoying yourself?"

"Yes." She wouldn't think about what he was, not now. Soon enough the night would be over and tomorrow would have to be faced. While the music played and he held her, she would only think of what he meant to her. "Very much."

The dreamy tone of her voice almost undid him. "Apparently Dimitri entertained you well."

"Mmm. He's a very nice man."

"You moved easily from his arms to mine."

Something in his tone pried through the pleasure she felt. Carefully she drew back so that she could see his face. "I don't think I know what you mean."

"I believe you do."

She was tempted to laugh, but there was no humor in Stephen's eyes. Rebecca felt her stomach knot as it always did when she was faced with a confrontation. "If I do, then I'd have to think you ridiculous. Maybe we'd better go back to the table."

"So you can be with him?" Even as the words came out he realized the unfairness, even the foolishness, of them.

She stiffened, retreating as far as she could from anger. "I don't think this is the place for this kind of discussion."

"You're quite right." As furious with himself as he was with her, he pulled her from the dance floor.

CHAPTER EIGHT

"Stop it." By the time he'd dragged her to the elevators, Rebecca had gotten over her first shock. "What's gotten into you?"

"I'm simply taking you to a more suitable place for our discussion." He pulled her into the elevator, then punched the button for their floor.

"You have guests," she began, but he sent her a look than made her feel like a fool. Falling back on dignity, she straightened her shoulders. "I prefer to be asked if I want to leave, not dragged around as though I were a pack mule."

Though her heart was pounding, she sailed past him

when the doors opened, intending to breeze into her own rooms and slam the door in his face. In two steps he had her arm again. Rebecca found herself guided, none too gently, into Stephen's suite.

"I don't want to talk to you," she said, because she was certain her teeth would begin to chatter at any moment. She didn't argue well in the best of circumstances. Faced with Stephen's anger, she was certain she would lose.

He said nothing as he loosened his tie and the first two buttons of his shirt. He went to the bar and poured two brandies. He was being irrational and he knew it, but he seemed unable to control it. That was new, he decided. But there had been many new emotions in him since Rebecca.

Walking back to Rebecca, he set one snifter by her elbow. When he looked at her…he wanted to shout, to beg, to demand, to plead. As a result, his voice was clipped and hard.

"You came to Athens with me, not with Dimitri or any other man."

She didn't touch the snifter. She was certain her hands would shake so hard that it would slip out of her grip. "Is that a Greek custom?" It amazed her—and bolstered her confidence—to hear how calm her voice was. "Forbidding a woman to speak to another man?"

"Speak?" He could still see the way Dimitri had bent his head close to hers. Dimitri, who was smooth and practiced. Dimitri, whose background would very likely mirror Rebecca's. Old money, privileged childhoods, quiet society. "Do you allow every man who speaks to you to hold you, to touch you?"

She didn't blush. Instead, the color faded from her cheeks. She shook, not with fear but with fury. "What I do, and with whom I do it, is my business. Mine."

Very deliberately he lifted his snifter and drank. "No."

"If you think that because I came here with you you have the right to dictate to me you're wrong. I'm my own person, Stephen." It struck her even as she said it that it was true. She was her own person. Each decision she made was her own. Filled with a new sense of power, she stepped forward. "No one owns me, not you, not anyone. I won't be ordered, I won't be forced, I won't be pressured." With a flick of her skirts, she turned. He had her again quickly, his hands on both of her arms, his face close.

"You won't go back to him."

"You couldn't stop me if that was what I wanted." She tossed her head back challengingly. "But I have no intention of going back downstairs to Dimitri, or anyone else." She jerked her arms free. "You idiot. Why should I want to be with him when I'm in love with you?"

She stopped, her eyes wide with shock, her lips parted in surprise. Overwhelmed by a combination of humiliation and fury, she spun around. Then she was struggling against him. "Leave me alone! Oh, God, just leave me alone!"

"Do you think I could let you go now?" He caught her hair in his hand, dragging it back until her eyes met his. In them she saw triumph and desire. "I feel as though I've waited all my life to hear you say those words." He rained kisses over her face until her struggles ceased. "You drive me mad," he murmured. "Being with you, being without you."

"Please." Colors, shapes, lights were whirling in her head. "I need to think."

"No. Ask me for anything else, but not more time." Gathering her close, he buried his face in her hair. "Do you think I make a fool of myself over every woman?"

"I don't know." She moaned when his lips trailed down her throat. Something wild and terrifying was happening inside her body. "I don't know you. You don't know me."

"Yes, I do." He pulled away just far enough to look down at her. "From the first moment I saw you, I knew you. Needed you. Wanted you."

It was true. She knew it, felt it, but she shook her head in denial. "It's not possible."

"I've loved you before, Rebecca, almost as much as I do now." He felt her go still. The color fled from her face again, but her eyes stayed steady on his.

"I don't want you to say what isn't real, what you're not sure of."

"Didn't you feel it, the first time I kissed you?" When he saw the acknowledgment in her eyes, his grip tightened. He could feel her heart thundering, racing to match the rhythm of his own. "Somehow you've come back to me, and I to you. No more questions," he said, before she could speak. "I need you tonight."

It was real. She felt the truth and the knowledge when his mouth found hers. If it was wrong to go blindly into need, then she would pay whatever price was asked. She could no longer deny him...or herself.

There was no gentleness in the embrace. It was as

it had been the first time, lovers reunited, a hunger finally quenched. All heat and light. She gave more than she'd known she had. Her mouth was as avid as his, as seeking. Her murmurs were as desperate. Her hands didn't shake as they moved over him. They pressed, gripped, demanded. Greedy, she tugged the jacket from his shoulders.

Yes, he'd come back to her. If it was madness to believe it, then for tonight she'd be mad.

The taste of her, just the taste of her, was making his head swim and his blood boil. He nipped at her lip, then sucked until he heard her helpless whimper. He wanted her helpless. Something fierce and uncivilized inside him wanted her weak and pliant and defenseless. When she went limp in his arms he dived into her mouth and plundered. Her response tore at him, so sweet, so vulnerable, then suddenly so ardent.

Her hands, which had fluttered helplessly to her side, rose up again to pull at his shirt, to race under it to warmed flesh. She could only think of how right it felt to touch him, to press against him and wait for him to light new fires inside her.

With an oath, he swept her up into his arms and carried her to the bedroom.

The moon was waning and offered only the most delicate light. It fell in slants and shadows on the bed, dreamlike. But the vibrating of Rebecca's pulse told her this was no dream. There was the scent of jasmine from the sprigs in the vase beside the bed. It was a scent she would always remember, just as she would remember how dark and deep were the color of his eyes.

Needful, desperate, they tumbled onto the bed.

He wanted to take care with her. She seemed so small, so fragile. He wanted to show her how completely she filled his heart. But his body was on fire, and she was already moving like a whirlwind beneath him.

His mouth was everywhere, making her shudder and arch and ache. Desires she'd never known sprang to life inside her and took control. Delirious, she obeyed them, reveled in them, then searched for more.

They rolled across the bed in a passionate war that would have two victors, touching, taking, discovering. Impatient, he peeled the dress from her, moaning as he found her breasts with his hands, his lips, his teeth. Unreasoning desire catapulted through him when he felt her soar.

Her body felt like a furnace, impossibly hot, impossibly strong. Sensations rammed into her, stealing her breath. Mindless and moaning, she writhed under him, open for any demand he might make, pulsing for any new knowledge he might offer.

Finally, finally, she knew what it was to love, to be loved, to be wanted beyond reason. Naked, she clung to him, awash in the power and the weakness, the glory and the terror.

He raced over her as if he already knew what would make her tremble, what would make her yearn. Never before had she been so aware, so in tune with another.

She made him feel like a god. He touched, and her skin vibrated under his hand. He tasted, and her flavor was like no other. She was moist, heated, and utterly willing. She seemed to explode beneath him, lost in pleasure, drugged by passion. No other woman had ever driven him so close to madness. Her head was thrown back, and one hand was flung out as her fingers dug into the sheets. Wanton, waiting, wild.

With her name on his lips, he drove into her. His breath caught. His mind spun. Her cry of pain and release echoed in his head, bringing him both triumph and guilt. His body went rigid as he fought to claw his way back. Then she seemed to close around him, body, heart, soul. As helpless as she, he crossed the line into madness and took her with him.

CHAPTER NINE

Aftershocks of passion racked her. Stunned and confused, she lay in the shadowed light. Nothing had prepared her for this. No one had ever warned her that pleasure could be so huge or that need could be so jagged. If she had known... Rebecca closed her eyes and nearly laughed out loud. If she had known, she would have left everything behind years ago and searched the world for him.

Only him. She let out a quiet, calming sigh. Only him.

He was cursing himself, slowly, steadily, viciously. Innocent. Dear God. She'd been innocent, as fresh and untouched as spring, and he'd used her, hurt her, taken her.

Disgusted with himself, he sat up and reached for a cigar. He needed more than tobacco. He needed a drink, but he didn't trust his legs to carry him.

The flick of his lighter sounded like a gunshot. For an instant his face, hardened by anger and self-loathing, was illuminated.

"Why didn't you tell me?"

Still floating on an ocean of pleasure, she blinked her eyes open. "What?"

"Damn it, Rebecca, why didn't you tell me you hadn't been with a man before? That this—that I was your first?"

There was an edge of accusation in his voice. For the first time, she realized she was naked. Her cheeks grew hot as she fumbled for the sheet. One moment there was glory; the next, shame. "I didn't think of it."

"Didn't think of it?" His head whipped around. "Don't you think I had a right to know? Do you think this would have happened if I had known?"

She shook her head. It was true that she hadn't thought of it. It hadn't mattered. He was the first, the last, the only. But now it occurred to her that a man like him might not want to make love with an inexperienced woman. "I'm sorry." Her heart seemed to shrivel in her breast. "You said that you loved me, that you wanted me. The rest didn't seem to matter."

She'd cried out. He'd heard the shock and pain in her voice. And he hadn't been able to stop himself. Yes, he needed a drink. "It mattered," he tossed back as he rose and strode into the other room.

Alone, she let out a shuddering breath. Of course it mattered. Only a fool would have thought otherwise. He'd thought he was dealing with an experienced, emotionally mature woman who knew how to play the game. Words like *love* and *need* and *want* were interchangeable. Yes, he'd said he loved her, but to many love was physical and physical only.

She'd made a fool of herself and she'd infuriated him, and all because she'd begun a relationship built on illusions.

She'd knowingly taken the risk, Rebecca reminded herself as she climbed out of bed. Now she'd pay the price.

He was calmer when he started back to the bedroom. Calmer, though anger still bubbled inside him. First he would show her how it should have been, how it could be. Then they had to talk, rationally, coherently.

"Rebecca…" But when he looked at the bed it was empty.

She was wrapped in a robe and was hurling clothing into her suitcase when she heard him knock. With a shake of her head, she rubbed the tears from her cheeks and continued her frenzied packing. She wouldn't answer…. She wouldn't answer and be humiliated again.

"Rebecca." The moment of calm he'd achieved had vanished. Swearing through gritted teeth, he pounded on the door. "Rebecca, this is ridiculous. Open this door."

Ignoring him, she swept bottles and tubes of toiletries off the bureau and into her bag. He'd go away, she told herself, hardly aware that she'd begun to sob. He'd go away and then she'd leave, take a cab to the airport and catch the first plane to anywhere.

The sound of splintering wood had her rushing into the parlor in time to see the door give way.

She'd thought she'd seen fury before, but she'd been wrong. She saw it now as she stared into Stephen's face. Speechless, she looked from him to the broken door and back again.

Elana, tying the belt of her robe, rushed down the hall. "Stephen, what's happened? Is there a—"

He turned on her, hurling one short sentence in clipped Greek at her. Her eyes widened and she backed away, sending Rebecca a look that combined sympathy and envy.

"Do you think you have only to walk away from me?" He pushed the door back until it scraped against the battered jamb.

"I want—" Rebecca lifted a hand to her throat as if to push the words out. "I want to be alone."

"The hell with what you want." He started toward her, only to stop dead when she cringed and turned away. He'd forgotten what it was like to hurt, truly hurt, until that moment. "I asked you once if you were afraid of me. Now I see that you are." Searching for control, he dipped his hands into the pockets of the slacks he'd thrown on. She looked defenseless, terrified, and tears still streaked her cheeks. "I won't hurt you again. Will you sit?" When she shook her head, he bit off an oath. "I will."

"I know you're angry with me," she began when he'd settled into a chair. "I'll apologize if it'll do any good, but I do want to be alone."

His eyes had narrowed and focused. "You'll apologize? For what?"

"For…" What did he expect her to say? Humiliated, she crossed her arms and hugged her elbows. "For what happened…for not…explaining," she finished lamely. "For whatever you like," she continued as the tears started again. "Just leave me alone."

"Sweet God." He rubbed a weary hand over his face. "I can think of nothing in my life I've handled as badly as this." He rose, but stopped again when she automatically retreated. "You don't want me to touch you." His voice had roughened. He had to swallow to clear his throat. "I won't, but I hope you'll listen."

"There's nothing more to say. I understand how you feel and why you feel it. I'd rather we just left it at that."

"I treated you inexcusably."

"I don't want an apology."

"Rebecca—"

"I don't." Her voice rose, stopping his words, stopping her tears. "It's my fault. It's been my fault all along. No, no, no!" she shouted when he took another step. "I don't want you to touch me. I couldn't bear it."

He sucked in his breath, then let it out slowly. "You twist the knife well."

But she was shaking her head and pacing the room now. "It didn't matter at first—at least I didn't think it would matter. I didn't know who you were or that I would fall in love with you. Now I've waited too long and ruined everything."

"What are you talking about?"

Perhaps it was best, best for both of them, to lay out the truth. "You said you knew me, but you don't, because I've done nothing but lie to you, right from the first moment."

Slowly, carefully, he lowered himself to the arm of a chair. "What have you lied to me about?"

"Everything." Her eyes were drenched with regret when she looked at him. "Then, tonight… First I found out that you own hotels. *Own* them."

"It was hardly a secret. Why should it matter?"

"It wouldn't." She dropped her hands to her sides. "If I was what I'd pretended to be. After we'd made love and you—I realized that by pretending I'd let you have feelings for someone who didn't even exist."

"You're standing in front of me, Rebecca. You exist."

"No. Not the way you think, not the way I've let you think."

He prepared himself for the worst. "What have you done? Were you running away from America?"

"No. Yes." She had to laugh at that. "Yes, I was running." She gathered what composure she had left and folded her hands. "I did come from Philadelphia, as I told you. I've lived there all my life. Lived there, went to school there, worked there." She found a tissue in the pocket of her robe. "I'm an accountant."

He stared at her, one brow lifting, as she blew her nose. "I beg your pardon?"

"I said, I'm an accountant." She hurled the words at him, then whirled away to face the window. Stephen started to rise, then thought better of it.

"I find it difficult to imagine you tallying ledgers, Rebecca. If you'd sit down, maybe we could talk this through."

"Damn it, I said I'm an accountant. A CPA, specializing in corporate taxes. Up until a few weeks ago I worked for McDowell, Jableki and Kline in Philadelphia."

He spread his hands, taking it all in. "All right. What did you do? Embezzle?"

She tossed back her head and nearly exploded with laughter. If she said yes he'd probably be intrigued. But the time for intrigue was over. The time for the truth was now. "No. I've never done anything illegal in my life. I've never even had a parking ticket. I've never done anything at all out of the ordinary until a few weeks ago."

She began to pace again, too agitated to keep still. "I'd never traveled, never had a man send a bottle of champagne to my table, never walked along the beach in the moonlight, never had a lover."

He said nothing, not because he was angry or bored but because he was fascinated.

"I had a good job, my car was paid for, I had good, conservative investments that would have ensured me a comfortable retirement. In my circle of friends I'm known as dependable. If someone needs a sitter they know they can call Rebecca. If they need advice or someone to feed their fish while they're on vacation they don't have to worry. I was never late for work, never took five minutes extra for lunch."

"Commendable," he said, and earned a glare.

"Just the type of employee I imagine you'd like to hire."

He swallowed a chuckle. He'd been prepared for her to confess she had a husband, five husbands, a prison record. Instead she was telling him she was an accountant with an excellent work record. "I have no desire to hire you, Rebecca."

"Just as well." She turned away and started to prowl the room again. "You'd undoubtedly change your mind after I tell you the rest."

Stephen crossed his ankles and settled back. God, what a woman she was. "I'm anxious to hear it."

"My aunt died about three months ago, suddenly."

"I'm sorry." He would have gone to her then, but he could see she was far from ready. "I know how difficult it is to lose family."

"She was all I had left." Because she needed something to do, she pushed open the balcony doors. Warm, fragrant night air rushed in. "I couldn't believe she was gone. Just like that. No warning. Of course, I handled the funeral arrangements. No fuss, no frills. Just the way Aunt Jeannie would have wanted. She was a very economical woman, not only in finances but in dress, in speech, in manner. As long as I can remember, people compared me to her."

Stephen's brow lifted again as he studied the woman being buffeted by the breeze—the short red silk robe, the tousled hair.

"Soon after her death—I don't know if it was days or a week—something just snapped. I looked at myself, at my life, and I hated it." She dragged her hair back, only to have the wind catch it again. "I was a good employee, just like my aunt, a good credit risk, a dependable friend. Law-abiding, conservative and boring. Suddenly I could see myself ten, twenty, thirty years down the road, with nothing more than I had at that moment. I couldn't stand it."

She turned around. The breeze caught at the hem of her robe and sent it dancing around her legs. "I quit my job, and I sold everything."

"Sold?"

"Everything I owned—car, apartment, furniture, books, absolutely everything. I turned all the cash into traveler's checks, even the small inheritance from my aunt. Thousands of dollars. I know it might not sound like a lot to you, but it was more than I'd ever imagined having at once."

"Wait." He held up a hand, wanting to be certain he understood everything. "You're telling me that you sold your possessions, *all* your possessions?"

She couldn't remember ever having felt more foolish, and she straightened her shoulders defensively. "Right down to my coffeepot."

"Amazing," he murmured.

"I bought new clothes, new luggage, and flew to London. First-class. I'd never been on a plane before in my life."

"You'd never flown, but took your first trip across the Atlantic."

She didn't hear the admiration in his voice, only the amusement. "I wanted to see something different. To *be* something different. I stayed at the Ritz and took pictures of the changing of the guard. I flew to Paris and had my hair cut." Self-consciously she lifted a hand to it.

Because he could see that she was overwrought, he was careful not to smile. "You flew to Paris for a haircut."

"I'd heard some women discussing this stylist, and I— Never mind." It was no use trying to explain that she'd gone to the same hairdresser, to the same shops, for years. The same everything. "Right after Paris, I came here," she went on. "I met you. Things happened. I let them happen." Tears threatened. She could only pray he didn't see them. "You were exciting, and attracted to me. Or attracted to who you thought I was. I'd never had a romance. No one had ever looked at me the way you did."

Once more he chose his words carefully. "Are you saying that being with me was different? An adventure, like flying to a Paris salon?"

She would never be able to explain what being with him had meant to her. "Apologies and explanations really don't make any difference now. But I am sorry, Stephen. I'm sorry for everything."

He didn't see the tears, but he heard the regret in her voice. His eyes narrowed. His muscles tensed. "Are you apologizing for making love with me, Rebecca?"

"I'm apologizing for whatever you like. I'd make it up to you if I could, but I don't know how, unless I jump out the window."

He paused, as if he were considering it. "I don't think this requires anything quite that drastic. Perhaps if you'd sit down calmly?"

She shook her head and stayed where she was. "I can't handle any more of this tonight, Stephen. I'm sorry. You've every right to be angry."

He rose, the familiar impatience building. But she was so pale, looked so fragile, sounded so weary. He hadn't treated her gently before. At least he could do so now.

"All right. Tomorrow, then, after you've rested." He

started to go to her, then checked himself. It would take time to show her that there were other ways to love. Time to convince her that love was more, much more than an adventure. "I want you to know that I regret what happened tonight. But that, too, will wait until tomorrow." Though he wanted to touch a hand to her cheek, he kept it fisted in his pocket. "Get some rest."

She had thought her heart was already broken. Now it shattered. Not trusting her voice, she nodded.

He left her alone. The door scraped against the splintered jamb as he secured it. She supposed there might have been a woman somewhere who'd made a bigger fool of herself. At the moment, it didn't seem to matter.

At least there was something she could do for both of them. Disappear.

CHAPTER TEN

It was her own fault, she supposed. There were at least half a dozen promising accounting positions in the want ads. Not one of them interested her. Rebecca circled them moodily. How could she be interested in dental plans and profit sharing? All she could think about, all she'd been able to think about for two weeks, was Stephen.

What had he thought when he'd found her gone? Relief? Perhaps a vague annoyance at business left unfinished? Pen in hand, Rebecca stared out of the window of the garden apartment she'd rented. In her fantasies she imagined him searching furiously for her, determined to find her, whatever the cost. Reality, she thought with a sigh, wasn't quite so romantic. He would have been relieved. Perhaps she wasn't sophisticated, but at least she'd stepped out of his life with no fuss.

Now it was time to get her own life in order.

First things first. She had an apartment, and the little square of lawn outside the glass doors was going to make her happy. That in itself was a challenge. Her old condo had been centrally located on the fifth floor of a fully maintained modern building.

This charming and older development was a good thirty miles from downtown, but she could hear the birds in the morning. She would be able to look out at old oaks and sweeping maples and flowers she would plant herself. Perhaps it wasn't as big a change as a flight to Paris, but for Rebecca it was a statement.

She'd bought some furniture. *Some* was the operative word. Thus far she'd picked out a bed, one antique table and a single chair.

Not logical, Rebecca thought with a faint smile. No proper and economical living room suite, no tidy curtains. Even the single set of towels she'd bought was frivolous. And exactly what she'd wanted. She would do what she'd secretly wanted to do for years—buy a piece here, a piece there. Not because it was a good buy or durable, but because she wanted it.

She wondered how many people would really understand the satisfaction of making decisions not because they were sensible but because they were desirable. She'd done it with her home, her wardrobe. Even with her hair, she thought, running a hand through it. Outward changes had led to inner changes. Or vice versa.

Either way, she would never again be the woman she'd been before.

Or perhaps she would be the woman she'd always been but had refused to acknowledge.

Then why was she circling ads in the classifieds? Rebecca asked herself. Why was she sitting here on a beautiful morning planning a future she had no interest in? Perhaps it was true that she would never have the one thing, the one person, she really wanted. There would be no more picnics or walks in the moonlight or frantic nights in bed. Still, she had the memories, she had the moments, she had the dreams. There would be no regrets where Stephen was concerned. Not now, and not ever. And if she was now more the woman she had been with him, it had taken more than a change in hairstyle.

She was stronger. She was surer. She was freer. And she'd done it herself.

She could think of nothing she wanted less than to go back into someone else's firm, tallying figures, calculating profit and loss. So she wouldn't. Rebecca sank into the chair as the thought struck home.

She wouldn't. She wouldn't go job hunting, carrying her résumé, rinsing sweaty palms in the rest room, putting her career and life in someone else's hands again. She'd open her own firm. A small one, certainly. Personalized. Exclusive, she decided, savoring the word. Why not? She had the skill, the experience, and—finally—she had the courage.

It wouldn't be easy. In fact, it would be risky. The money she had left would have to go toward renting office space, equipment, a phone system, advertising. With a bubbling laugh, she sprang up and searched for a

legal pad and a pencil. She had to make lists—not only
of things to do but of people to call. She had enough
contacts from her McDowell, Jableki and Kline days.
Maybe, just maybe, she could persuade some of her
former clients to give her a try.

"Just a minute," she called out when she heard the
knock on the door. She scribbled a reminder to look for
file cabinets as she went to answer. She'd much rather
have some good solid oak file cabinets than a living
room sofa.

She knew better than to open the door without checking the security peephole, but she was much too involved with her plans to think about such things. When
she opened the door, she found herself face-to-face with
Stephen.

Even if she could have spoken, he wasn't in the mood
to let her. "What in the hell do you think you're doing?"
he demanded as he slammed the door behind him. "Do
you deliberately try to drive me mad, or does it come
naturally to you?"

"I—I don't—" But he was already yanking her
against him. Whatever words she might have spoken
dissolved into a moan against his lips. Her pad fell to
the floor with a slap. Even as her arms came up around
him he was thrusting her away.

"What kind of game are you playing, Rebecca?"
When she just shook her head, he dug his hands into
his pockets and paced the wide, nearly empty room. He
was unshaven, disheveled and absolutely gorgeous. "It's
taken me two weeks and a great deal of trouble to find
you. I believe we'd agreed to talk again. I was surprised

to discover you'd not only left Athens, but Europe." He swung back and pinned her with a look. "Why?"

Still reeling from his entrance, she struggled not to babble. "I thought it best that I leave."

"You thought?" He took a step toward her, his fury so palatable that she braced herself. "You thought it best," he repeated. "For whom?"

"For you. For both of us." She caught herself fiddling with the lapels of her robe and dropped her hands. "I knew you were angry with me for lying to you and that you regretted what had happened between us. I felt it would be better for both of us if I—"

"Ran away?"

Her chin came up fractionally. "Went away."

"You said you loved me."

She swallowed. "I know."

"Was that another lie?"

"Please don't." She turned away, but there was nowhere to go. "Stephen, I never expected to see you again. I'm trying to make some sense out of my life, to do things in a way that's not only right but makes me happy. In Greece, I guess, I did what made me happy, but I didn't think about what was right. The time with you was…"

"Was what?"

Dragging both hands through her hair, she turned to him again. It was as if the two weeks had never been. She was facing him again, trying to explain what she feared she could never explain. "It was the best thing that ever happened to me, the most important, the most unforgettable, the most precious. I'll always be grateful for those few days."

"Grateful." He wasn't sure whether to laugh or murder her. Stepping forward, he surprised them both by slipping his hands lightly around her throat. "For what? For my giving you your first fling? A fast, anonymous romance with no consequences?"

"No." She lifted a hand to his wrist but made no attempt to struggle. "Did you come all this way to make me feel more guilty?"

"I came all this way because I finish what I begin. We'd far from finished, Rebecca."

"All right." Be calm, she told herself. When a man was this close to the edge, a woman's best defense was serenity. "If you'll let me go, we'll talk. Would you like some coffee?"

His fingers tightened reflexively, then slowly relaxed. "You've bought a new pot."

"Yes." Was that humor in his eyes? she wondered. "There's only one chair. Why don't you use it while I go into the kitchen?"

He took her arm. "I don't want coffee, or a chair, or a pleasant conversation."

It seemed serenity wouldn't work. "All right, Stephen. What do you want?"

"You. I'd thought I'd made that fairly obvious." When she frowned, he glanced around the apartment. "Now tell me, Rebecca, is this what you want? A handful of rooms to be alone in?"

"I want to make the best of the rest of my life. I've already apologized for deceiving you. I realize that—"

"Deceiving me." He held up a finger to stop her. "I've wanted to clear that point up myself. How did you deceive me?"

"By letting you think that I was something I'm not."

"You're not a beautiful, interesting woman? A passionate woman?" He lifted a brow as he studied her. "Rebecca, I have too much pride to ever believe you could deceive me that completely."

He was confusing her—deliberately, she was sure. "I told you what I'd done."

"What you'd done," he agreed. "And how you'd done it." He brought his hand to her throat again, this time in a caress. His anger hadn't made her knees weak. She felt them tremble now at his tenderness. "Selling your possessions and flying to Paris for a new hairstyle. Quitting your job and grabbing life with both hands. You fascinate me." Her eyes stayed open wide when he brushed his lips over hers. "I think the time is nearly over when you'll be so easily flattered. It's almost a pity." He drew her closer, slowly, while his mouth touched hers. Relief coursed through him as he felt her melt and give. "Do you think it was your background that attracted me?"

"You were angry," she managed.

"Yes, angry at the idea that I had been part of your experiment. Furious," he added before he deepened the kiss. "Furious that I had been of only passing interest." She was heating in his arms, just as he remembered, just as he needed, softening, strengthening. "Shall I tell you how angry? Shall I tell you that for two weeks I couldn't work, couldn't think, couldn't function, because you were everywhere I looked and nowhere to be found?"

"I had to go." She was already tugging at his shirt to find the flesh beneath. To touch him again, just for a moment. To be touched by him. "When you said you regretted making love…" Her own words brought her back. Quickly she dropped her hands and stepped away.

He stared at her for a moment, then abruptly swore and began to pace. "I've never thought myself this big a fool. I hurt you that night in a much different way than I'd believed. Then I handled it with less finesse than I might the most unimportant business transaction." He paused, sighing. For the first time she saw clearly how incredibly weary he was.

"You're tired. Please, sit down. Let me fix you something."

He took a moment to press his fingers to his eyes. Again he wanted to laugh—while he strangled her. She was exactly what he needed, what he understood. Yet at the same time she baffled him.

"You weaken me, Rebecca, and bring out the fool I'd forgotten I could be. I'm surprised you allowed me to set foot into your home. You should have—" As quickly as the anger had come, it faded. As quickly as the tension had formed, it eased. Everything he'd needed to see was in her eyes. Carefully now, he drew a deep breath. A man wasn't always handed so many chances at happiness.

"Rebecca, I never regretted making love with you." He stopped her from turning with the lightest of touches on her shoulder. "I regretted only the way it happened. Too much need and too little care. I regret, I'll always regret, that for your first time there was fire but no warmth." He took her hands in his and brought them to his lips.

"It was beautiful."

"In its way." His fingers tightened on hers. Still so

innocent, he thought. Still so generous. "It was not kind or patient or tender, as love should be the first time."

She felt hope rise in her heart again. "None of that mattered."

"It mattered, more than I can ever tell you. After, when you told me everything, it only mattered more. If I had done what my instincts told me to do that night you would never have left me. But I thought you needed time before you could bear to have me touch you again." Slowly, gently, he drew the tip of her finger into his mouth and watched her eyes cloud over. "Let me show you what I should have shown you then." With her hands locked in his, he looked into her eyes. "Do you want me?"

It was time for the truth. "Yes."

He lifted her into his arms and heard her breath catch. "Do you trust me?"

"Yes."

When he smiled, her heart turned over. "Rebecca, I must ask you one more thing."

"What is it?"

"Do you have a bed?"

She felt her cheeks heat even as she laughed. "In there."

She was trembling. It reminded him how careful he had to be, how precious this moment was to both of them. The sun washed over the bed, over them, as he lay beside her. And kissed her—only kissed her, softly, deeply, thoroughly, until her arms slipped from around him to fall bonelessly to her sides. She trembled still as he murmured to her, as his lips brushed over her cheeks, her throat.

He had shown her the desperation love could cause, the sharp-edged pleasure, the speed and the fury. Now he showed her that love could mean serenity and sweetness.

And she showed him.

He had thought to teach her, not to learn, to reassure her but not to be comforted. But he learned, and he was comforted. The need was there, as strong as it had been the first time. But strength was tempered with patience. As he slipped his hands down her robe to part it, to slide it away from her skin, he felt no need to hurry. He could delight in the way the sun slanted across her body, in the way her flesh warmed to his touch.

Her breath was as unsteady as her hands as she undressed him. But not from nerves. She understood that now. She felt strong and capable and certain. Anticipation made her tremble. Pleasure made her shudder. She gave a sigh that purred out of her lips as she arched against his seeking hands. Then he nipped lightly at her breast and she bounded from serenity to passion in one breathless leap.

Still he moved slowly, guiding her into a kind of heated torment she'd never experienced. Desire boiled in her, and his name sprang to her lips and her body coiled like a spring. Chaining down his own need, he set hers free and watched as she flew over the first peak.

"Only for me," he murmured as she went limp in his arms. "Only for me, Rebecca." With his own passions strapped, he slipped into her, determined to watch her build again. "Tell me you love me. Look at me and tell me."

She opened her eyes. She could barely breathe.

Somehow the strength was pouring back into her, but so fast, so powerfully. Sensation rolled over sensation, impossibly. She moved with him, pressed center to center, heart to heart, but all she could see were his eyes, so dark, so blue, so intense. Perhaps she was drowning in them.

"I love you, Stephen."

Then she was falling, fathoms deep, into his eyes, into the sea. With her arms locked around him, she dragged him under with her.

He pulled her against him so that he could stroke her hair and wait for his pulse to level. She'd been innocent. But the surprise, the one he'd been dealing with for weeks, was that until Rebecca he'd been just as innocent. He'd known passion, but he'd never known intimacy, not the kind that reached the heart as fully as the body. And yet...

"We've been here before," he murmured. "Do you feel it, too?"

She linked her fingers with his. "I never believed in things like that until you. When I'm with you it's like remembering." She lifted her head to look at him. "I can't explain it."

"I love you, Rebecca, only more knowing who you are, why you are."

She touched a hand to his cheek. "I don't want you to say anything you don't really feel."

"How can a woman be so intelligent and still so stupid?" With a shake of his head, Stephen rolled on top of her. "A man doesn't travel thousands of miles for this, however delightful it may be. I love you, and though it annoyed me for quite some time I'm accustomed to it now."

"Annoyed you."

"Infuriated." He kissed her to cut off whatever retort she might make. "I'd seen myself remaining free for years to come. Then I met a woman who sold her coffeepot so she could take pictures of goats."

"I certainly have no intention of interfering with your plans."

"You already have." He smiled, holding her still when she tried to struggle away. "Marriage blocks off certain freedoms and opens others."

"Marriage?" She stopped struggling but turned her head to avoid another kiss.

"Soon." He nuzzled her neck. "Immediately."

"I never said I'd marry you."

"No, but you will." With his fingertips only, he began to arouse her. "I'm a very persuasive man."

"I need to think." But she was trembling again. "Stephen, marriage is very serious."

"Deadly. And I should warn you that I've already decided to murder any man you look at for more than twenty seconds."

"Really?" She turned her head back, prepared to be angry. But he was smiling. No one else had ever smiled at her in quite that way. "Really?"

"I can't let you go, Rebecca. Can't and won't. Come back with me. Marry me. Have children with me."

"Stephen—"

He laid a finger to her lips. "I know what I'm asking you. You've already started a new life, made new plans. We've had only days together, but I can make you happy. I can promise to love you for a lifetime, or however many lifetimes we have. You once dived into the sea on impulse. Dive with me now, Rebecca. I swear you won't regret it."

Gently she pressed her lips to his fingertip, then drew his hand away. "All my life I've wondered what I might find if I had the courage to look. I found you, Stephen." With a laugh she threw her arms around him. "When do you want to leave?"

* * * * *

THE NAME OF THE GAME

To Faye Ashley.

Now you'll have to leave me the bracelet.

CHAPTER ONE

"Marge Whittier, this is your chance to win *ten thousand dollars*. Are you ready?"

Marge Whittier, a forty-eight-year-old schoolteacher and grandmother of two from Kansas City, squirmed in her chair. The lights were on, the drum was rolling and the possibility of her being sick was building. "Yes, I'm ready."

"Good luck, Marge. The clock will start with your first pick. Begin."

Marge swallowed a lump of panic, shuddered with excitement and chose number six. Her sixty seconds began to dwindle, and the tension grew as she and her celebrity partner picked their brains for the right answers. They leaped over such questions as who founded psychoanalysis and how many yards in a mile, then came to a screeching halt. What element do all organic compounds contain?

Marge went pale, and her lips quivered. She was an English teacher and a bit of a history and movie buff, but science wasn't her long suit. She looked pleadingly at her partner, who was better known for her wit than for her wisdom. Precious seconds ticked away. As they fumbled, the buzzer sounded. Ten thousand dollars flowed through Marge's sweaty fingers.

The studio audience groaned their disappointment.

"Too bad, Marge." John Jay Johnson, the tall, sleekly polished host, laid a sympathetic hand on her shoulder. His rich, rolling voice expressed just the right combination of disappointment and hope. "You were so close. But with eight correct answers you add another eight hundred dollars to your total. An impressive one." He smiled at the camera. "We'll be back after this break to total up Marge's winnings and to give you the correct answer to the stumper. Stay with us."

The music was cued. John Jay kept his avuncular smile handy. He used the timed ninety-second break to come on to the pretty celebrity panelist.

"Pompous jerk," Johanna muttered. The pity was that she was too aware his smooth looks and slick manner were keeping *Trivia Alert* up in the ratings. As producer, she'd learned to accept John Jay as part of the set. She checked the second hand of her watch before walking over to the losers. Putting on a smile of her own, she commiserated and congratulated as she eased them along. She needed them in camera range for the finish.

"Coming up on five," she announced, and signaled for applause and music. "And cue."

John Jay, his arm around Marge and his three-thousand-dollar caps gleaming, closed the show.

They were one big happy family as the assistant director shut off his stopwatch. "That's a wrap."

Kiki Wilson, Marge's partner and the current star of a popular situation comedy, chatted a few moments longer with Marge in a way that would have the schoolteacher remembering her warmly for years to come. When Kiki rose, her smile was still firmly in place as she walked the few steps to John Jay.

"If you ever pull something like that again," she said quietly, "you'll need a paramedic."

Knowing she was referring to his quick—and, if he did say so, clever—hand maneuver just before the end of the break, John Jay smiled. "Just part of the service. About that drink, sweetheart…"

"Kiki." In a smooth move that didn't appear nearly as rushed and harassed as it was, Johanna swung over and scooted the actress away. "I want to thank you again for agreeing to do the show. I know how hectic your schedule must be."

Johanna's warm voice and soothing manner brought Kiki's blood pressure down slightly. "I enjoyed it." Kiki pulled out a cigarette and tapped it absently against an enameled case. "It's a cute show, moves fast. And God knows the exposure never hurts."

Though Johanna didn't smoke, she carried a small

gold lighter. Pulling it out, she lit Kiki's cigarette. "You were wonderful. I hope you'll consider coming back."

Kiki blew out smoke and regarded Johanna. The lady knew her job, Kiki admitted. Even though she looked like some cuddly little model for shampoo or yogurt. It had been a long day, but the catered dinner break had been first-class, the studio audience generous with their applause. In any case, her agent had told her that *Trivia Alert* was *the* up-and-coming game show of the year. Considering that, and the fact that Kiki had a good sense of humor, she smiled.

"I just might. You've got a good crew, with one notable exception."

Johanna didn't have to turn to know where Kiki's narrowed gaze had landed. With John Jay it was either love or disgust, with little middle ground. "I have to apologize for any annoyance."

"Don't bother. There are plenty of jerks in the business." Kiki studied Johanna again. Quite a face, she decided, even with the minimal makeup. "I'm surprised you don't have a few fang marks."

Johanna smiled. "I have very thick skin."

Anyone who knew her would have attested to that. Johanna Patterson might have looked soft and creamy, but she had the energy of an Amazon. For eighteen months she had slaved, hustled and bargained to get and keep *Trivia Alert* on the air. She wasn't a novice in the entertainment business, and that made her all the more aware that behind the scenes and in the boardrooms it was still a man's world.

That would change eventually, but eventually was too long a wait. Johanna wasn't patient enough to wait for doors to open. When she wanted something badly enough, she gave them a push. For that she was willing to make certain adjustments herself. The business of entertainment was no mystery to her; nor were the deals, the concessions or the compromises. As long as the end product was quality, it didn't matter.

She'd had to swallow pride and sacrifice a principle or two to get her baby off and running. For example, it wasn't her name, but her father's logo that flashed importantly at the end of the show: Carl W. Patterson Productions

His was the name the network brass related to, and his was the one they trusted. So she used it—grudgingly—then ran things her way.

Thus far, the uneasy marriage was into its second year and holding its own. Johanna knew the business—and her father—too well to take for granted that it would continue.

So she worked hard, tying up loose ends, hammering out solutions to problems and delegating carefully what couldn't be handled personally. The success or failure of the show wouldn't make or break her, financially or professionally, but she had more than money and reputation tied up with it. She had her hopes and her self-esteem.

The studio audience had been cleared. A few technicians remained on the set, either gossiping or tidying up last-minute business. It was just past eight o'clock, and moving into hour fourteen for Johanna.

"Bill, do you have the dupes?" She accepted the copies of the day's tape from her editor. Five shows were produced and recorded in one full-day session. Five costume changes for the celebrity panelists—Johanna had a policy against referring to them as guest stars. Five wardrobe trips for John Jay, who insisted on a change from underwear out for each show. His natty suits and coordinated ties would be sent back to the Beverly Hills tailor who provided them free in exchange for the plug at the end of each show.

His job was over, but Johanna's was just beginning. The tapes would be reviewed, edited and carefully timed. Johanna would oversee each step. There would be mail to go through, letters from home viewers who hoped to be chosen as contestants, more letters from people who disagreed with certain answers. She'd go head-to-head with her research coordinator to check facts and select new questions for upcoming shows. Though she couldn't personally interview and screen each potential contestant, she would go over her contestant coordinator's selections.

The game-show scandals of the fifties were long over, but no one wanted a repeat of them. Standards and Practices was very strict, their rules and regulations very clear. Johanna made it a habit never to relax her own, and to check each detail herself.

When screened contestants arrived at the studio for a day's taping, they were turned over to staff members who sequestered them from the crew, the audience and their prospective partners. They were entertained and soothed, literally cut off from the show until their turn came to participate.

Questions were locked in a safe. Only Johanna and her personal assistant had the combination.

Then, of course, there were the celebrities to deal

with. They would want their favorite flowers and choice of beverage in their dressing rooms. Some would go with the flow and make her life easier, and others would be difficult just to show they were important. She knew—and they knew she knew—that most of them appeared on morning game shows not for the money or the fun but for the exposure. They were plugging series and specials, placating their networks or scrambling to keep their face familiar to the public.

Fortunately, a good percentage of them had fun once the ball was rolling. There were still more, however, who required pampering, cajoling and flattery. She was willing, as long as they helped her keep her show on the air. When a woman had grown up with artistic temperaments and the wheeling and dealing of the entertainment business, very little surprised her.

"Johanna."

Regretfully Johanna put her fantasy of a hot bath and a foot massage on hold. "Yes, Beth?" She slipped the tapes into her oversize tote and waited for her assistant. Bethany Landman was young, sharp and energetic. Just now she seemed to be bubbling over. "Make it good. My feet are killing me."

"It's good." A bouncy dark contrast to Johanna's cool blond looks, Bethany gripped her clipboard and all but danced. "We've got him."

Johanna secured the tote on the shoulder of her slim violet-blue jacket. "Who have we got and what are we going to do with him?"

"Sam Weaver." Beth caught her lower lip between her teeth as she grinned. "And I can think of a lot of things we could do with him."

The fact that Bethany was still innocent enough to be impressed by a hard body and tough good looks made Johanna feel old and cynical. More, it made her feel as though she'd been born that way. Sam Weaver was every woman's dream. Johanna wouldn't have denied him his talent, but she was long past the point where sexy eyes and a cocky grin made her pulse flutter. "Why don't you give me the most plausible?"

"Johanna, you have no romance in your soul."

"No, I don't. Can we do this walking, Beth? I want to see if the sky's still there."

"You read that Sam Weaver's done his first TV spot?"

"A miniseries," Johanna added as they wound down the studio corridor.

"They aren't calling it a miniseries. Promotion calls it a four-hour movie event."

"I love Hollywood."

With a chuckle, Bethany shifted her clipboard. "Anyway, I took a chance and contacted his agent. The movie's on our network."

Johanna pushed open the studio door and breathed in the air. Though it was Burbank air and therefore far from fresh, it was welcome. "I'm beginning to see the master plan."

"The agent was very noncommittal, but…"

Johanna stretched her shoulders, then searched for her keys. "I think I'm going to like this *but*."

"I just got a call from upstairs. They want him to do it. We'll have to run the shows the week before the movie and give him time to plug it every day." She paused just long enough to give Johanna a chance to nod. "With that guarantee they'll put on the pressure and we've got him."

"Sam Weaver," Johanna murmured. There was no denying his drawing power. Being tall, lanky and handsome in a rough sort of way didn't hurt, but he had more than that. A bit part in a feature film five, maybe six years before had been a springboard. He'd been top-billed and hot box office ever since. It was more than likely he'd be a pain in the neck to work with, but it might be worth it. She thought of the millions of televisions across the country, and the ratings. It would definitely be worth it.

"Good work, Beth. Let's get it firmed up."

"As good as done." Bethany stood by the spiffy little Mercedes as Johanna climbed in. "Will you fire me if I drool?"

"Absolutely." Johanna flashed a grin as she turned the key. "See you in the morning." She drove the car out of the lot like a bullet. Sam Weaver, she thought as she turned the radio up and let the wind whip her hair. Not a bad catch, she decided. Not bad at all.

Sam felt like a fish with a hook through his mouth, and he didn't enjoy the sensation. He slumped in his agent's overstuffed chair, his long, booted legs stretched out and a pained scowl on the face women loved to love.

"Good Lord, Marv. A game show? Why don't you tell me to dress like a banana and do a commercial?"

Marvin Jablonski chomped a candied almond, his current substitute for cigarettes. He admitted to being forty-three, which made him a decade older than his client. He was trim and dressed with a subtle flair that spoke of wealth and confidence. When his office had consisted of a phone booth and a briefcase, he'd dressed the same. He knew how vital illusions were in this town. Just as he knew it was vital to keep a client happy while you were manipulating him.

"I thought it was too much to expect that you'd be open-minded."

Sam recognized the touch of hurt in Marv's tone— the poor, self-sacrificing agent, just trying to do his job. Marv was far from poor and he'd never been into personal sacrifice. But it worked. With something like a sigh, Sam rose and paced the length of Marv's glitzy Century City office. "I was open-minded when I agreed to do the talk-show circuit."

Sam's easy baritone carried a hint of his native rural Virginia, but his reputation in Los Angeles wasn't that of a country gentleman. As he paced, his long-legged stride made the observer think of a man who knew exactly where he was going.

And so he did, Marv thought. Otherwise, as a selective and very successful theatrical agent he would never have taken the struggling young actor on six years before. Instinct, Marv was wont to say, was every bit as important as the power breakfast. "Promotion's part of the business, Sam."

"Yeah, and I'll do my bit. But a game show? How is guessing what's behind door number three going to boost the ratings for *Roses*?"

"There aren't any doors on *Trivia*."

"Thank God."

Marv let the sarcasm pass. He was one of the few in the business who knew that Sam Weaver could be ma-

neuvered with words like *responsibility* and *obligation*.
"And it'll boost the ratings because millions of sets are
tuned in to that half-hour spot five days a week. People
love games, Sam. They like to play, they like to watch
and they like to see other people walk out with a free
lunch. I've got miles of facts and figures, but let's just
say that most of those sets are controlled by women."
His smile spread easily, shifting his trim, gray-flecked
mustache. "Women, Sam, the ones who buy the bulk
of the products the sponsors are hyping. And that fizzy
little soft drink that's the major sponsor for *Roses* also
buys time on *Trivia*. The network likes that, Sam. Keeps
things in the family."

"That's fine." Sam hooked his thumbs in the pockets
of his jeans. "But we both know I didn't take the TV
deal to sell soda pop."

Marv smiled and ran a hand over his hair. His new
toupee was a work of art. "Why did you take the deal?"

"You know why. The script was gold. We needed
the four hours to do it right. A two-hour feature would
have meant hacking it to bits."

"So you used TV." Marv closed his fingers together
lightly, as if he were shutting a trap. "Now TV wants
to use you. It's only fair, Sam."

Fair was another word Sam had a weakness for.

A short four-letter epithet was Sam's opinion. Then
he said nothing as he stared out at his agent's lofty view
of the city. He wasn't so many years off the pavement
that he'd forgotten what it felt like to have the heat bake
through his sneakers and frustration run through his
blood. Marv had taken a chance on him. A calculated

risk, but a risk nonetheless. Sam believed in paying his dues. But he hated making a fool of himself.

"I don't like to play games," he muttered, "unless I set the rules."

Marv ignored the buzzer on his desk; it was the prerogative of a man in demand. "You talking politics or the show?"

"Sounds to me like they've been lumped together."

Marv only smiled again. "You're a sharp boy, Sam."

Sam turned his head just a fraction. Marv had been hit by the power of those eyes before. They were one of the reasons he'd signed an unknown when he'd been in a position to refuse the business of well-established luminaries. The eyes were big, heavy lidded and blue. Electric blue, with the power of a lightning bolt. Intense, like his long-boned, narrow face and firm mouth. The chin wasn't so much cleft as sculpted. The kind of chin that looked as though it could take a punch. The nose was a bit crooked, because it had.

California sun had tanned the skin a deep brown and added the interest of faint lines. The kind that made a woman shiver, imagining the experiences that had etched them there. There was a mystery about his face that appealed to females, and a toughness that drew approval from other men. His hair was dark and left long enough to go its own way.

It wasn't a face for a poster in a teenager's room, but it was the kind that haunted a woman's secret dreams.

"How much choice do I have on this?" Sam asked.

"Next to none." Because he knew his client, Marv decided it was time to bare the truth. "Your contract with the network ties you to promotion work. We could get around it, but it wouldn't be good for you, this project or any future ones."

Sam didn't give a damn if it was good for him. He rarely did. But the project was important. "When?"

"Two weeks from today, I'll move the paperwork through. Keep it in perspective, Sam. It's one day out of your life."

"Yeah." One day, he thought, could hardly make much difference. And it wasn't easy to forget that a decade before he'd have considered an offer to do a game show as much of a miracle as manna from heaven. "Marv…" He paused at the door. "If I make an ass out of myself, I'm going to dump Krazy Glue on your hairpiece."

It was strange that two people could have business in the same building, often ride the same elevator, but never cross paths. Sam didn't make the trip from Malibu to his agent's office often. Now that his career was on the rise he was usually tied up in rehearsals, script meetings or location shoots. When he had a few weeks, as he did now, he didn't waste it battling L.A.'s traffic or closing himself up inside Century City's impressive walls. He preferred the seclusion of his ranch.

Johanna, on the other hand, made the trip to her Century City office daily. She hadn't taken a personal vacation in two years, and she put in an average of sixty hours a week on her show. If anyone had tagged her as a workaholic she would have shrugged off the label. Work wasn't an illness, as far as Johanna was concerned; it was a means to an end. The long hours and dedication justified her success. She was determined that no one accuse her of riding on Carl Patterson's coattails.

The offices maintained by *Trivia*'s staff were comfortable but understated. Her own was large enough to prevent her from feeling claustrophobic and practical enough to make the statement that this was a place of business. She arrived like clockwork at eight-thirty, broke for lunch only if it included a meeting, then worked straight through until she was finished. Besides her almost maternal devotion to *Trivia*, she had another concept on the back burner. A word game this time, an idea that was nearly refined enough to take to the network brass.

Now she had her jacket slung over her chair and her nose buried in a week's worth of potential questions passed on to her by Research. She had to get close to the words because she refused to wear the reading glasses she needed.

"Johanna?"

With little more than a grunt, Johanna continued to read. "Did you know Howdy Doody had a twin brother?"

"We were never close," Bethany said apologetically.

"Double Doody," Johanna informed her with a nod. "I think it's a great one for the speed round. Did you catch today's show?"

"Most of it."

"I really think we should try to lure Hank Loman back. Soap stars are a big draw."

"Speaking of big draws..." Bethany set a stack of papers on Johanna's desk. "Here's the contract for Sam

Weaver. I thought you'd like to look it over before I run it up to his agent."

"Fine." She shuffled papers before drawing the contract close enough to focus on it. "Let's send him a tape of the show."

"The usual fruit and cheese for the dressing room?"

"Mmm-hmm. Is the coffee machine fixed?"

"Just."

"Good." She took a casual glance at her watch. It was a simple affair with a black leather band. The diamond-encrusted one her father's secretary had picked out for her last birthday was still in its box. "Listen, you go on to lunch. I'll run these up."

"Johanna, you're forgetting how to delegate again."

"No, I'm just delegating me." Rising, she shook the creases out of her pale rose jacket. After picking up the remote channel changer from her desk, she aimed it at the television across the room. Both picture and sound winked off. "Are you still seeing that struggling screenwriter?"

"Every chance I get."

Johanna grinned as she shrugged into her jacket. "Then you'd better hurry. This afternoon we need to brainstorm over the home viewer's contest. I want that rolling by next month." She picked up the contracts and slipped them and a cassette into a leather portfolio. "Oh, and make a note for me to slap John Jay's wrist, will you? He charged a case of champagne to the show again."

Bethany wrote that down enthusiastically and in capital letters. "Glad to do it."

Johanna chuckled as she swung out the door. "Results of the contestant screening by three," she continued. "That tech's wife—Randy's wife—she's in Cedars of Lebanon for minor surgery. Send flowers." Johanna grinned over her shoulder. "Who says I can't delegate?"

On the ride up in the elevator, Johanna smiled to herself. She was lucky to have Beth, she thought, though she could already foresee the time when her assistant would be moving up and out. Brains and talent rarely settled for someone else's dream. She liked to think she'd proved that theory for herself. In any case, Johanna had Beth now, and with the rest of her bright young staff, Johanna was on her way to establishing her own niche in the competitive world of daytime television.

If she could get her new concept as far as a pilot, she had no doubt she could sell it. Then maybe a daytime drama, something with as much action as heartache. That story was already in its beginning stages. In addition to that, she was determined to have a nighttime version of *Trivia* syndicated to the independents. She was already on the way to achieving her five-year goal of forming her own production company.

As the elevator rose, Johanna automatically smoothed down her hair and straightened the hem of her jacket. Appearances, she knew, were as important as talent.

When the doors opened, she was satisfied that she looked brisk and professional. She passed through the wide glass doors into Jablonski's offices. He didn't believe in understatement. There were huge Chinese-red urns filled with feathers and fans. A sculpture of what might have been a human torso gleamed in brushed brass. The carpet was an unrelieved white and, Johanna's practical mind thought, must be the devil to keep clean.

Wide chairs in black and red leather were arranged beside glass tables. Trade magazines and the day's papers were set in neat piles. The setup told her Jablonski didn't mind keeping clients waiting.

The desks in the reception area followed the theme in glossy red and black. Johanna saw an attractive brunette seated at one. Perched on the corner of the desk and leaning close to the brunette was Sam Weaver. Johanna's brow lifted only slightly.

She wasn't surprised to see him flirting with one of the staff. Indeed, she expected that kind of thing from him and others like him. After all, her father had had an affair with every secretary, receptionist and assistant who had ever worked for him.

He'd been the tall, dark and handsome type, too, she thought. Still was. Her only real surprise at running into Sam Weaver was that he was one of that rare breed of actor who actually looked better in the flesh than on the screen.

He packed a punch, an immediate one.

Snug jeans suited him, she acknowledged, as did the plain cotton shirt of a working man. No gold flashed, no diamonds winked. He didn't need them, Johanna decided. A man who could look at the receptionist the way Sam was looking at that brunette didn't need artifice to draw attention to him.

"She's beautiful, Gloria." Sam bent closer to the snapshots the receptionist was showing off. From Johanna's angle it looked as though he were whispering endearments. "You're lucky."

"She's six months old today." Gloria smiled down at the photograph of her daughter, then up at Sam. "I was lucky Mr. Jablonski gave me such a liberal maternity leave, and it's nice to be back at work, but boy, I miss her already."

"She looks like you."

The brunette's cheeks flushed with pride and pleasure. "You think so?"

"Sure. Look at that chin." Sam tapped a finger on Gloria's chin. He wasn't just being kind. The truth was, he'd always gotten a kick out of kids. "I bet she keeps you busy."

"You wouldn't believe—" The still-new mother might have been off and running if she hadn't glanced up and seen Johanna. Embarrassed, she slid the pictures into her drawer. Mr. Jablonski had been generous and understanding, but she didn't think he'd care to have her spending her first day back on the job showing off her daughter. "Good afternoon. May I help you?"

With a slight inclination of her head, Johanna crossed the room. As she did, Sam swiveled on the desk and watched her. He didn't quite do a double take, but damn near.

She was beautiful. He wasn't immune to beauty, though he was often surrounded by it. At first glance she might have been taken for one of the hordes of slim and leggy California blondes who haunted the beaches and adorned glossy posters. Her skin was gold—not bronzed, but a very pale and lovely gold. It set off the smoky blond hair that fluffed out to tease the shoulders of her jacket. Her face was oval, the classic shape given drama by prominent cheekbones and a full mouth. Her eyes, delicately shaded with rose and violet, were the clear blue of a mountain lake.

She was sexy. Subtly sexy. He was used to that in women as well. Maybe it was the way she moved, the way she carried herself inside the long loose jacket and straight skirt, that made her seem so special. Her shoes were ivory and low-heeled. He found himself noticing even them and the small, narrow feet they covered.

She didn't even glance at him, and he was glad. It gave him the chance to stare at her, to absorb the sight of her, before she recognized him and spoiled the moment.

"I have a delivery for Mr. Jablonski."

Even her voice was perfect, Sam decided. Soft, smooth, just edging toward cool.

"I'll be happy to take it." Gloria gave her most co-operative smile.

Johanna unzipped her portfolio and took out the contracts and tape. She still didn't look at Sam, though she was very aware he was staring. "These are the Weaver contracts and a tape of *Trivia Alert*."

"Oh, well—"

Sam cut her off neatly. "Why don't you take them in to him, Gloria? I'll wait."

Gloria opened her mouth, then shut it again to clear her throat as she rose. "All right. If you'd just give me a moment," she said to Johanna, then headed down the corridor.

"Do you work for the show?" Sam asked her.

"Yes." Johanna gave him a small and purposefully disinterested smile. "Are you a fan, Mr.—?"

She didn't recognize him. Sam had a moment to be both surprised and disconcerted before he saw the humor of it and grinned. "It's Sam." He held out a hand, trapping her into an introduction.

"Johanna," she told him, and accepted the handshake. His easy reaction made her feel petty. She was on the verge of explaining when she realized he hadn't released her hand. His was hard and strong. Like his face, like his voice. It was her reaction to them, her quick and intensely personal reaction to them, that drove her to continue the pretense and blame it on him.

"Do you work for Mr. Jablonski?"

Sam grinned again. It was a fast, crooked grin that warned a woman not to trust him. "In a manner of speaking. What do you do on the show?"

"A little of this, a little of that," she said, truthfully enough. "Don't let me keep you."

"I'd rather you did." But he released her hand because she was tugging at it. "Would you like to have lunch?"

Her brow lifted. Five minutes ago he'd been cuddling up to the brunette; now he was inviting the first woman who came along to lunch. Typical. "Sorry. I'm booked."

"For how long?"

"Long enough." Johanna glanced past him to the receptionist.

"Mr. Jablonski will have the contracts signed and returned to Ms. Patterson by tomorrow afternoon."

"Thank you." Johanna shifted her portfolio and turned. Sam laid a hand on her arm and waited until she looked back at him.

"See you."

She smiled at him, again disinterestedly, before she walked away. She was chuckling when she reached the elevators, unaware that she'd tucked the hand he'd held into her pocket.

Sam watched her until she'd turned the corner. "You know, Gloria," he said, half to himself, "I think I'm going to enjoy playing this game after all."

CHAPTER TWO

On the day of a taping, Johanna was always on the set by nine. It wasn't that she didn't trust her staff. She did. She simply trusted herself more. Besides, last week they'd had a few mechanical glitches with the moving set that swung the contestants and their counters stage center for play, then off again for the championship round. Small problems like that could delay taping anywhere from five minutes to two hours. By checking everything through personally beforehand, she sweetened the odds.

All the lights on the display board had to be tested, and the dressing rooms had to be primped and fresh coffee and cookies arranged for the prospective contestants.

They weren't due until one, but experience told Johanna that most would arrive early so they could chew their nails in the studio. Soothing them was one job she gladly delegated. The celebrities were also due at one so they could do a run-through and still have plenty of time for hair, makeup and wardrobe.

John Jay would arrive at two to complain about the suits that had been selected for him. Then he would close himself in his dressing room to sulk before his makeup call. When he was suited up, powdered and sprayed he would emerge, ready to shine for the cameras. Johanna had learned to ignore his artistic temperament—for the most part—and to tolerate the rest. There was no arguing with his popularity quotient. It was largely due to him that the line would form outside the studio for tickets for the day's taping.

Johanna checked off her duties one by one, then double-checked everyone else's. Over the years, efficiency had grown from a habit to an obsession. At noon she downed something that resembled a shrimp salad. The taping should start at three and, if God was in his heaven, be over by eight.

Fortunately, the female celebrity was a repeater who had done *Trivia* at least a dozen times, along with numerous other game shows. That gave Johanna one less headache. She hadn't given Sam Weaver a thought.

So she told herself.

When he arrived, she would turn him and his entourage over to Bethany. It would give her assistant a thrill and keep God's gift to women out of her hair.

She only hoped he could handle the game. The questions were fun, for the most part, but they weren't always easy. More than once she'd had a celebrity grumble and complain because an inability to answer had made him or her look stupid. Johanna made it a policy to see that each show's batch of questions contained the obvious and amusing, as well as the challenging.

It wouldn't be her fault if Sam Weaver turned out to have an empty head. He would only have to smile to gain the audience's forgiveness.

She remembered the way he'd smiled at her when she'd asked if he worked for Jablonski. Yes, that was all it would take to make every woman at home and in the studio turn to putty—except her, of course.

"Check the bell." Johanna stood in the middle of the set and directed her sound technician. At her signal the bright, cheery beep of the winning bell rang. "And the buzzer." The flat drone of the loser sounded. "Bring up the lights in the winner's circle." She nodded in satisfaction as the bulbs flashed.

"The contestants?"

"Sequestered." Bethany checked her clipboard. "We have the accountant from Venice returning from last week. He's a three-game winner. First challenger's a housewife from Ohio in town visiting her sister. Nervous as hell."

"Okay, see if you can help Dottie keep them calm. I'll give the dressing rooms a last check."

Mentally calculating her time as she went, Johanna scooted down the corridor. Her female celebrity was Marsha Tuckett, a comfortable, motherly type who was part of the ensemble of a family series in its third year.

A nice contrast for Sam Weaver, she thought. Johanna made sure there were fresh pink roses on the dressing table and plenty of club soda on ice. Satisfied the room was in order, she walked across the narrow hall to the next room.

Because she hadn't thought roses appropriate for Sam Weaver, she'd settled on a nice leafy fern for the corner. As a matter of course she checked the lights, plumped the pillows on the narrow daybed and made certain the towels were fresh and plentiful. A last look showed her nothing he could find fault with. Carelessly she stole a mint from the bowl on the table and popped it into her mouth, then turned.

He was in the doorway.

"Hello again." He'd already decided to make it his business to find her, but he hadn't expected to be quite so lucky. He stepped into the room and dropped a garment bag negligently over a chair.

Johanna pushed the candy into the corner of her mouth. The dressing room was small, but she couldn't recall feeling trapped in it before. "Mr. Weaver." She put on her best at-your-service smile as she offered a hand.

"It's Sam. Remember?" He took her hand and stepped just close enough to make her uncomfortable. They both knew it wasn't an accident.

"Of course. Sam. We're all delighted you could join us. We'll have our run-through shortly. In the meantime, you can let me or one of the staff know if you need anything." She looked past him, puzzled. "Are you alone?"

"Was I supposed to bring someone?"

"No." Where was his secretary, his assistant, his gofer? His current lover?

"According to my instructions, all I needed was five changes. Casual. Will this do to start?"

She studied the navy crewneck and the buff-colored slacks as though it mattered. "You look fine."

She'd known who he was all along, Sam thought. He wasn't so much annoyed as curious. And she wasn't comfortable with him now. That was something else to think about. Making a woman comfortable wasn't always a goal. After reaching for a mint himself, he rested a hip against the dressing table. It was a move that brought him just a little closer. Her lipstick had worn off, he noticed. He found the generous and unpainted shape of her mouth appealing.

"I watched the tape you sent."

"Good. You'll have more fun if you're familiar with the format. Make yourself comfortable." She spoke quickly but not hurriedly. That was training. But she wanted out, and she wanted out now. That was instinct. "One of the staff will be along to take you to Makeup."

"I also read credits." He blocked the door in an offhand way. "I noticed that a Johanna Patterson is executive producer. You?"

"Yes." Damn it, he was making her jittery. She couldn't remember the last time anyone had been able to make her nervous. Cool, controlled and capable. Anyone who knew her would have given that description. She glanced deliberately at her watch. "I'm sorry I can't stay and chat, but we're on a schedule."

He didn't budge. "Most producers don't hand-deliver contracts."

She smiled. Though on the surface it was sweet, he

saw the ice underneath and wondered at it. "I'm not most producers."

"I won't argue with that." It was more than attraction now, it was a puzzle that had to be solved. He'd managed to resist any number of women, but he'd never been able to resist a puzzle. "Since we missed lunch before, how about dinner?"

"I'm sorry. I'm—"

"Booked. Yeah, so you said." He tilted his head just a bit, as if to study her from a new angle. It was more than the fact that he was used to women being available. It was the fact that she seemed bound and determined to brush him off, and not very tactfully. "You're not wearing any rings."

"You're observant."

"Involved?"

"With what?"

He had to laugh. His ego wasn't so inflated that he couldn't take no for an answer. He simply preferred a reason for it. "What's the problem, Johanna? Didn't you like my last movie?"

"Sorry. I missed it," she lied, smiling. "Now if you'll excuse me, I've got a show to see to."

He was still standing at the door, but this time she brushed past him. And against him. Both felt a jolt, unexpected and tingling.

Annoyed, Johanna kept walking.

Intrigued, Sam kept watching.

She had to admit, he was a pro. By the middle of the taping of the first show, Sam had gotten in a casual and very competent plug for his new miniseries *No Roses for Sarah*. So effective, that Johanna knew she'd tune in herself. The sponsors and the network brass would be delighted. He'd charmed his partner, the mother of two from Columbus, who had walked onto the set so tense that her voice had come out in squeaks. He'd even managed to answer a few questions correctly.

It was hard not to be impressed, though she worked at it. When the lights were on and the tape was rolling he was the embodiment of that elusive and too often casually used word: *star*. John Jay's posturing and flashing incisors shifted to the background.

Not all entertainers were at ease in front of a live audience. He was. Johanna noted that he was able to turn on just the right amount of enthusiasm and enjoyment when the cameras were rolling, but also that he played to the studio audience during breaks by joking with his competitor and occasionally answering a question someone shouted out at him.

He even seemed to be genuinely pleased when his partner won five hundred in cash in the bonus speed round.

Even if he was just putting on a good face, Johanna couldn't fault him for it. Five hundred dollars meant a great deal to the mother of two from Columbus. Just as much as her moment in the sun with a celebrated heartthrob.

"We've got a very tight game going here, folks." John Jay smiled importantly at the camera. "This final question will determine today's champion, who will then go to the winner's circle and try for ten thousand dollars. Hands on your buzzers." He drew the card from the slot on his dais. "And the final question, for the championship, is…who created Winnie the Pooh?"

Sam's finger was quick on the trigger. The woman from Columbus looked at him pleadingly. John Jay called for a dramatic silence.

"A. A. Milne."

"Ladies and gentlemen, we have a new champion!"

As the cheers got louder and his partner threw her arms around his neck, Sam caught Johanna's look of surprise. It was easy to read her mind and come up with the fact that she didn't see him as a man who could read and remember storybooks—especially not classic children's books.

John Jay said the official goodbyes to the accountant from Venice and broke for a commercial. Sam had to all but carry his partner to the winner's circle. As he settled back in his chair, he glanced at Johanna.

"How'm I doing?"

"Sixty seconds," she said, but her voice was friendlier because she saw he was holding his partner's hand to calm her.

When the minute was up, John Jay managed to make the woman twice as nervous as he ran down the rules and the possibilities. The clock started on the first question. They weren't so difficult, Sam realized. It was the pressure that made them hard. He wasn't immune to it himself. He really wanted her to win. When he saw she was beginning to fumble, he blanked out the lights and the camera the way he did during any important scene. The rules said he could answer only two questions for her. Once he did, letting her keep her viselike grip on his hand, she was over the hump.

There were ten seconds left when John Jay, his voice

pitched to the correct level of excitement, posed the last question. "Where was Napoleon's final defeat?"

She knew it. Of course she knew it. The problem was to get the word out. Sam inched forward in the impossibly uncomfortable swivel chair and all but willed her to spit out the word.

"Waterloo!" she shouted, beating the buzzer by a heartbeat. Above their heads, *10,000* began to flash in bold red lights. His partner screamed, kissed him full on the mouth, then screamed again. While they were breaking for a commercial, Sam was holding her head between her knees and telling her to take deep breaths.

"Mrs. Cook?" Johanna knelt down beside them and monitored the woman's pulse. This wasn't the first time a contestant had reacted so radically. "Are you going to be all right?"

"I won. I won ten thousand dollars."

"Congratulations." Johanna lifted the woman's head far enough to be certain it was merely a case of hyperventilation. "We're going to take a fifteen-minute break. Would you like to lie down?"

"No. I'm sorry." Mrs. Cook's color was coming back. "I'm all right."

"Why don't you go with Beth? She'll get you some water."

"Okay. I'm fine, really." Too excited to be embarrassed, Mrs. Cook managed to stand, with Johanna taking one arm and Sam the other. "It's just that I've never won anything before. My husband didn't even come. He took the kids to the beach."

"You'll have a wonderful surprise for him," Johanna said soothingly, and kept walking. "Take a little breather, then you can start thinking about how you're going to spend that money."

"Ten thousand dollars," Mrs. Cook said faintly as she was passed over to Beth.

"Do you get a lot of fainters?" Sam asked.

"Our share. Once we had to stop taping because a construction worker slid right out of his seat during the speed round." She watched a moment longer until she was satisfied Bethany had Mrs. Cook under control. "Thanks. You acted quickly."

"No problem. I've had some practice."

She thought of women fainting at his feet. "I'll bet. There'll be cold drinks and fresh fruit in your dressing room. As long as Mrs. Cook's recovered, we'll start the tape in ten minutes."

He took her arm before she could move away. "If it wasn't my last movie, what is it?"

"What is what?"

"All these little barbs I feel sticking into my heart. You have a problem with me being here?"

"Of course not. We're thrilled to have you."

"Not we. You."

"I'm thrilled to have you here," she corrected, wishing he didn't make it a habit to stand almost on top of her. Her low heels brought her eyes level with his mouth. She discovered it wasn't the most comfortable view. "This series of contests, like your movie, will be shown during the May sweeps. What could be better?"

"A friendly conversation, over dinner."

"You're persistent, Mr. Weaver."

"I'm puzzled, Ms. Patterson."

Her lips very nearly twitched. There was something

cute about the way he drawled her last name. "A simple no shouldn't puzzle a man who obviously thinks so well on his feet." Deliberately she looked at her watch. "Half your break's up. You'd better change."

Because things ran smoothly, they were able to tape three shows before the dinner break. Johanna began to have fantasies about finishing on time. She kept them to herself, knowing how easy it was to jinx success. The dinner spread wasn't elaborate, but it was plentiful. Johanna didn't believe in pinching pennies over such minor matters as food. She wanted to keep her celebrities happy and her contestants at ease.

During the break she didn't sit, but grabbed a plate and a few essentials and kept herself available. The audience had been cleared, and new ticketholders would be allowed in for the two final tapings. All she had to do was avoid any crises, keep the energy level up and make certain John Jay didn't proposition any of the females on set.

With the first in mind, Johanna kept her eyes on the new challenger, a young woman from Orange County who appeared to be about six months pregnant.

"Problem?"

She'd forgotten that her other prerequisite had been to avoid Sam Weaver. Reminding herself to keep the celebrities happy, she turned to him as she plucked a small chilled shrimp from her plate. "No, why?"

"You don't relax, do you?" Without expecting an answer, he chose a slim carrot stick from her plate. "I've noticed you're watching Audrey like a hawk."

She wasn't surprised that he already knew the expectant mother by her first name. "Just being cautious." She bit into the shrimp and unbent enough to smile at him. After all, the day was nearly over. "During one of my early shows we had an expectant mother go into labor in the winner's circle. It's not an experience you forget."

"What did she have?" he asked, testing.

"A boy." Her smile became more generous as her eyes met his. It was one of her best memories. "By the time she was halfway to the hospital the staff had a pool going." She swallowed the last of the shrimp. "I won."

So she liked to bet. He'd keep that in mind. "I don't think you have to worry about Audrey. She's not due until the first part of August." He caught Johanna's curious look. "I asked," he explained. "Now, can I ask you a question? Professional," he added when he sensed her withdrawal.

"Of course."

"How often do you have to wind John Jay up?"

She had to laugh, and she didn't bother to object when he snitched a cube of cheddar from her plate. "Wind down's more like it. He's harmless, really. Only he thinks he's irresistible."

"He told me the two of you were...cozy."

"Really?" She glanced briefly over in the show's host's direction. The haughty look was so casual and innate that Sam grinned. "He's also an optimist."

He was glad to hear it. Very glad. "Well, he does his job. Somehow he manages to hit the note between cheerleader and father confessor."

Covering her personal opinion with her professional one was an old habit. To her, entertainment was first and last a business. "Actually, we're lucky to have him. He hosted another show about five years back, so he's not only familiar but also has a strong appeal to the home viewer."

"Are you going to eat that sandwich?"

Without answering, Johanna took half of the roast-beef-and-Swiss and handed it to him. "Are you enjoying yourself so far?"

"More than I'd expected." He took a bite. So she had a taste for hot mustard. He was fond of spice himself, and in more than food. "Will you be offended if I tell you I kicked a bit about doing it?"

"No. I'm the first to admit that the show isn't Shakespeare, but it serves its purpose." Leaning against a wall, she watched one of the crew heap on a second helping. "What have you found appealing about it?"

He avoided the obvious answer. Her. The one he gave was equally true. "I got a kick out of seeing those people win. Of course, I developed a soft spot for Mrs. Cook. Why do you do it?"

She avoided several possible answers. The one she settled on was true enough. "I enjoy it." When he offered her his glass of sparkling water and lime, she accepted without thinking. She was relaxed, optimistic about the rest of the day and, though she didn't realize it, comfortable in his company.

"I hesitate to point this out, but it looks like we're having dinner after all."

She looked at him again, slowly, gauging him and her reaction to him. If she'd had a different background, different memories, fewer disillusionments, she would have been flattered. More, she would have been tempted. He had a way of looking at her as though they were alone; as though, if they'd been in a room with hundreds of other people, he would have picked her, and only her, out.

Trick of the trade, she told herself, disliking her own cynicism.

"Isn't it handy we got that out of the way?" She handed him back his glass.

"Yeah. It should make it easier for us to do it again."

Casually she signaled to the crew to begin clearing up. "I don't want to rush you, but we'll start taping again in fifteen minutes."

"I never miss my cue." He shifted his body just enough to prevent her from walking by him. He had the moves, Johanna thought. Very smooth. Very slick. "I get the impression you like to play games, Johanna."

There was a dare in his voice. She caught it, and was trapped. Though her voice was cool again, she stood her ground and met his gaze. "Depends on the stakes."

"Okay, how's this? If I win the next two games you'll have dinner with me. I set the time and the place."

"I don't like those stakes."

"I haven't finished. If I lose I come back on the show within six months. No fee." That had her attention, he noted, pleased with himself. He hadn't misjudged her dedication to her show or her weakness for a dare.

"Within six months," she repeated, studying him to assess whether he could be trusted. Not an inch, she decided, on many matters. But she didn't see him as a man to welsh on a bet.

"Deal?" He made his voice deliberately challenging as he held out a hand.

It was too good a bet to turn down. His eyes were too mocking to ignore. "Deal." She set her palm against his, then removed it and stepped away. "Ten minutes, Mr. Weaver."

Johanna had a very bad feeling when Sam and his teammate took the first game. Since the conception of the show, she'd had a strict personal policy against rooting for either side. It didn't matter that no one could read her thoughts. She knew them, and prejudice of any kind was unprofessional. She certainly would never have imagined herself actually rooting against a certain team. She did now.

It was because she wanted him back on the show, she told herself when the last taping of the day began. The producer, not the woman, had made the bet. It was ridiculous to think that she was afraid, even uneasy, about having a meal with him. That would only be a small annoyance—like a spoonful of bad-tasting medicine.

But she stood behind camera two and cheered inwardly when the opposing team took the lead.

He didn't show nerves. Sam was much too skilled an actor to show nerves in front of a camera. But they dogged him. It was the principle, he told himself. That was the only reason he was so determined to win and make Johanna pay the price. He certainly wasn't infatuated. He'd been around too long to be infatuated just because a woman was beautiful. And aloof, his mind added. And contrary and stubborn. And damn sexy.

He wasn't infatuated. He just hated to lose.

By the beginning of the final round, the two teams were neck and neck. The studio audience was loud and raucous, the contestants wired. Johanna's stomach was in knots. When Sam turned and winked at her during the commercial break she nearly bared her teeth.

Positions jockeyed back and forth. Professionally Johanna knew that when the show aired it would pull the television audience in. That was, after all, the name of the game. Personally, she'd hoped for a landslide, however boring.

When the final question came up, she held her breath. Sam was quick to push the button, but his partner was quicker. He nearly swore. The expectant mother from Orange County had more than her own fate in her hands.

"Surrender, Dorothy!" she shouted. When the lights went on, Sam took her face in his hands and kissed her. Hard. Audrey would be able to dine out on the moment for months. Sam kept his arm around her as they walked toward the winner's circle. Once she was settled, he strolled casually over to Johanna and bent closer to her ear.

"Saturday night, seven. I'll pick you up."

She only nodded. It was hard to speak when your teeth were clenched.

Johanna found several vital tasks to perform after the taping was completed. She did not, as was her habit, say a personal thank-you to both guest stars. That job was handed over to Bethany. She made herself scarce for thirty minutes so that she could be sure Sam Weaver was off and out of her hair. Until Saturday.

She couldn't quite drum up the job-well-done mood the end of the day usually brought her. Instead she made a list of details to see to the following day that would keep her occupied from the time she got up until she crawled back home again. Business as usual, she told herself, and broke the tip off her pencil.

"Everybody's happy," Beth told her. "The questions we didn't use in the speed round are locked back in the safe. The contestants we didn't get to are ready and willing to come back next week. Your dupes." She handed Johanna the tapes. "We've got some great shows. Especially the last one. Even the techs were getting into it. They loved Sam." Bethany pushed back a lock of hair. "And you know how jaded techs can be. Anyway, it's nice to know that besides being gorgeous and sexy he's got some smarts."

Johanna grunted and dropped the tapes in her carryall.

Bethany tilted her head. "I was going to ask you if you wanted to take some of the leftover fruit home, but it looks more like you'd prefer raw meat."

"It's been a long day."

"Uh-huh." Beth knew her boss better. Johanna had pulled a roll of antacids out of her bag and had popped two of them. A sure sign of trouble. "Want to have a drink and talk about it?"

Johanna had never made it a habit to confide in anyone. There simply hadn't been enough people in her life she could trust. Johanna knew Beth. Her assistant was young and energetic, but she was also trustworthy. She was also the closest thing Johanna had ever had to a foul-weather friend.

"I'll pass on the drink, but how about walking me out to my car?"

"Sure."

The sun hadn't set. Johanna found something reassuring about that after having been inside all day. She'd put the top down, she thought, and take the drive home through the Hills fast. Maybe a bit recklessly. She had a taste for the reckless, a taste she usually controlled. It came from her father. But tonight it might do her good to give in to it for a little while.

"What did you think of Sam Weaver?"

Bethany cocked a brow. "Before or after I stopped drooling?"

"After."

"I liked him," she said simply. "He didn't expect the red carpet, he wasn't condescending and he wasn't snickering behind his hand at the contestants."

"Those are all negative virtues," Johanna pointed out.

"Okay, I liked the way he joked around with the crew. And the way he signed autographs as though he wanted to instead of acting as though he were granting a favor." She didn't add that she'd asked for one herself. "He acted like somebody without making sure everybody remembered that *somebody* was in all capital letters."

"Interestingly said," Johanna murmured. "Are you still keeping that little book with the list of celebrity panelists?"

Beth colored a bit. She was in the business, but that didn't stop her from being a fan. "Yeah. Sam gets five stars."

Johanna's lips twitched a bit at her assistant's top rating. "I guess I should be relieved to hear it. I'm having dinner with him on Saturday."

Bethany's mouth went into the *O* position. There

were stars in her eyes. She simply couldn't help it. "Wow."

"It's confidential."

"Okay," Bethany said, and Johanna knew she was as good as her word. "Johanna, I know you were raised in the business and Cary Grant probably bounced you on his knee, but doesn't it give you a tingle?"

"It gives me a pain," Johanna stated bluntly as she pulled open her car door. "Actors aren't my type."

"Too general."

"Okay, blue-eyed lanky actors with a drawl aren't my type."

"You're sick, Johanna. Very, very sick. You want me to go as proxy?"

She chuckled as she lowered herself into the car. "No. I can handle Sam Weaver."

"Lucky you. Listen, not to pry or anything..."

"But?"

"You will remember the details? I might want to write a book or something."

"Go home, Beth." The engine sprang to life as she twisted the key. Yes, she definitely wanted power and speed tonight.

"Okay, just let me know if he always smells so good. I can live on that."

Shaking her head, Johanna roared out of the lot. She hadn't been interested enough to notice what Sam Weaver had smelled like.

Like a man, her memory informed her. He'd smelled very much like a man.

CHAPTER
THREE

It was only dinner. Nothing to worry about. Certainly nothing, after several days to put it in perspective, to be annoyed about. They would no doubt go to one of L.A.'s flashier restaurants, where Sam could see and be seen. Between the pâté and the double chocolate mousse he would greet and chat with the other glamorous types who patronized that kind of eatery.

Meat houses, her second stepmother had called such places. Not because of the menu but because of the flesh exposed. Darlene had been one of the most honest and least affected of her father's attachments.

If she wanted to stretch a point, Johanna could consider it a business dinner. She found she wanted to stretch a point. She could tolerate this, as she had tolerated many other meals, as a part of the game everyone who wanted to remain part of the business learned to play. Since it was business, she would be charming and chatty, even gracious, until it was over and she could close the door on the entire episode.

She didn't like persistent men.

She didn't like men with reputations.

She didn't like Sam Weaver.

That was before the flowers arrived.

Johanna had spent Saturday morning gardening and half-hoping Sam Weaver wouldn't find her address. He hadn't called to ask her for it or to confirm plans. Waiting for him to do just that had left her jumpy and out of sorts all week. That was just one more sin to lay at his door.

It was her habit whenever she worked outside to take her cordless phone with her. Business could crop up even on weekends. Today, however, she pretended to have forgotten it and spent a warm and pleasant morning tending a plot of columbine.

This was her respite, even her vice, in a way. The flowers she planted were nurtured and cared for. They rewarded her by renewing themselves year after year. Their continuity soothed her. This, as was the case in other areas of her life, was something she'd done with her own hands. Whatever rewards she reaped, whatever failures she suffered, were her own.

The flowers lasted. The people in her life rarely did.

Her jeans were scruffy at the knees and her hands

stained with mulch when the delivery man pulled up. Johanna shaded her eyes as she rose.

"Miz Patterson?"

"Yes."

"Sign here, please." The deliveryman met her half-way across her lawn, handing her first his clipboard and then a long white box embossed with a florist's name and tied with a red satin ribbon. "Nice garden you got there," he said with a tip of his hat as he climbed back into the truck.

She was a sucker for flowers. Without waiting to go in and wash up, Johanna opened the box. They were roses. Not a dozen red or two dozen pink, but one long-stemmed sample of every color she'd ever seen, from the purest white to the deepest red, and all the pinks and golds between. Charmed, she lowered her face to the box to draw in their scent.

Heady. Roses were always heady, lush and unashamedly sensual.

It wasn't her birthday. In any case, her father—or rather her father's secretary—wasn't imaginative enough to have thought of such a sweet and charming gift. Though her fingertips were soiled, she pulled open the card that had come with the box. I don't know your favorite color. Yet. Sam.

She wanted to shrug it off. Pretty gestures came so easily to some. It would have taken only a casual order to an assistant to have them delivered. How well she knew it. So he'd found her, she thought with a shrug as she started back across the lawn. The deal was still on, and she'd live up to her end of it.

She tried, really tried, to set them aside and go back to work on the buds she'd planted herself. But she couldn't dismiss the roses, didn't have the heart to dampen her own pleasure. She was smiling when she sniffed the flowers again. Smiling still when she went into the house to arrange them.

He hadn't looked forward to an evening quite so much in a long time. It was easy to compare it to a winning poker hand or a successful day at the track. He'd never cared half as much for the purse as for the winning. He'd have preferred to think of it in those terms, but the truth was that he was looking forward to spending a few hours in Johanna Patterson's company.

Maybe he was intrigued because she was so disinterested. Sam took a turn sharp and fast while the radio blared through the open windows. What man didn't appreciate a challenge? If she'd taken him at his word on their first meeting, they might have enjoyed a pleasant lunch and an easy hour. He'd never know if that would have been the end of it. The fact that she'd refused, and had continued to refuse, only made him more determined to wear her down.

Women came easily to him. Too easily. Sam wouldn't deny he'd gone through a stage when he'd taken advantage of that. But his background, and what many might have considered the rather quaint and traditional values that had gone into it, had surfaced again.

The press could beat the drum of his romantic adventures all they liked. The truth was, he *was* a romantic. Rolling from one bed to the next had never been his style.

There were two Sam Weavers. One was intensely private, guarded about matters like family and relationships, the things that really mattered. The other was an actor, a realist who accepted that the price of fame was public consumption. He gave interviews, didn't bother to dodge the paparazzi and was always willing to sign an autograph. He'd learned to shrug off whatever reports were exaggerations or outright lies. They were the public Sam's problem. The private one couldn't have cared less.

He wondered, given what he now knew about Johanna Patterson's background, which Sam Weaver she would understand.

She was the only child of the respected producer Carl Patterson, the product of his first, and reportedly most tempestuous marriage. Her mother had disappeared or, as some reports put it, "gone into seclusion," after the marriage had failed. Johanna had grown up in the luxury of Beverly Hills, had attended the best schools. Some rumors stated that she adored her father, others that there was no love lost between them. In either case, she was the only offspring Patterson had after four marriages and numerous affairs.

He was surprised that she lived back in the Hills. He'd expected some slick condo in the city or a wing in her father's Beverly Hills estate. The sharp professional woman he'd met seemed out of place so far from the action. He was more surprised when he found the house.

It was tiny. Like a dollhouse, but without the gingerbread. Hardly more than a cabin, it was rustic and sturdy, with the wood unpainted and the panes of glass sparkling in the evening sun. There wasn't much land before the trees and the hills took it over. What was there was uneven and rocky. To compensate—more, to enhance it—flowers and budding vines were everywhere. The dashing little Mercedes parked in the driveway looked as though it had been left there by mistake.

Hands in pockets, he stood beside his own car and looked again. She didn't have any close neighbors, and the view was nothing to write home about, but it seemed as though she'd carved out her own corner of the mountainside. He knew about that. Appreciated it.

When he reached the door, he caught the scent of sweet peas. His mother planted them each spring, outside the kitchen windows. Johanna opened the door and found him smiling.

"Brigadoon," he said, and watched her polite smile turn to an expression of puzzlement. "I was trying to think what your place reminded me of. Brigadoon. Like it's only here once every hundred years."

Damn him, she thought, feeling almost resigned. She'd barely managed to put the roses in perspective and here he was, charming her again. "I wasn't sure you'd find it."

"I have a good sense of direction. Most of the time." He glanced toward the flowers that flanked both sides of her house. "From the looks of things, the roses were overkill."

"No." It would have been petty not to let him know they'd pleased her. "It was sweet of you to send them." He wasn't wearing a dinner suit, but a breezy linen shirt and pleated slacks. Johanna was glad she'd guessed right when she'd bypassed glitz for the subtler lines of a slim-skirted white dress. "If you'd like to come in a minute, I'll get my jacket."

He did, though he thought it would be a shame to cover up her arms and shoulders. The living room was small enough to be cozy. She'd arranged deep chairs by a white bricked fireplace and had added dozens of pillows. It made Sam think that when Johanna was finished with work she liked to take off her shoes and snuggle in.

"This isn't what I expected."

"No?" She pulled on a sizzling tomato-red jacket. "I like it."

"I didn't say I didn't like it, I said it wasn't what I expected." He noted his roses had been given a place of honor on the mantel, tucked prettily in a clear, wide-mouthed vase that glinted at the bottom with colored pebbles. "Do you have a favorite?"

She glanced at the roses. "No. I just like flowers." The clusters of rubies at her ears glinted as she adjusted them. "Shall we go?"

"In a minute." He crossed to her, noticing with some interest the way she stiffened up. Despite it, he took her hand. "Are you going to be a good sport about this?"

She let out a little sigh. "I've thought about it."

"And?" It was the easy curving of his lips that made her relax.

"I decided I might as well."

"Are you hungry?"

"Some."

"Mind a bit of a ride?"

Curious, she tilted her head. "No, I suppose not."

"Good." He kept her hand in his as they walked outside.

* * *

She should have known he was up to something. They didn't drive into the city as she'd expected. Rather than comment, Johanna let the conversation flow as she wondered how to handle him. Actors were a tricky bunch. They knew how to set the stage, how to read their lines, how to put on whatever face was most appropriate to the situation. At the moment, it seemed Sam had chosen to be the casually friendly companion a woman could relax with. Johanna wasn't ready to give him an inch.

He drove fast, just faster than the law allowed and just under the edge of safety. Even when they left the freeway for a road that was rough and sparsely populated, he continued at the same steady clip.

"Mind if I ask where we're going?"

Sam negotiated a lazy turn. He'd wondered how long it would take before she asked. "To dinner."

Johanna turned to study the landscape. The land rolled by, wide and dusty. "Something over an open fire?"

He smiled. She'd used her haughty tone again, and damned if he didn't enjoy hearing it. "No, I thought we'd eat at my place."

His place. The thought of dining privately with him didn't alarm her. She was too confident of her ability to handle whatever situation cropped up. She was more curious about the fact that he would have a *place* this far from the glitz. "You have a cave?"

Because there was amusement in her voice now, his smile widened. "I can do a little better than that. I only eat in restaurants when it's necessary."

"Why?"

"Because you end up doing business, or being stared at. I wasn't in the mood for either tonight." Pebbles spit from under the tires as he turned to drive through a plain wooden gate.

"That's part of the game, isn't it?"

"Sure, but there has to be a reason to play it." He whizzed by a pretty white house with blue shutters, giving two blasts of his horn. "My foreman and his family live there. If he knows it's me he won't come looking for trespassers."

They passed barns and sheds, and she was surprised that they looked as though they had a purpose other than a decorative one. She spotted paddocks with split-rail fencing and dark, rich dirt. A dog—or what sounded like a pair of them—began to bark.

The road forked, and then she saw the ranch house. It, too, was white, but the shutters were gray and the three chimneys it boasted were brick weathered to a dusky rose. It was low and spreading, shaped like an *H* turned on its side. For all its size, it didn't overpower. There were rockers on the porch, sturdy wooden ones that gave the impression that someone sat in them often. Window boxes had been freshly painted a bright, sassy red. Tumbling out of them were pansies and bushy impatiens. Though the air here was hot and dry, they were thriving and well tended.

Johanna stepped out of the car to turn a slow circle. It certainly looked like a working ranch. "Quite a place."

"I like it," he said, mimicking her earlier remark.

She acknowledged that with a quick, though cautious, smile. "It must be inconvenient to commute."

"I keep a place in L.A." He shrugged it off as though it were no more than a storage closet. "The best thing about finishing a film is being able to come back here and dig in for a while. Before I got hooked on acting, I'd wanted to come west and work on a ranch." He took her arm as they walked up the two wooden steps to the porch. They creaked. For some reason, Johanna found that endearing. "I was lucky enough to do both."

She glanced at the pansies, with their arrogant Alice-in-Wonderland faces. "Do you raise cattle?"

"Horses." He'd left the door unlocked. It was a habit he'd grown up with. "I bought the place about three years ago. Convinced my accountant that it'd be a great tax shelter. It made him feel better."

The hardwood floors were polished to a high gloss, scattered with hand-hooked rugs in muted pastels. In the entrance a collection of pewter—bowls, spoons, mugs, even a dented candlestick—was arranged on a waist-high table. The early twilight crept through the windows.

It had a good feel, a solid feel. Though she would never had admitted it out loud, Johanna had always felt strongly that houses had their own personalities. She'd selected her own house because it had made her feel warm and comfortable. She'd left her father's because it had been possessive and dishonest.

"Do you get to stay here often?" she asked him.

"Not often enough." He glanced around at the walls, which he'd painted himself. The house, like his career, was something he never took for granted. Though he'd never known poverty, he'd been taught to appreciate security, and that nothing replaced sweat for earning it. "Would you like a drink, or would you rather go for dinner?"

"Dinner," she said firmly. She knew better than to drink, socially or otherwise, on an empty stomach.

"I was hoping you'd say that." In the casual way he had, he took her hand and led her down the hall. The wing of the house ran straight. At the end it opened up into a large country kitchen. Copper pots hung from hooks over a center island. The room was flanked by counters and cabinets on one side and a small stone hearth on the other. A ribbon of windows gave an open view of dusk settling over a brick terrace and a mosaic pool. She'd thought to find a servant or two busily preparing the evening meal. Instead, all she found was the scent of cooking.

"It smells wonderful."

"Good." Scooping up two hot pads, Sam bent down to the oven. "I left it on warm." He drew out a casserole of bubbly lasagna.

Food wasn't something that usually excited her, but now the scent alone drew her over to his side. How long had it been since she'd seen someone take a homemade meal out of an oven? "It looks wonderful, too."

"My mother always told me food tastes better if it looks good." He picked up a long loaf of Italian bread and began slicing.

"You didn't cook this."

"Why not?" He glanced over his shoulder, amused that she was frowning again. She looked so thoughtful that he was tempted to run a fingertip down the faint line that formed between her brows. "Cooking's a very manageable skill if you approach it properly and have the right incentive."

Johanna stuck with carryout or prepackaged microwave meals. "And you have both?"

"I wanted to be an actor, but I didn't have any desire to be a starving actor." He poured garlic butter over the bread, set the oven, then slid it in. "After I came to California, I kicked around from audition to audition and from greasy spoon to greasy spoon. A couple of months of that and I called home and asked my mother for some recipes. She's a great cook." Sam drew the cork from a bottle of wine, then set it aside to breathe. "Anyway, it took me a lot less time to figure out how to sauté trout than it did for me to get a memorable part."

"Now that you've had a number of memorable parts, what's your incentive?"

"To cook?" He shrugged and took a leafy spinach salad from the refrigerator. "I like it. We're about ready here. You want to grab the wine? I thought we'd eat outside."

The trouble with Hollywood, Johanna thought as she followed him out, was that things were never what they seemed. She'd been sure she had Sam Weaver pegged. But the man she'd assessed and dismissed wouldn't have copied recipes from his mother.

Nor was he the type, she thought as she set the wine down, who would have prepared a charming dinner for two, alfresco, with pretty blue stoneware plates and thick yellow candles. It was every bit as friendly as it was romantic. The romance she'd expected, and she knew just how to discourage it. The offer of friendship was another matter.

"Light those candles, will you?" He glanced around briefly, checking the way a man did when he was already certain things were just as he wanted them to be. "I'll get the rest."

Johanna watched him go back inside. Did someone who walked like that, she wondered—as though he were heading toward a shoot-out—really prepare spinach salad? She struck a match and held it to the wick of the first candle. Apparently so. There were more important things to lie about than cooking. She held the match to the second candle, then deliberately blew it out. She wouldn't have called avoiding three on a match superstitious. Just practical.

She heard the music he put on, something low and bluesy, with a lot of sax. While he brought out the rest of the meal, she poured the wine.

His instincts had been right, Sam thought as they settled at the wicker table. He'd been on the verge of making dinner reservations at some tony restaurant when he'd pulled back. He'd cooked for women before, but never here. He never brought anyone to the ranch, because the ranch was home. Private. Off limits to the press and the public, it was both refuge and sanctuary from a world he was a voluntary member of—when he chose to be. At the time, he hadn't been sure why he'd wanted to break his own rule with Johanna. Now he began to understand.

At the ranch he could be himself—no pretenses, no roles. Here he was Sam Weaver from Virginia, and here he was most comfortable. He didn't have to be *on* here. And he wanted to be himself with Johanna.

She wasn't without pretenses, he mused as he

watched her. Not entirely. Unless he missed his guess, most of her resentment had faded, but not her distrust. He'd already decided to ease his curiosity and find the reason for it.

Maybe she'd been stung in an affair that had gone sour. Broken hearts often mended jaggedly. If she had been betrayed by a man she'd cared for and trusted, it would be logical that she would put up some defenses. It might take some time before he could wear them down, but he had a feeling it would be worth it. He'd start with what he believed was the focus of her life: her work.

"Were you happy with the taping the other day?"

"More than." She was too fair-minded not to give him his due. "You were really good, not just as far as the answers went, but overall. A lot of times you can have people zip right through the questions and be a dead bore." She broke off a piece of bread, then nibbled at the crust. He'd hit the right tone. It was always easy for her to relax when the subject was business. "And, of course, it was a coup to have you."

"I'm flattered."

She studied him again with those cool blue eyes. "I doubt it would be that easy to flatter you."

"An actor always wants to be wanted. Well, to a point, anyway," he added with another quick grin. "Do you know how many game shows I've turned down in the last couple of days?"

She smiled and sipped her wine. "Oh, I could hazard a guess."

"How'd you get into it? Producing?"

"Heredity." Her lips tightened only briefly. After taking a second sip, she set her glass down. "I guess you could say I like pulling the strings."

"You'd have learned young with Carl Patterson as your father." He saw it, very briefly but very clearly. More than resentment, less than pain. "He's produced some of the best, and most successful television shows, as well as an impressive number of features. Being second-generation can be a strain, I imagine."

"You get past it." The lasagna was cheesy and rich with spices. Johanna concentrated on it. "This really is terrific. Your mother's recipe?"

"With some variations." So her father was off limits. He could respect that—for now. "How about the show itself? How did that get started?"

"With the flu." At ease again, she smiled and took another bite.

"Care to elaborate?"

"I had the flu, a nasty bout of it, a couple of years ago. I had to stay in bed for a week, and since it hurt my eyes to read, I lay there hour after hour and watched television. The game shows hooked me." She didn't object when he topped off her glass. The wine was very mellow and dry, and she knew her limit right down to the swallow. "You get involved, you know, in the games, and the people playing them. After a while you start rooting for them, tensing up in an effort to help them. When someone wins, the vicarious thrill is automatic. And then you have the advantage of almost always being smarter at home, because there's no pressure. That's a nice smug feeling."

He watched her as she spoke. She was animated now, the way she'd been while she'd rushed around the set making sure things fell into place. "So after your bout with the flu you decided to produce one."

"More or less." She could remember running into the brick wall of the network brass and ultimately having to appeal to her father. "In any case, I had the concept, and the experience in producing. I'd done a couple of documentaries for public television and had worked on a prime-time special. With a little string-pulling, we got a pilot done. Now we're only a couple of ratings points from being on top. I'm waiting for the go-ahead to start evening syndication."

"What happens then?"

"The demographics open. You get the kids who've finished their homework, the business crowd who want to put their feet up for a half hour. You up the ante. Give away some cars, bigger bucks."

She was surprised to discover she'd cleared her plate. Usually she ate a few bites, then ended up picking at the rest, impatient for the meal—and the time sitting down—to be over.

"Want some more?"

"No. Thanks." She picked up her wine as she studied him. "I know I lost the bet, but it looks as though I got the best part of the deal."

"Not from where I'm sitting."

The shades came down. Just like that. One compliment, however offhand, and she pulled back. Seeing it, Sam rose and offered a hand. "Want to walk? There's enough moonlight."

There was no point in being ungracious, Johanna told herself. She hated it when she became prickly over something unimportant. "All right. The only ranches I've ever seen have been on the back lot."

He bundled up the last of the bread, then handed it to her. "We'll go by the pond. You can feed the ducks."

"You have ducks?"

"Several overfed ducks." He slipped an arm around her shoulders to steer her. She smelled like the evening they walked through, quiet and promising. "I like looking at them in the morning."

"Your Jake in *Half-Breed* would have eaten them for breakfast."

"So you did see my last movie."

She took a quick nip at the tip of her tongue. "Oh, was that your last one?"

"Too late. You've already boosted my ego."

When she looked at him, his smile was appealing and too easy to respond to. *He* was too easy to respond to. In self-defense she looked back at the house.

"It's lovely from out here, too. You live all alone?"

"I like a little solitude now and then. Of course, I've got a few hands who look after things while I'm working, and Mae comes in a couple times a week to scoop at the dust." His hand slipped down to take hers. "My family comes out a few times a year and shakes everything up."

"Your parents visit you here?"

"Them, my brother, my two sisters, their families. Assorted cousins. The Weavers are a large and loud bunch."

"I see." But she didn't. She could only imagine. And envy. "They must be proud of you."

"They were always supportive, even when they thought I was crazy."

The pond was almost a quarter mile from the house, but the going was easy. It was obvious he walked the path often. She caught the scent of citrus, then the stronger scent of water. The moonlight struck it, highlighting the grass which had been left to grow ankle-high. Sensing an audience, several brown and speckled ducks paddled over to the water's edge.

"I've never had the nerve to come out here empty-handed," he told her. "I think they'd follow me home."

Johanna opened the linen cloth and broke off a crust of bread. It didn't even hit the water before it was gobbled up. She laughed; it was a low, delighted sound deep in her throat. Immediately she tore off another piece and, tossing this one farther out, watched a drake zoom in on it.

"I've always wanted to watch them from underneath so I could see their feet scramble." She continued to break off and toss. Ducks pursued the bread in groups and squabbled over it with bad-tempered quacks and competitive pecks. "My mother and I used to go out and feed the ducks. We'd give them silly names, then see if we could tell them apart the next time."

She caught herself, amazed that the memory had surfaced, stunned that she'd shared it. Her hand closed into a fist over the bread.

"There was a pond about five miles away when I was a kid," Sam said, as if he hadn't noticed her change in mood. "We used to ride our bikes to it during the summer, after we'd stolen a pack of crackers or whatever from the kitchen. We'd toss it out for the ducks—and a couple of pushy swans—and accidentally fall in as often as possible." He glanced out over the water. "Looks like someone's had a family."

She followed his gaze and saw a brown duck gliding along, trailed by a long shadow. As it came closer, Johanna saw that the shadow wasn't a shadow, it was fluffy ducklings. "Oh, aren't they sweet?" She crouched down for a closer look, forgetting about the hem of her skirt. The babies followed Mama on their evening swim, straight as an arrow. "I wish there was more light," she murmured.

"Come back when there is."

Johanna tilted her head up. In the moonlight his face was stronger, more attractive, than it had a right to be. The eyes, eyes that invariably drew women in, were as dark as the water. And, as with the water, Johanna didn't know what lay beneath the surface. Turning away again, she continued shredding the bread and tossing it.

He liked the way her hair haloed around her face, stopping just inches from her shoulders. A man could fill his hands with it. It would be soft, like the hand she rarely offered but he continued to take. It would carry that same subtle scent.

Her skin would be like that, on the back of her neck beneath all that heavy blond hair. He had an urge to touch it now, to skim his fingers over it and see if she trembled.

The ducks stopped their chatter when the last of the bread was consumed. A few hopefuls hung around the edge of the pond for a minute longer, then, satisfied the treat was done, glided away. Into the sudden silence came a night bird's song, and the rustle of a rabbit running into the brush.

"It's a lovely spot," she said, rising and brushing the crumbs from her fingers. "I can see why you like it so much."

"I want you to come back."

It was said very simply, so it shouldn't have meant so much. Johanna didn't back away, because that would have been admitting it did. If her heart was beating a little faster, she could pretend otherwise. She reminded herself that things often seemed more important in the moonlight than they did in the day.

"We had a bet. I lost." She said it lightly, already aware that the tone wouldn't matter. "But that's been paid up tonight."

"This has nothing to do with bets or games." He touched her hair as he'd wanted to. "I want you to come back."

She should have been able to shrug it off, to nip it before whatever was beginning to grow would blossom. It wasn't as easy as it should have been to dredge up the cool smile and the careless refusal. She looked at him, really looked at him, and could think of only one thing to say.

"Why?"

His lips curved. She watched the smile move slowly over his face, the angles shifting, the shadows playing. "Damned if I know. But when you do come back, maybe we'll both have an answer. Meanwhile, why don't we get this one question out of the way?"

He leaned toward her. She'd told herself she didn't want to be kissed. She wouldn't like it. She wasn't a demonstrative person, and for her a kiss wasn't merely a touching of lips. Even though she'd grown up in a world where a kiss was nothing more than a handshake—and often less binding—to her it was a personal thing that meant affection, trust, warmth.

She'd told herself she wouldn't be kissed. But that had been before the moonlight and the bird's song. That had been before he'd touched her.

Her eyes were wary. He saw that even as he brushed his lips lightly over hers. He'd meant it to be light, casual, hardly more than a peace offering. She was so cool and lovely, and so firmly on guard, that he'd been unable to resist.

An easy kiss. A friendly kiss. That was where he'd meant to begin and end it. That was before he'd tasted her.

He drew back, not quite sure of his footing. He hadn't been prepared for whatever had rushed into him, not for the punch of it. With the water lapping beside them, he stared down at her. Moonlight was on her face, and he touched her cheek where the light played. She didn't move. He couldn't know that her own stunned reaction had left her rooted to the spot.

He touched her again, drawing his fingers back through her hair until they gripped it. Still she didn't move. But when his lips came to hers again, hard, hungry, she met passion with passion.

She'd never wanted it to be like this. Desire raced through her, pushing her to keep pace with it. His mouth ran along her jaw, across her face, making her shiver with pleasure, but she twisted until their lips joined again.

A craving she'd never known she had…a dream she'd

never allowed into her waking hours...that was what he was. Wherever his hands touched, they lingered, as if he couldn't get enough. Lost in the first wave of pleasure, she pressed against him.

No, he couldn't get enough. He pulled her head back and deepened the kiss. She tasted like the night, dark, haunted. The thin silk under her jacket teased and shifted until he had to force back the urge to tear it away. He wanted her, all of her. There, in the tall, damp grass, he wanted to discover all her secrets and make them his own.

She was breathless when they drew apart. That frightened her. Caution and control had been hard-learned lessons, and she always, without exception, applied them to all the areas of her life. She'd lost them both in the flash of an instant, in the brush of his lips.

She had to remember what he was: an artist, both in his craft and with his women. More, she had to remember what *she* was. There was no room in her life for reckless passion in the moonlight.

He reached for her again, just to trace his knuckles along her cheek. Because even that affected her, she moved aside.

"This isn't the answer for either of us." She didn't like hearing the strain in her own voice, or the lingering huskiness he'd caused.

"It was a lot more than I bargained for," he admitted. The defenses were going up again. He took her hand before she could withdraw behind them completely. "I felt something the first time I saw you. Now I begin to see why."

"Lust at first sight?"

"Damn it, Johanna."

She'd hated herself the moment she'd said it, but she couldn't back down. If she backed down, she'd give in. "Let's let it go, Sam. I'll be honest and say that was more than nice, but I'm just not interested in the sequel."

Anger stirred. He knew his own temper well enough to take things slow. He'd never decked a woman. Yet. "What are you interested in?"

She recognized barely restrained fury when she heard it. It was almost a relief. If he'd been kind, if he'd been the least bit persuasive, she would have crumbled. "My job." She tried for a smile and almost managed it. "That's really enough complications for me."

"Lady, anybody who can kiss like that is just asking for complications."

She hadn't known she could kiss like that. She certainly hadn't known she'd wanted to. And what was even more unnerving was that she wanted to kiss him again. "I suppose that's a compliment. Shall we just say it was an interesting evening and leave it at that?"

"No."

"That's the best I can do."

He touched her hair again. It wasn't a testing gesture this time, it was a possessive one. "Okay. You'll learn as you go along."

She couldn't pretend to be amused, because he was frightening her. It wasn't a fear that he would drag her to the ground and finish what they'd both started, but it was a fear that he would prove to be stronger-willed and much more determined than she.

Stay out of his way, her mind warned her. And get started on it now.

"It was much too nice an evening to end it with an argument. I appreciate the meal and the walk. Now it's getting late, and since it's a long drive, we should be going."

"All right." He was much too annoyed to fight with her. Better, he thought, that he do exactly as she asked, then reevaluate the situation. Turning homeward, he reached out to guide her so that she wouldn't stumble. When she jerked at his touch, he smiled again, and most of his annoyance left him.

"The longest trips are often the most eventful, don't you think?"

She thought it best to leave that question unanswered.

CHAPTER FOUR

"Just how many cases of Diet Zing do we have?" Johanna waited for Bethany to run down her list.

"Considering what the crew pinched, about a hundred and fifty cases. We're square on the porto-vacs and the gift certificates and, of course, the encyclopedias." Bethany turned over the list of parting gifts. Though she thought it odd that Johanna was staring out the window rather than checking off her own list, she didn't comment. "About the home viewers' contest," Bethany began.

"Hmmm?"

"The home viewers' contest?"

"Oh." Johanna swore at herself, then pulled her gaze away from the window and her mind away from Sam Weaver. Daydreaming was always a waste of time, but it was a sin during office hours. "I want to get that nailed down this morning." She unlocked the top drawer of her desk and pulled out a file. "I have several potential questions. Research put in a lot of extra time on it last week. The idea is to have John Jay announce a different one every day, somewhere during the program." She glanced down the list again to satisfy herself. "I don't want him to do it at the same time every day, particularly not at the beginning. If we're going to draw people in, I want them to watch all day, all week. Is the deal on the car set?"

"Almost. We're going with the American product and tying it in with the drawing the week of the Fourth of July."

"Fine, but I want two."

"Two what?"

"Two cars, Beth. Watch *Trivia Alert* and win." She smiled a bit and tapped the end of her pencil on the desk. "Two luxury cars. One should be a convertible. People in Omaha with two kids don't usually buy convertibles. Let's make it a red one, at least for the ads. We'll have the full-sized car in white and John Jay in a blue suit."

"Hit them over the head with patriotism?"

"Something like that. See if we can bring the total value up to fifty thousand."

"Sure." Bethany blew her bangs away from her eyes. "I'll use charm. And if that doesn't work I'll use Mongo the enforcer."

"Use the ratings," Johanna suggested. "I want a big

ad in the *TV Guide* and the Sunday supplements. Black and white for the guide, color for the supplements." She waited while Bethany made her notes. "The ten-second spot at ten is already set. We'll tape it as soon as the cars are delivered. We have to pick five questions from the list." She handed Bethany a copy. "And the list doesn't go out of this office."

Bethany skimmed down. "Where did Betty meet the leader of the pack?" Lips pursed, she glanced up. "Betty who?"

"Brush up on your girl groups. Early-sixties rock and roll."

Bethany merely made a face. "These are pretty tough."

That was exactly what she'd wanted to hear. "They're worth fifty thousand."

Giving a quiet murmur of agreement, she checked another question. "Johanna, how could anyone know how many witches were burned at the stake in Salem?"

"None." Sitting back, Johanna ran the pencil through her fingers. "They were hanged."

"Oh. Well, so far I'm batting a thousand." When Johanna's phone rang, Bethany took another hard look at the questions.

"Mr. Weaver's on the line, Ms. Patterson."

Johanna opened her mouth and was surprised when nothing came out.

"Ms. Patterson?"

"What? Oh, tell Mr. Weaver I'm in a meeting."

When she hung up, Beth glanced over. "I wouldn't have minded waiting."

"I doubt he's calling to discuss the show." Telling

herself to dismiss it, Johanna picked up her list and made her eyes focus. "What do you think about number six?"

"I don't know that answer, either. Johanna…" Outgoing and candid herself, Bethany nonetheless understood and respected her boss's restraint. "Did everything go okay the other night?"

It would have been foolish to pretend to misunderstand. "It went fine. Very pleasant." Johanna dug into her pocket for a roll of antacids. "I'm leaning toward numbers one, four, six, nine and thirteen."

Beth looked at each one, decided she might have an inkling about question thirteen, then nodded. "Let's go for them." She handed the list back so that Johanna could lock them up. "Could we pretend we're out of the office, maybe at home with our feet up and a nice bottle of wine already half-gone?"

Johanna turned the key and pocketed it. "Do you have a problem, Beth?"

"No, but I'd swear you did."

"I'm fine." Johanna began to stack and straighten papers on her desk. "We had a friendly dinner, some pleasant conversation, and that was that. I have no idea why Sam's calling me at the office, but I don't have time to chat with him."

"I didn't mention Sam," Bethany pointed out. "You did. I only mentioned a problem." She smiled sympathetically. "I get the feeling they're the same thing."

Johanna rose and, with her hands in the deep pockets of her skirt, walked to the window. "He just can't get it through his head that I'm not interested."

"Are you? Not interested, I mean," Bethany supplied when Johanna turned her head.

"I don't want to be interested. It's the same thing."

"No. If you weren't interested you'd be able to smile, maybe pat him on the head and say thanks but no thanks. Not wanting to be interested means you are and you get around it by avoiding phone calls and making excuses."

Johanna pushed a thumb into the ivy geranium hanging in a basket at her window. The soil was moist. She'd watered it herself that morning. "How did you get to be an expert?"

"Unfortunately, most of it comes from observation rather than execution. He seems like a nice guy, Johanna."

"Maybe, but I don't have room for men right now, and less than none for actors."

"That's a hard line."

"It's a hard town."

Bethany wasn't willing to buy that. True, she'd only lived in L.A. for three years, but it still fascinated her. To her it remained the town where dreams could be chased and caught. "I hope you're not going to break my heart and tell me he's a jerk."

"No." With a reluctant smile, Johanna turned again. "No, he's not a jerk. Actually, you're right, he's a very nice guy, charming, easy to talk to—" She caught herself. "For an actor."

"He makes my insides tingle," Bethany confessed, unashamed and artless.

Mine, too, Johanna thought. Which was precisely why she wasn't going to see him again. "You're supposed to be concentrating on your screenwriter," she said briskly, then stopped when she saw Beth's expression. "Trouble?"

"He dumped me." She shrugged her shoulders in an unconcerned gesture. Johanna only had to look at Beth's eyes to see how much she was hurting. "It's no big deal, really. We weren't serious."

Maybe he wasn't, Johanna thought with a mixture of sympathy and resignation. "I'm sorry. Everyone has spats, Beth."

Bethany understood that, had even expected it. She hadn't expected deceit. "We went a little beyond that. It's better this way, really it is. I thought he was interested in me, you know, but when I found out he was more interested in my position—" She caught herself, swore silently, then smiled. "Doesn't matter. He was just one of the many toads you have to go through to find the prince."

"What about your position?" It never took Johanna long to put two and two together. Screenwriter, assistant producer. Toss in ambition and it added up perfectly. "Did he want you to hawk a script?"

Uncomfortable, Bethany shifted. "Not exactly."

"Spit it out, Beth."

"All right. He had the idea that I could influence you to influence your father to produce his screenplay. When I told him it wouldn't work, he got mad, then I got mad, and one thing led to another." She didn't add that it had been ugly. She didn't have to.

"I see." Why were there so many creeps in this world? Johanna wondered. So many users. "I am sorry, Beth."

"Bruises fade," Beth said easily, though she was aware hers would last a long time. "Besides, I've got the satisfaction of hoping he sells nothing but commercial jingles for the next ten or twenty years."

"Do yourself a favor," Johanna advised her. "Fall in love with an insurance salesman." She glanced toward the door as her secretary popped a head in.

"Telegram, Ms. Patterson."

With a murmured thank-you, Johanna took it. Stupid, she told herself as her fingers tensed on the paper. It had been almost twenty-five years since she'd gotten that brief and heartbreaking telegram from her mother. She hadn't even been old enough to read it herself. Shoving back the memory, she tore the envelope open.

I can be as stubborn as you. Sam.

Johanna scowled at the single line, read it twice, then crumpled it into a ball. But instead of tossing it in the wastebasket, she shoved it into her pocket.

"Bad news?" Bethany asked.

"A weak threat," Johanna said, picking up her remote. "The show's starting."

The damn woman was making him crazy. Sam groomed the mare, who'd been bred only hours before to his prize stud. She was still skittish and prone to nip. High-strung, pedigreed and temperamental, she reminded Sam of Johanna. That made him smile, if a bit grimly. He didn't think Johanna would appreciate being compared to a horse, not even a purebred.

She hadn't returned one of his calls. *Miss Patterson is unavailable. Miss Patterson is in a meeting.*

Miss Patterson is avoiding you like the plague.

He was beginning to feel like a gawky teenager with a crush on the class princess. More than once he'd told himself to write her off, to find some less complicated woman to spend an evening with.

The mare turned her head and took aim at his shoulder. Sam merely shifted out of range and continued to stroke and soothe. He didn't want to spend the evening with a less complicated woman. He wanted to spend it with Johanna. Just a test, he told himself, to see if whatever had happened by the pond would happen again. And if it did, what the hell was he going to do about it?

He was better off not seeing her again. A man had a lot more freedom when he cluttered up his life with many women than when he found himself concentrating on only one. He wasn't trying to concentrate on her, he reminded himself. He just couldn't get her out of his head.

What secrets did she have tucked away inside her? He had to find out.

When she'd kissed him…there had been no secrets there. She'd been open, passionate and as honest as a man could hope for. It hadn't been ordinary. He knew what it was to kiss a woman for pleasure, for obligation or because the script called for it. That moment with Johanna had been nothing so simple as pleasure, and it had been nothing so casual as obligation. The reaction—his *and* hers—hadn't been in any script.

She'd been as stunned as he was, and as unnerved. Didn't she want to know why?

The hell with what she wanted, Sam decided as he shut the stall door. *He* had to know why. Whether she wanted to or not, Johanna was going along for the ride.

* * *

She was beat. Johanna downed two aspirin and a carton of yogurt at her kitchen sink. Her afternoon had been taken up by back-to-back meetings, and though she should have been celebrating the nighttime syndication of *Trivia*, she'd opted for a quiet evening at home. She'd have to set up a party for the crew next week. They deserved it. And she'd see that Beth got a raise. For tonight, she didn't want to think about production meetings or sponsors. Her flowers needed tending.

The sun was warm on her face and arms as she walked outside to her garden. The roses that climbed the trellis along the side of the house needed pinching off. Snapdragons and hollyhocks needed weeding. Some of the taller and heavier-bloomed plants would require staking. Pleased with the scents and colors, she dug in.

She'd spent many quiet afternoons with the gardener on her father's estate, learning the names of the plants and the care they required. He'd let her have a plot of her own and had shown her how to turn soil and plant seeds, how to separate at the roots and prune. She'd learned how to blend plants for color, texture, height and flowering periods from him. On rainy days, or during cold snaps, he'd let her explore the greenhouse, where fragile seedlings had been nursed or exotic bulbs forced for early blooming.

The scents there had never been forgotten, the sultriness, the heat, even the damp smell of watered soil. He'd been a kind man, a little stoop-shouldered and thick through the middle. During one brief fantasy she'd imagined he was her father and they'd gone into business together.

She hadn't known until she'd heard him talking with another servant that he'd felt sorry for her.

All the servants had felt sorry for her—the little girl who was only brought out and paraded at her father's whim. She'd had a three-story dollhouse, a tea set of English china and a white fur coat. There had been ballet lessons and piano lessons and French taught by a private tutor. Other little girls would have dreamed of having what Johanna had only had to lift a hand for.

At six, her picture had been splashed across the press. She'd worn a red velvet dress that had skimmed her ankles and a tiny diamond tiara as flower girl at her father's second wedding. A Hollywood princess.

The bride had been an Italian actress who enjoyed having tantrums. Her father had spent a good deal of that two-year union on the Italian Riviera. Johanna had spent most of it in the gardens of his Beverly Hills estate.

There had been a scandal and a mudslinging divorce. The actress had kept the Italian villa, and her father had had a blistering affair with the lead in his next production. Johanna, at age eight, had already developed a cool and all-too-adult view of relationships.

She preferred her flowers. She didn't like wearing gloves. She felt that she got a better sense of the soil and the fragile roots with her hands uncovered. When she managed to squeeze in time for a manicure, she was usually met with shock and dismay. As a matter of routine, Johanna kept her nails clipped short and didn't bother with enamel.

Unfeminine. That was what Lydia had called her. Lydia had been one of her father's more vocal and lon-

ger-lasting distractions. Lydia had been palely beautiful and unceasingly selfish. Fortunately, she hadn't
wanted to marry Carl Patterson any more than he had
wanted to marry her.

*Send the girl to the nuns in Switzerland, darling.
Nothing like nuns for teaching a girl a little feminin-
ity and grace.*

Johanna, at twelve, had lived in terror that she would
be sent away, but Lydia had been replaced before she'd
managed to pressure Carl into paying the tuition.

Unfeminine. The word still cropped up in Johanna's
head from time to time. She usually ignored it; she'd
found her own style of womanhood. But now and again,
like an old scar, the word caused an itch.

On her hands and knees, she brushed through her
patio dahlias, back to the freesia that would bloom in
another few weeks. With care and precision, she pulled
out any weeds that had had the audacity to sprout. It had
been a dry spring, and after testing the soil she decided
she'd give everything a good soak before calling it a day.

She heard the car but didn't bother to glance up, because she expected it to drive by. When it didn't, Johanna had just enough time to look around before Sam
swung out of the driver's side.

She said nothing and remained kneeling, speechless.

He was furious. The long drive from his ranch had
given him plenty of time to work on his temper. Here
he was chasing after some cool-eyed go-to-hell blonde
and all he could think of when he saw her was how she'd
looked in the moonlight.

It was dusk now, the light soft and tenuous. She was
kneeling in front of a bank of flowers like some pagan

virgin sacrifice. She didn't rise, and her hands were stained with soil and grass. The air smelled like sin, dark and rich.

"Why the hell do you have a secretary and an answering machine if you don't intend to answer messages?"

"I've been busy."

"What you are is rude."

She hated that. Hated knowing it was true. "I'm sorry." She put on her coolest and most professional smile. "The show's going into syndication and I've been tied up with meetings and paperwork. Was there something important?"

"You know damn well it's important."

She spent the next ten seconds carefully wiping the worst of the dirt from her hands onto her jeans and staring at his boots. "If there's a problem with your contract—"

"Cut it, Johanna. We've done our business. That's over."

She looked at him then. "Yes, that's right."

He stuck his hands in his pockets. If he'd had them free much longer he might have throttled her. "I don't like feeling like a fool."

"I'm sure you don't." She rose, careful to keep an arm's length of distance between them. "I'm losing the light, Sam. If there's nothing else…" The rest of the words slid down her throat when he grabbed her by her shirtfront.

"You're going to turn away from me once too often," he said quietly. Much too quietly. "I've always considered myself fairly even-tempered. Seems I was wrong."

"Your temperament's not my problem."

"The hell it isn't." To prove his point, he yanked her against him. Her hands came up automatically for balance and defense. But his mouth was already on hers.

There was no testing kiss this time, no friendly overture. There was only the outpouring of urgency and demand that had clawed inside him for days. She didn't struggle. He hated to think of what he might have done if she had. Instead, she went very still, and for a moment nearly fooled them both into thinking she was unaffected.

Then she moaned. The sound went from her mouth into his, filled with surrender and despair. Before the sound had died her arms were around him, her fingers digging into his shoulders.

Twilight deepened, cooling the air, but she felt only the heat from his body as she pressed against him. He smelled of horses and leather. Dazed, she thought that the scent must be part of some deeply buried fantasy. Knight on white charger. But she didn't want to be rescued. Like a fool, she'd thought she could escape, from him, from herself. It only took a moment to show her how firmly she was already bound.

He brushed his mouth across her face, drawing in the taste, the softness. Her lips skimmed his jaw as she, too, searched for more. He tightened his arms around her. He'd thought he'd understood what it was to ache for a woman. Nothing had ever come close to this. He hurt everywhere, with a pain more erotic than anything he'd ever imagined. The more he touched, the more he hurt. The more he hurt, the more he was driven to touch.

"I want you, Johanna." His hands were in her hair

now, as if he couldn't trust them to wander over her again. "I haven't been able to stop thinking about you for days. For nights. I want to be with you. Now."

She wanted it, too. A shudder ran through her as she clung to him. She wanted him. She wanted to let go of her control, of her caution, and just feel—the way he could make her feel. Somehow she already knew that he could bring her things she'd never believed in. Once he did, she'd never be the same.

For a moment longer, she held on. Regret, more than she'd ever known, replaced desire as she drew away. With an effort she managed a smile as she glanced at the smudges on his shoulders. "My hands were dirty."

He took them both. "Let's go inside."

"No." Gently she drew her hands from his. "It wouldn't work, Sam. *We* wouldn't work."

"Why?"

"Because I wouldn't want it to. I wouldn't let it work."

He took her chin in his hand. "Bull."

"I wouldn't." She wrapped her fingers around his wrist. The pulse was fast there, as fast as her own. "I'm attracted to you, I won't deny that. But it can't lead anywhere."

"It already has."

"Then it can't lead any farther. Believe me when I say I'm sorry, but we're both better off facing up to it now."

"I'm sorry, too, but I can't accept it." He moved his hand to her cheek in a gesture that pierced her with its tenderness. "If you're expecting me to walk away and leave you alone, you're going to be disappointed."

She took a deep breath and met his eyes squarely. "I'm not going to sleep with you."

His brow lifted. "Now, or ever?"

The last thing she'd expected to do was laugh, but the chuckle bubbled out. "Good night, Sam."

"Hold on. We're not finished." There was amusement in his voice as he gestured toward her front steps. "Why don't we sit down? It's a nice night." When she hesitated, he lifted his hands, palms out. "No contact."

"All right." She wasn't completely at ease with it but felt perhaps she owed them both that much. "Would you like a drink?"

"What have you got?"

"This morning's coffee."

"I'll skip it, thanks." He settled comfortably next to her, hip to hip. "I do like your place, Johanna," he began, wondering if he would be able to understand her better through it. "It's quiet, private, well looked-after. How long have you had it?"

"About five years."

"Did you plant all this?"

"Yes."

"What are those?"

She looked over to the edge of one of her borders. "Soapwort."

"Ugly name for such a pretty thing." The little pink flowers looked delicate, but he could see that they spread exactly as they chose. "You know, it occurs to me that we don't know each other very well." He leaned back against the next step, stretching his legs out. Johanna thought he looked very much at home.

"No," she said cautiously. "I suppose we don't."

"You believe in dating?"

She hooked her hands around her knees and smiled. "It's a nice occupation for teenagers."

"You don't figure adults can pull it off?"

On guard again, she moved her shoulders. "Most people I know have lovers, not boyfriends."

"And you don't have either."

"I like it that way."

The way she said it made him glance back at the little pink flowers again. "Why don't we shoot for another term, like companion?" He turned to study her profile. "We could try being companions for a while. That's an easy, uncomplicated term. No strings."

It sounded that way, but she knew better. "I meant what I said before."

"I'm sure you did." He crossed his feet at the ankles. "That's why I figured you wouldn't be afraid to get to know me better."

"I'm not afraid," she said immediately, showing him that he'd hit the right button.

"Good. There's a benefit Friday night at the Beverly Wilshire. I'll pick you up at seven."

"I don't—"

"You support raising funds for the homeless, don't you?"

"Of course I do, but—"

"And since you're not afraid, it wouldn't bother you to be my companion. It's formal," he continued smoothly. "I don't care much for that kind of evening myself, but it's for a good cause."

"I appreciate the offer, but I simply couldn't manage to get home from work and change in time for a formal function at the Wilshire by seven." And that, she thought, should be the end of that.

"All right, I'll pick you up at your office. That way we can make it seven-thirty."

She let out a huge breath, then shifted so that she could look at him directly. "Sam, why are you trying to maneuver me this way?"

"Johanna..." He took her hand and kissed her fingers, too quickly for her to object. "I can maneuver much better than this."

"I'll just bet."

Delighted, he grinned. "I love it when you use that tone. It's so proper. Makes me want to muss you up."

"You didn't answer my question."

"Which question? Oh, that one," he finished when she narrowed her eyes. "I'm not trying to maneuver you, I'm trying to make a date with you. No, not a date," he corrected. "No dates for adults. We can't call it a meeting, that's too businesslike. How about encounter? You like encounter?"

"I don't think so."

"One thing I've found out about you already, Johanna, is that you're a hard woman to please." He stretched out again with a sigh. "But that's all right. I can sit right here until you come up with the right choice of words. Stars are coming out."

Involuntarily she glanced up. She often sat out by herself in the evening. She'd been content to look at the stars alone. Somehow the night seemed more appealing with him there, and that worried her. Depending on someone else for your contentment was a big mistake.

"It's getting chilly," she murmured.

"Are you asking me in?"

She smiled, then rested her elbow on her knee. "It's not that chilly." They were silent for a moment. Then the silence was broken by a nighthawk. "Why aren't you down in the city at some club being seen with some up-and-coming actress with lots of teeth?"

As if he were thinking it through, Sam rested his elbows on the back of the step. "I don't know. Why aren't you down in the city at some club being seen with some hotshot director with a perfect tan?"

Still pouting a bit, she kept her head still but shifted her gaze over to him. "I asked you first."

"I love acting," he said after a moment. His voice was so calm and serious that she turned her head again. "I really love it when it all comes together—the script, the moves, the crew. And I don't mind being paid well for it, either. I've got a couple of weeks before we start shooting. Once we do, there are going to be a lot of very long and very demanding days. I don't want to waste the little time I have in a club." He touched her hair. They both remembered he'd promised there would be no contact, but she didn't object. "Are you going to come back and feed my ducks, Johanna?"

It was a mistake, she told herself as she smiled at him. A stupid one. At least she was making it with her eyes open. "I think I can make it Friday night, if you don't mind leaving the benefit a bit early. I'll have put in a full day at the office."

"Seven-thirty, at your office?"

"Fine. No strings?"

"Deal."

The minute he leaned toward her, she held up a hand. "Don't kiss me, Sam."

He backed off, not without effort. "Now, or ever?"

She rose and brushed off the seat of her jeans. "Now, anyway. I'll see you tomorrow."

"Johanna." She paused at the top of the steps and looked back. "Nothing," he told her. "I just wanted to look at you again. Night."

"Drive carefully. It's a long trip."

He threw her a grin over his shoulder. "It's getting shorter all the time."

CHAPTER
FIVE

By five-thirty the offices were like a tomb. Johanna was happy enough to have an extra hour to herself. Paperwork that never seemed to diminish during the normal working day could be gotten through in an un-interrupted hour. Questions for Monday's taping had been chosen and checked, but Johanna took the time to go over them herself to be certain they were as en-tertaining as they were educational.

She answered a pile of memos, read and signed let-ters and approved a stack of bills. The beauty of game shows, she thought as she worked, was that they were cheap to produce. In a big week they could give away over fifty thousand dollars and still come in at a fraction of the cost of a thirty-minute situation comedy.

She was still determined to get her other concept on the air, and was ready to make her pitch for the pilot so that when things clicked the show could debut in the fall. And they would click, Johanna promised herself. One more success, one more solid success, and her own production company could begin its struggle for survival.

Garden Variety Productions. She could already see the logo. Within two years others would see it, as well. And remember it.

She'd continue to do the games, of course, but she'd begin to expand her own horizons, as well. A daytime drama, a couple of prime-time movies, a weekly series. She could already see it building, step by step. But for now she had to concentrate on getting through the rest of the day. And the evening.

After her desk was cleared, Johanna brought out her secret. She'd hidden the bag in her bottom drawer, behind the office stationery. There'd been enough commotion over her bringing an evening dress to the office. Now Johanna pulled the box from the bag, opened it, then read the instructions through twice. It didn't seem that complicated. She'd make it an adventure, she told herself, even if it was silly. She'd told herself it was silly even as she'd let the clerk talk her into buying them.

Johanna set her equipment in orderly lines, with the instructions handy, then examined her hands, back, then palms. The clerk hadn't been wrong about her nails being a mess. And what was wrong with trying something new? Johanna picked up the first fake fingernail and began to file it. She tested it often, placing it on her short, unpainted thumbnail until she was satisfied that the length wasn't extravagant. Only nine more to go, she thought, and began to attack the rest.

As she worked, she slipped out of her shoes and curled her legs under her. It was a position she never would have permitted herself to take if anyone had been in the office. Alone, she switched to it without thinking. Once she had ten uniformly filed nails on her blotter, she went on to the next stage.

The instructions told her it was easy, quick and neat. Johanna peeled off the adhesive and pressed it against her nail. Easy. With the tweezers she carefully caught the tip of the backing and began to peel it off. The adhesive rolled into a ball. Patiently Johanna removed it and tried again. The third time she managed to make it stick. Pleased, she picked up the first nail and aligned it carefully over her own. After pressing down, she examined the result.

It didn't look like her thumb, but it was rather elegant. After she painted it with the Shell-Pink Fizz enamel the clerk had sold her, no one would know the difference.

It took her twenty minutes to complete one hand, and she had to resort to digging out her reading glasses— something else she never would have done unless completely alone. She was swearing at the clerk, at herself and at the manufacturer when the phone rang. Johanna hit line one and popped the nail off her index finger.

"Johanna Patterson," she said between her teeth.

"It's John Jay, honey. I'm so glad you're a workaholic."

Johanna glared at her naked index finger. "What is it?"

"I've got a teeny little problem, sweetheart, and need you to come to my rescue." When she said nothing, he cleared his throat. "Listen, it seems my credit card's at the limit and I'm in a bit of an embarrassment. Would you mind talking to the manager here at Chasen's? He says he knows you."

"Put him on." Disgusted, she ran her hand through her hair and popped off another nail. It took less than two minutes to squeeze John Jay out of his embarrassment. After she hung up the phone, Johanna looked at her hand. Two of the nails she'd meticulously placed were gone, and her fingers were smeared with adhesive. Letting out a long breath, she began to remove the rest.

She was an intelligent, capable woman, she reminded herself. She was a hop and a skip away from being thirty and she held down a complex and demanding job. She was also probably the only woman in the country who couldn't attach fake nails.

The hell with it. She dumped everything, including the bottle of enamel, into the trash.

She did what she could with her hair in the women's lounge. Then, because she was feeling unfeminine and klutzy, she went dramatic with her makeup. Dressed only in thigh-high stockings and tap pants, she unzipped the garment bag. She'd only worn the gown once before, a year ago. It was strapless and clingy, a far cry from her usual style. With a shrug, Johanna stepped into it, and shimmied it up, then fought to reach the zipper. She swore again and wondered why she'd allowed herself to be talked into going out at all. Once the dress was secured, she tried to see as much of herself as possible in the waist-high mirrors.

It was a good fit, she decided as she turned to the side. And the color—which, she remembered grimly, would have matched the enamel now in the trash—was flattering. Though she couldn't see it, the hem skimmed her knees in the front, then graduated down to full-length in the back. Johanna changed her everyday earrings for pearl-and-diamond circles, then clasped on a matching choker.

As good as it gets, she thought, and zipped her office clothes in the bag. She'd have her secretary send them to the cleaners on Monday. With the bag slung over her arm, she started back to her office. She'd been wise to have Sam meet her here, Johanna decided. Not only did it make it less like a date, there was the added security that she'd have to be dropped off back in the parking garage so that she could drive herself home.

The coward's way. She shrugged her shoulders with a touch of annoyance as she walked. The safe way, she corrected. Whatever she was feeling for Sam was a little too fast and a little too intense. Having an affair wasn't in her plans, professionally or personally. She'd simply lived through too many of her father's.

Her life would never be like his.

As far as Sam Weaver was concerned, she would be sensible, cautious and, above all, in complete control of the situation.

Oh, God, he looked wonderful.

He was standing in her office by the window, his hands in the pockets of his tux and his thoughts on something she couldn't see. Pleasure, hardly comfortable, slammed into her. If she'd believed in happily-ever-afters, she would have believed in him.

He hadn't heard her, but he'd been thinking about her hard enough, deeply enough, that he'd known the moment she'd stepped into the doorway. He turned, and his image of her dissolved and reassembled.

She looked so fragile with her hair swept up off her neck and her shoulders bare. The business-first office had suited the woman he'd first met. The pretty garden and isolated house had suited the woman who'd laughed with him beside the pond. But this was a new Johanna, one who seemed too delicate to touch.

As ridiculous as it made him feel, he had to catch his breath. "I thought you'd skipped out."

"No." When she realized her knuckles were turning white clutching her summer bag, she relaxed them. "I was changing." Because she wanted badly to act natural, she made herself move to the closet. "I'm sorry if I'm a bit behind. I got caught up. Work," she said, and with a quick glance made certain the fiasco of plastic nails and polish was out of sight.

"You look wonderful, Johanna."

"Thanks." She shut the closet door, trying to take the compliment with the same ease with which it was given. "So do you. I'm ready whenever you are."

"I need another minute." He crossed to her, catching the quick surprise in her eyes just before he covered her bare shoulders with his hands and kissed her. He lingered over the kiss, struggling to keep the pressure light, the demand minimal. "Just wanted to see if you were real," he murmured.

She was real, all right, so real that she could feel her own blood pumping hot and quick. "We should go."

"I'd rather stay here and neck. Well, maybe some other time," he added when he saw her brow lift. With her hand in his, he started out of the office toward the elevators. "Listen, if this is really boring we could leave early. Take a drive."

"Hollywood galas are never boring." She said it so dryly that he laughed.

"You don't like them."

"I don't often find it necessary to attend them." She stepped into the elevator as the door opened.

"It's hard to be a part of a world and ignore it at the same time."

"No, it's not." She'd been doing it for years. "Some of us do better behind the scenes. I saw one of the early ads for your miniseries," she continued, changing the subject before he had a chance to probe. "It looked good, very classy, very sexy."

"That's marketing," he said dismissively as the elevator reached the underground parking garage. "It's not really sexy. It's romantic. There's a difference."

There was indeed, but it surprised her that he knew it. "When you've got your shirt off and your chest is gleaming, people think sex."

"Is that all it takes?" He opened the passenger door of his car. "I can be out of this cummerbund in under five seconds."

She swung her legs into the car. "Thanks, but I've already seen your chest. Why television?" she asked when he'd joined her. "At this point in your career, I mean."

"Because the majority of people won't sit still in a

theater for four hours, and I wanted to do this movie. The small screen's more personal, more intimate, and so was this script." The car's engine echoed in the nearly empty garage as he backed up and began to drive out. "The character of Sarah is so fragile, so tragic. She's so absolutely trusting and naive. It knocked me out the way Lauren pulled it off," he added, referring to his co-star. "She really found the essence of that innocence."

And, according to the press, he and Lauren had had as many love scenes away from the cameras as they had in front of them. It would be wise, Johanna reminded herself, to remember that. "It's not usual to hear an actor talk about a character other than his own."

"Luke's a bastard," Sam said simply as he stopped at a light. "An opportunist, a womanizer and a heel. A very charming, glib-tongued one."

"Did you capture his essence?"

He studied Johanna before the light changed. "You'll have to watch and tell me."

Deliberately she turned away. "What's your next project?"

"It's a comedy."

"I didn't know you did comedy."

"Obviously you missed my tour de force as the Raisin Crunch man a few years ago."

The chuckle welled up. "I'm embarrassed to say I did."

"That's all right. I'm embarrassed to say I didn't. That was right before I did the Mano cologne commercials. 'What woman can resist a man who smells like a man?'"

She would have laughed again if she hadn't remembered her own reaction to everything about him, including his scent. "Well, no one can say you haven't paid your dues."

"I like to think I have, and I'm also aware that the Mano campaign got me a reading for *Undercover*."

She was sure it had. Johanna hadn't missed those particular ads. In them, Sam had been blood-pumpingly sexy, intensely male and cocky enough to make a woman's mouth water. His character in *Undercover* had been precisely the same, but with an underlying depth that had surprised both the audience and the critics.

"Those kind of breaks don't happen very often," she said aloud. "When they do, they're usually deserved."

"Well…" He drew the word out. "I think that was a compliment."

She shrugged. "I've never said you weren't good at what you do."

"Maybe we could turn that around and say the problem from the outset has been that I am." She said nothing, but he thought that was answer enough.

Her brow creased a bit as they drove up to the well-lit limousine-adorned Beverly Wilshire. "Looks like quite a crowd."

"We can still go back to your office and neck."

She gave him a brief, very bland look as one of the uniformed staff opened her door. The moment she was on the curb, strobe lights and cameras flashed.

She hated that. She didn't have the words to explain even to herself how much she hated it. With a gesture that could be taken for one of aloofness rather than panic, she turned away. Sam slipped an arm around her and by doing so caused a dozen more flashes.

"They hound you less if you smile and cooperate," he murmured in her ear.

"Mr. Weaver! Mr. Weaver! What can you tell us about your upcoming television miniseries?"

Sam aimed his answer at the crowd of reporters and personalized it with a smile even as he started to walk. "With a quality script and a cast that includes Lauren Spencer, I think it speaks for itself."

"Is your engagement to Miss Spencer off?"

"It was never on."

One of the reporters got close enough to grab Johanna's arm. "Could we have your name, Miss?"

"Patterson," she said, and shook him off.

"Carl Patterson's girl," she heard someone in the crowd say. "That's the old man's daughter. Ms. Patterson, is it true your father's marriage is on the rocks? How do you feel about him being linked with a woman half his age?"

Saying nothing, Johanna swept through the front doors into the lobby.

"Sorry." Sam kept his arm around her. She was trembling a bit with what he took for anger.

"You had nothing to do with it." She only needed a moment, she thought, to calm down. Yes, there was anger, but there was also that stomach-churning distress that swooped down on her whenever she was confronted with cameras and demanding questions about her father. It had happened before and would happen again, as long as she was the daughter of Carl W. Patterson.

"You want to slip into the bar and get a drink? Sit in a dark corner for a minute?"

"No. No, really, I'm fine." As the tension eased, she

smiled up at him. "I'd hate to go through that as often as you must."

"It's part of the job." But he lifted her chin with a finger. "Are you sure you're okay?"

"Of course. I think I'll just—"

But her plans for a brief escape were scotched when several people walked over to greet Sam.

She knew them, some by sight, others by reputation. Sam's co-star in his last feature was with her husband and happily pregnant with her first child. The elite of the press who had been permitted inside took the photo opportunity.

As they inched their way to the ballroom, others came by to renew an acquaintance or be introduced. Through her father she knew a great many of them herself. There were cheeks to be kissed, hugs to be given, hands to be shaken. A veteran actor with a silver mane of hair and a face that still graced billboards squeezed her. With an affection she felt for few, Johanna hugged him back. She'd never forgotten how he had come up to her room and entertained her with stories long ago, during one of her father's parties.

"Uncle Max, you're even more handsome than ever."

His laugh was low and gravelly as he kept his arm around her. "Jo-Jo. Looking at you makes me feel old."

"You'll never be old."

"Mary will want to see you," he said, speaking of his longtime and only wife. "She's run off with a safari to the ladies' room." He kissed her cheek again, then turned to size up Sam. "So you've finally broken down and taken on an actor. At least you've chosen a good one. I've admired your work."

"Thank you." After six years in the business, Sam had thought he was immune to being starstruck. "It's an honor to meet you, Mr. Heddison," he said, and he meant it. "I've seen everything you've ever done."

"Little Jo-Jo always had taste. I'd like to work with you sometime. Not many of this generation I'd say that to."

"Tell me when and where."

With his eyes narrowed, Max gave a slow nod. "I've a script I've been considering. Maybe I'll send it along and let you have a look. Jo-Jo, I'd like to see your pretty face more often." He kissed her again, then strode off to find his wife.

"I believe you're speechless," Johanna commented when Sam only continued to watch Max's back.

"There's not another actor alive I admire more than Max Heddison. He doesn't socialize much, and the couple of times I've seen him I didn't have the nerve to wangle an introduction."

"You, shy?"

"Intimidated is a mild way to put it."

Johanna took his hand again, touched that he could be. "He's the kindest man I know. Once for my birthday he gave me a puppy. My father was furious—he hates dogs—but he couldn't say anything because it was from Uncle Max."

"Jo-Jo?"

She shot him a look. "Uncle Max is the only one who has ever, or who will ever, call me that."

"I like it." He ran a finger down her nose. "It makes me wonder how you'd look in pigtails and a straw hat. Oh, God." She saw his expression change from one of amusement to resignation just before he was enveloped by slim white arms.

"Oh, Sam, I just can't believe how long it's been." The woman with the gypsy mane of red curls turned her face just enough to let the camera get her best side. "Darling, where *have* you been hiding?"

"Here and there." He managed, with considerable skill, to untangle himself. "How are you, Toni?"

"Well, how do I look?" She threw back her magnificent head and laughed. Johanna noted that her dress was cut to the lowest degree that the law would allow. "I've been so terribly busy I've lost touch. I've just started filming and could barely fit this little event into my schedule. It's so boring not being able to see friends."

"Johanna Patterson, Toni DuMonde."

"It's nice to meet you." Johanna knew DuMonde's reputation as a mediocre actress who traded more on sex appeal than talent. She'd married well twice, and both husbands had boosted her career.

"Any friend of Sam's—" she began, then stopped. "You aren't Carl's daughter, are you?" Before Johanna could answer, she threw her head back again, making sure her hair cascaded as she laughed. "What a riot! Darling, I've just been dying to meet you!" Placing a hand on Johanna's shoulder, she scanned the room. Her eyes, sharp and tawny, skimmed over minor celebrities, smiled at those worth noticing and narrowed when focused on a rival. When she found her objective, her smile turned up several hundred kilowatts. Johanna noticed the flashy diamond on her left hand as she signaled.

"This is such a happy coincidence," Toni continued.

"I'm sure you'll understand how very delighted I am. Sweetheart, look who I found."

Johanna looked at her father as Toni snuggled against him. The move was calculated so that the diamond on her finger winked hard and cold and in plain sight.

"Johanna, I didn't realize you were attending." Carl brushed his cheek against hers, as he would have with any of his hundreds of acquaintances.

He was a tall man, with broad shoulders and a flat stomach. He'd allowed his face to line because he had a fear of going under the knife, even cosmetically. But he'd never permitted his body to sag. At fifty-five, Carl W. Patterson was in his prime. Women were as drawn to him now as they had been thirty years before. Perhaps more, as power added to his sex appeal.

"You're looking well," Johanna told him. Sam noted that there was none of the warmth here that there had been when she'd greeted Max Heddison. "Carl Patterson, Sam Weaver."

"A pleasure." Carl took Sam's hand in his hefty, well-manicured one. "I've kept my eye on your career. Word is you're starting a film with Berlitz soon. We go back a ways."

"I'm looking forward to it."

"Isn't this cozy?" Toni put in, clipping her free hand through Sam's arm. "The four of us running into each other this way. We'll have to get a table together, won't we, Carl? After all, I'll want to get to know your daughter, now that we're going to be family."

Johanna didn't freeze. She didn't even react. By this time she was past being surprised by her father. "Congratulations." She winced only slightly when a camera flashed, catching the four of them together.

"We haven't set the date yet." Toni beamed up at Carl. "But we plan to make it soon—well, as soon as a few minor matters are taken care of."

Which would be the legal disposal of his fourth wife, Johanna surmised. Fortunately, she was no longer affected by the whims or variable presence of stepmothers. "I'm sure you'll be very happy."

"We intend to be." Carl patted Toni's hand, looking at her rather than at his daughter.

"Do let's get a table, Carl, and have a drink to celebrate." Toni kept a casual grip on both men. So casual that it was barely noticeable when Sam removed her hand and took Johanna's. Hers was ice-cold and rigid.

"I'm sorry, we can't stay long." Sam's smile was charming and faintly apologetic.

"Oh, pooh, you've time for one quick drink before this place turns into a zoo." Toni trailed her fingertips up Carl's arm. "Darling, you'll have to insist."

"No need to insist." She wouldn't be ill, Johanna told herself. She wouldn't even be upset. Neither did she smile as she looked up at her father. "The least I can do is drink to your happiness."

"Wonderful." Toni thought it more than wonderful to be seen with a man as important as Carl and a man as attractive as Sam at the same time. "Now, Johanna darling, you mustn't believe all those naughty things you must have read about Sam and me. You know how people in this town love to talk." She turned to be escorted inside and shot a smile over her shoulder, daring Johanna not to believe every word.

"Why in the hell are you doing this?" Sam demanded.

"Because it's part of the game." Chin up, Johanna stepped into the ballroom.

The room was full of babble. It glittered as such events are meant to, and it would make excellent copy in *People*. It would raise a great deal of money—a hundred, perhaps a hundred and fifty thousand dollars—while making the evening worth the price of the meal. And the food was lavish.

She didn't eat. Johanna barely noticed what was placed in front of her, though Toni cooed over each course and made noises about calories. The ring on her hand flashed triumphantly every time she moved her fingers. She made coy little remarks about Sam behaving like a gentleman with her almost-step-daughter, giggled delightedly about having a daughter the same age as herself and snuggled kisses on Carl's cheek when she wasn't flirting elsewhere.

He was dazzled by her. Johanna sipped champagne and watched her father preen whenever the redhead stroked his ego. She'd never known him to be dazzled by a woman before. Desirous, covetous, infuriated, but never dazzled.

"Just a teeny bit more," Toni said when Carl poured more wine. "You know how silly I get when I drink too much." She shot him an intimate look that promised she could get a great deal more than silly. "Isn't this a wild crowd?" She waved cheerily to someone at another table. "God, what a hideous dress. All those diamonds don't make up for plain bad taste, do they? Sam, darling, I heard Lauren's seeing some French race-car driver. Did she break your heart?"

"No," he said flatly, and shifted away when she patted his knee.

"That's because you always do the heartbreaking. Be very careful with this man, Johanna dear, better women than I have shed a tear over him."

"I'm certain," Johanna said sweetly, and sipped more champagne.

"Tell me, why haven't you had your daddy put you in the movies?" Toni gave her a cool woman-to-woman look over her glass.

"I don't act."

"What do you do?"

"Johanna produces daytime television," Carl put in. "The latest reports that crossed my desk were excellent, by the way."

"Thank you."

"Evening syndication is moving forward?"

"Yes, we just finalized it. I would have sent you a memo, but I thought you were out of town."

"We just spent two weeks on the most dismal location shoot in Arizona." Toni patted Carl's hand. "Thank God Carl was there to be sure I wasn't worn to a frazzle. Sam, I've heard the most marvelous things about your television thing. That'll be aired in a couple of weeks, won't it?"

He smiled at her again and nodded. He knew she'd tested for the part of Sarah and had yet to forgive him for not pulling strings to get it for her.

"We really should do a movie together, with Carl producing."

When hell freezes over, Sam thought. "I really hate to cut this short, but Johanna and I are already late." He rose before anyone could protest and offered a hand. "A pleasure meeting you, Mr. Patterson, and my compliments on your finest production." Taking Johanna by the hand, he grinned at Toni. "Don't ever change, darling."

"Good night," Johanna said to her father. "Best wishes." She didn't object to Sam's supporting arm as he guided her out of the ballroom. "You didn't have to cut your evening short on my account," she began.

"I didn't cut it short, and I'm not leaving only on your account. I don't like socializing with piranhas like Toni." He drew out the claim check for his car and handed it to the boy on the curb. "Besides, you look like you could use some fresh air."

"I'm not drunk."

"No, but you were heading there."

"I never get drunk, because I don't like to be out of control."

Truer words had never been spoken, he was certain. "Fine, but I'm going to get you something to eat anyway." He handed the boy who brought his car a twenty and ushered Johanna in himself. "Could you handle a burger?"

"I'm not hungry."

Stubborn, he thought, and just this side of sulking. "Okay, I want a burger."

She started to snap and realized just in time that she was being nasty. "Sam, I appreciate it, but I really don't want anything. Why don't you just drop me off so I can get my car?"

"You had five glasses of wine. I counted." He'd nursed one the moment he'd seen what kind of mood she was in. "I'm driving you home—after we eat."

"I can't leave my car in town."

"I'll have someone drop it off to you tomorrow."

"That's too much trouble. I can—"

"Johanna…" He pulled over to the curb and waited until she looked at him. "Let me be a friend, okay?"

She shut her eyes, wanting badly to do something else she never allowed herself. To cry, hard and long and for no reason at all. "Thanks. I guess I could use some food and some air."

In his tux, Sam ran into a bright fast-food restaurant, ordered burgers, fries and coffee, signed half a dozen autographs and ran out again. "Life's rarely simple anymore," he told Johanna as he tucked the bag between her feet. "The little girl behind the counter wanted to pay for them, and I know damn well she stuck her phone number in the bag. She must have been all of nineteen."

"You should have let me go in."

"We all have our crosses to bear." He headed out. "Johanna, I don't make it a habit to pay attention to what's said about me in print—unless it's a review— but I'd like to make an exception and tell you that Toni and I were never together."

"Sam, it's none of my business."

"Whether you think it's your business or not, I'd like you to believe me. If you've already got a picture of her and me, it's bad enough. When you add that to the fact that she's apparently going to marry your father, it's ludicrous."

Johanna opened her eyes and studied him as he

drove. It hadn't occurred to her before. She'd been too wrapped up in her own thoughts and feelings to notice. But she saw it now. "She embarrassed you. I'm sorry."

"I just didn't like her implying—" Implying, hell, he thought. She'd practically taken out an ad. "I'd feel better if you understood there'd never been anything between us." He wanted to say more but found it difficult to say what he thought about the woman who was going to become a part of Johanna's family. "Anyway, it wasn't quite the evening I had in mind."

In a little while he pulled up at the crest of a hill. Below, spread out like a game of lights, was the Los Angeles Basin. He put the top down. Far off in the distance she heard the call of a coyote.

"We're not dressed for burgers, but I got plenty of napkins." He reached down for the bag and the back of his hand brushed her calf. "Johanna, I have to tell you something."

"What?"

"You have incredible legs."

"Give me a hamburger, Sam," she said, and took off her shoes.

"Smells better than the veal medallions."

"Is that what we had?"

"No, that's what you didn't have. Here's the ketchup." He passed her a handful of little plastic bags, then waited until he was satisfied she was eating. If he'd ever seen anyone more miserable than Johanna had been at that pretty, flower-bedecked table with stars glittering in every corner, he couldn't remember. The worst of it was that she'd been struggling to be valiant about it.

"Want to talk about it?" When she only shrugged, he

pressed a little harder. "I take it you didn't know your father was planning to get married again."

"I didn't know he was planning to get divorced again. He doesn't check these things through with me."

"Are you fond of your current stepmother?"

"My father's current wife," she corrected automatically, which told him a great deal. "I don't know, I've only met her a couple of times. I think she moved back to New York a few weeks ago. I was just surprised because he doesn't usually stack one marriage on top of the other. Generally there's a space of a year or two between legal contracts."

"He'll have a few months to get to know Toni better. He could change his mind."

"I'm sure he knows exactly what she is. One thing Carl isn't is stupid."

"Sometimes if you tell someone when you're angry with them it loosens things up."

"I'm not angry with him, not really."

He brushed his knuckles along her cheek. "Hurt?"

She shook her head, unable to trust herself to speak for a moment. "He lives his own life. He always has. And that makes it easier for me to live mine."

"You know, I had some real matches with my father." He shook the bag of fries, urging them on her.

"Did you?"

"God, did we fight." With a laugh, Sam opened his coffee and began to sip. "The Weavers have tempers. We like to yell. I think I spent most of the years between fifteen and twenty going head-to-head with my old man. I mean, just because I plowed the car through

Greenley's fence was no reason to confiscate my license for six weeks, was it?"

"I imagine Greenley thought it was. Did you ever get your own way?"

"I figure that was about seventy-five, twenty-five, with him holding the lion's share. I probably got as much as I did because he was busy yelling at my brother or one of my sisters."

"It must be different, having a big family. I always imagined…"

"What?"

The wine cushioned embarrassment. Without it, she might never have said it out loud. "I sometimes thought it would be nice when I was little to have brothers and sisters… I don't know, grandparents to visit, family squabbles. Of course, I had stepsiblings from time to time. Things were usually finished before we'd gotten used to each other."

"Come here." He shifted over so he could put an arm around her. "Feel any better?"

"A lot." She sighed and rested her head. "I appreciate it."

Her hair smelled like the air outside the windows. Clean, quiet. The urge to turn his face into it was natural, and he did it without thinking. "I wish you hadn't had so much wine."

"Why?"

"Then it wouldn't be against the rules for me to seduce you."

She surprised herself by turning her face to his. She didn't like the word "seduce." It implied a lack of will.

But just now it sounded liberating, and more than tempting. "You live by the rules?"

"Not many of them." He brought his hand to her hair. "I want to make love with you, Johanna, but when I do I want you to have your wits about you. So for now I'll settle for a little less."

He nipped at her lower lip, testing its softness, experimenting with tastes. Here was warmth, just edging toward heat, and acceptance, only a step away from surrender.

Of all the visions and fantasies he'd already had of being with her, the one that was the strongest was of him just holding her like this, with the stars overhead and the night breezes blowing cool and clean.

She could have pulled away. His touch was so gentle she knew he would never have pushed. Not this time. There would be others. She already accepted that. On another night when the breeze was just ruffling the leaves he'd hold her like this, and his mood wouldn't be as patient. Nor, she was afraid, would hers. Something had taken root, no matter how hard she'd tried to pull it free. With a little sigh, she brought a hand to his face.

It was torture, but he ran his hand along her bare shoulders. He wanted to take the feel of her with him when he drew away. Just as he would take the taste of her, the scent of her skin, with him on the long, lonely trip home.

"I wish I knew what I was feeling," she murmured when she could speak again. It wasn't the wine. It would have been a lie to blame it on anything so ordinary. Her eyes were heavy, a bit dazed. Her mouth was soft. Just by looking at her Sam knew he could have her. One more easy nudge and they would be lovers.

He reminded himself about rules and fragile women.

"We're going to have to talk about it." He kissed her again, briefly. "Then we're going to have to do something about it. But right now I'm going to take you home."

CHAPTER
SIX

Johanna considered Saturdays the day the work force had been given to catch up on everything their jobs had forced them to ignore during the week. Rather than a day off, she thought of it as an alternate. Saturdays weren't for sleeping late—even if you were slightly hung over and punchy. They were for weeding the garden, marketing, dealing with personal correspondence and bookkeeping. Her Saturdays, like the rest of her days, had a routine she rarely varied. Johanna depended on organization because a well-ordered life was a safe one.

She dealt with the cleaning first. Though she'd never

thought of herself as particularly domestic, Johanna had never considered hiring someone to do the housekeeping. The house was her personal life, and as in all areas of that life, she preferred to handle it herself.

The vacuuming and dusting, the scrubbing down and polishing up, were never mundane chores. There was a certain basic pleasure in them, but more compelling was the feeling that her house, her things, deserved her attention. It was as simple as that. She could haul a bucket and dust rags from room to room with the same dedication and enjoyment she put into reading contracts or balancing budgets.

She preferred the radio loud so that she could hear it in whatever corner of the house she decided to tackle first. This was a day for both production and solitude. Over the years, Johanna had developed a dependency on both.

She did think about the car, and thinking of that naturally turned her thoughts to Sam. She hoped he didn't forget his promise to have someone drop it off, but if he did she'd simply forgo her Saturday marketing and have Bethany pick her up on Monday morning.

Johanna never depended on promises or other people's memories.

But she did think of him, and if her thoughts weren't completely comfortable she couldn't forget that he'd been kind, and gentler than she'd expected. She remembered, a little too well, how she'd felt when she'd kissed him. Full, edgy, tempted. Just a little more tempted each time she was with him to throw away the pact she'd made with herself so many years ago. The pact said no relationships that couldn't be controlled, by her, from the outset—no dependencies, no promises, long- or short-term.

It was a sensible pact, unwritten but binding. The fact that Sam had nearly lured her into forgetting it worried her. But it made her wonder more.

Just what was it about him that made her lose a bit of ground every time they were together? She could discount his looks, however delightful they were. She might appreciate a great physique, but she wouldn't swoon over one.

Not that she was swooning over Sam Weaver, Johanna reminded herself as she poured hot water into her bucket. She thought very little of women who built fantasies or relationships around cleft chins and bulging biceps.

Nor was it his reputation. That, in fact, worked against him. Johanna dunked her mop in hot, soapy water, then began to wash her kitchen floor. The fact that he was an actor was a strike against him. The fact that he was an actor with a reputation with women was a bigger one.

Of course, she knew that such reports were usually exaggerated and often outright lies. But there were times... There were times, Johanna thought as she swiped the mop back and forth, that the press didn't even come close to making rumor as outrageous as the truth.

The press had never known her truth. Her mother's truth. With the care and firmness of experience, she locked that thought away.

So it wasn't his looks or his reputed way with women. It certainly wasn't his fame. Growing up as she had, Johanna had had to tolerate vicarious fame all her life. It wasn't his talent, either, though she certainly respected that. She knew people were often drawn to talent and power. Her father, and the stream of women in his life, were proof of that. They were also drawn to wealth and position. Johanna was too ambitious and had spent too much time trying to perfect her own skills to be swayed by anyone else's.

So if it wasn't one of the attributes he was so obviously endowed with, just what was it that was making her think about him when she shouldn't?

It hadn't started with that first kiss. It would have been easy to blame it on basic sexual attraction, but Johanna preferred honest self-analysis. The seed of something had been there from that first meeting. If not, she wouldn't have gone out of her way to give him a hard time.

Defense mechanism, Johanna thought, recognizing and acknowledging it.

There was his charm, of course. She wrung out the mop and began to rinse. It wasn't stylized or deliberate. That she would have been immune to. It was natural, easy, even friendly. The roses had managed to turn the key in an old, well-guarded lock. The kiss had managed to blow it open briefly, just long enough to give her cause for alarm.

Alarm. Yes, that was what she'd felt overlaying every other emotion he'd drawn out of her. Now that she'd admitted it, she had to decide what to do about it.

She could ignore him. But she didn't believe that would do much good. She could—cautiously—go along with his suggestion that they get to know each other better. Slowly. And she could stick to her guns and not get involved beyond a wary friendship.

The solution had to be in there somewhere, she thought. She'd come up with it, and the next time she had to deal with him she'd be prepared.

She was incredible. Sam stood in the kitchen doorway and watched her mop the kitchen floor. He'd knocked, but the music she had blaring in the other room had drowned out the sound. Since the door hadn't been locked, he'd simply walked in and wandered through until he'd found her.

Johanna Patterson. She was just a bit different every time he saw her. Sophisticated one minute, wonderfully simple the next. Alluring, then cool. Nervous, then tough. A man could take years getting to know all of her. Sam figured he had time.

Right now she was dressed in faded cotton pants rolled up at the ankles and a big man-styled shirt pushed to her elbows. Her feet were bare, and her hair was pinned up untidily. She handled the mop with smooth, easy strokes, not skimming over the job and not swearing over it. He imagined she took to such things as housekeeping with the same steady drive she took to everything else. He liked that, and he liked her for it.

He knew exactly why he was attracted to Johanna. She was beautiful, but that wouldn't have been enough. She was smart, but though he respected a sharp mind that wouldn't have kept him coming back. She was vulnerable. Normally that would have made him take a cautious step back instead of these continued steps forward. She had an edge to her that in another few years might become hard. But now, just now, Johanna was a cautious woman with a few bruises who wasn't easily impressed by status. The combination was more than enough to keep pulling him toward her.

And she'd rather he didn't, Sam thought. On the surface, at least, she'd have preferred that he step out of her life and stay out. But deep down, he believed, she was looking for someone, for something, just as he was.

He wasn't naive enough to believe it was so just because that was what he wanted, but he was determined to find out.

He stood where he was as the strokes of the mop brought her closer. When she rammed into him, he took her arm to keep her from overbalancing.

Johanna whirled around, automatically gripping the mop like a weapon. The relief when she saw him turned quickly to anger.

"How the hell did you get in here?"

"The door," he told her easily. "It wasn't locked. I did knock. I guess you didn't hear me."

"No, I didn't." She was shouting to be heard over the music. "Apparently you took that as an invitation."

"I took it to mean you didn't hear me." He held up the keys she'd given him the night before. "I thought you'd want your car back."

"Thanks." She stuffed them in her pocket. It wasn't anger nearly as much as it was embarrassment. She didn't care to be sneaked up on unaware.

"You're welcome." He handed her a bouquet of painted daisies and snapdragons. As he'd suspected they would, her eyes softened. "I stole them from Mae's garden. I figured she wouldn't notice."

"They're pretty." With a sigh that was only partially

one of resignation, she took them. "I do appreciate you bringing my car back." She knew she was weakening, and she struggled not to. "You've caught me at a bad time. I can't even offer you a drink because the floor's wet, and I'm really busy."

"I'll take you out for one. Better, let's go have some lunch."

"I can't. I've only half finished here, and I'm not dressed to go out. Besides, I—"

"Look fine," he finished for her. "You'd better put those in water. They're starting to droop."

She could have been rude. Johanna knew she was capable of it, but she found she hadn't the heart. Instead, she said nothing. She plucked an old square bottle from a shelf and went into the bathroom to fill it. As she did, she heard the volume of the music go down several notches. He was in the living room studying her collection of antique glass when she came back.

"My mother used to have some plates like this green stuff here. Depression glass, right?"

"Yes."

"I thought that meant it made her sad. I could never figure out why she kept it."

She wouldn't be amused, Johanna told herself. At least not very. "Sam, you really shouldn't keep whoever followed you up waiting outside."

"No one followed me up." He hooked his thumbs in his pockets and smiled. Some might have thought the look sheepish, but Johanna wasn't fooled.

"Now I suppose you want me to drive you back."

"Sooner or later."

"I'll call you a cab," she said, turning to the phone. "I'll even pay for it."

He put his hand over hers on the receiver. "Johanna, you're being unfriendly again."

"You're being pushy."

"Yeah, but subtleties don't work with you." He reached over to stick a loose pin back in her hair. He'd have preferred to have pulled it out, and the rest of them besides, but bided his time. "So how about lunch?"

"I'm not hungry."

"So, we'll take a drive first." He skimmed his hand from her hair to her cheek. "I really think we should, because if we stay in here too much longer I'm going to want to make love with you, and since I figure you're not ready, a drive's a better idea."

Johanna cleared her throat and took another stab at persuasion. "I appreciate your logic, but I don't have time for a drive, either."

"You've got an appointment?"

"No," she said, then wished she could bite off her tongue. "That is, I—"

"You already said no." He watched her eyes narrow and thought she was almost as pretty annoyed as she was amused. You're already sunk waist-deep, Sam, he told himself. Another few steps and you're over your head. But what the hell. "It's too nice a day to stay indoors cleaning a house that's already clean enough."

"That's my business."

"Okay, then I'll wait for you to finish before we go out."

"Sam—"

"I'm persistent, Johanna. You told me so yourself."

"I'll drive you home," she said, giving up.

"Not good enough." He caught her again, this time by the shoulders. There was something about the way he spread his fingers over her, about the way his palm fit so truly over her. His expression had changed just enough to make her uneasy. The amusement was gone, but it hadn't been replaced by anger. She wouldn't have been uneasy about anger. This was determination, solid and unshakable. "I want to spend the day with you. You know damn well I want to spend the night with you, as well, but I'll settle for the day. Give me five reasons why not and I'll walk down to the freeway and hitch a ride."

"Because I don't want to."

"That's a statement, not a reason. And I don't buy it, anyway."

"Your ego won't buy it."

"Suit yourself." Refusing to be annoyed, he sat on the arm of her couch, absently picked up one of her pillows and began to toss it. "Look, I've got all day. I don't mind sitting around until you've stopped fussing with your imaginary dust. Hell, I'll even give you a hand, but then we're going to have to get out of here, because being alone with you for long periods of time isn't easy." She opened her mouth, but he continued before she could make a suggestion. "I keep wanting to touch you, Johanna, in all kinds of interesting places."

"We'll go out," she said quickly, before she could admit she wanted it, too.

"Good idea. Listen, why don't I drive?"

She started to protest even that—on principle—then decided he'd be less likely to give her trouble if he had his eyes on the road. "Fine." After switching off the radio, she dumped the keys back in his hands. "It'll take me a few minutes to change."

"You look fine," he said again, and took her hand. "I happen to like this Johanna every bit as much as the others I've met over the last couple of weeks."

She decided not to ask him what he was talking about. "We'll have to make it a very informal lunch, then."

"It will be." He opened the door of the car for her. "I promise."

He was as good as his word.

The hot dog dripped mustard, and the noise level was intense. Johanna sat almost in the shade and watched pink elephants circle overhead. It wasn't a dream, or the last remnants of a hangover. It was Disneyland.

"I don't believe this." She took another bite of the hot dog as a boy in mouse ears dashed by, yelling for his parents to hurry up.

"Pretty great, isn't it?" Sam wore sunglasses and a low-brimmed cowboy hat that Johanna was forced to admit suited him. So did the chinos and the simple T-shirt. The disguise wasn't very imaginative, and it would have been transparent as glass if anyone had looked closely enough. Sam had told her that the best place to be anonymous was a crowd. They certainly had one.

"You come here for lunch often?"

"Great hot dogs in Fantasyland." He took an enormous bite to prove his point. "Besides, I'm hooked on the Haunted Mansion. It's terrific, don't you think?"

"I don't know. I've never been in it."

"Never?" His tone of quick astonishment wasn't

feigned. Wanting a better look, he tipped down his tinted glasses and studied her. "You grew up here, didn't you?"

She only shrugged. Yes, she'd grown up a short drive from Anaheim, but neither her father nor her succession of stepmothers or "aunts," as she'd been taught to call the other women in her father's life, had been inclined to take a day trip to an amusement park.

"You're not telling me you've never been to Disney-land at all?"

"It's not a requirement."

He pushed his glasses back on his nose as she wiped her hands on a napkin. He remembered the impersonal non-kiss her father had given her the night before. His family was always, had always been, demonstrative, both physically and vocally. No, Disneyland, like other small pleasures, wasn't a requirement. But it should be.

"Come on, your education's lacking."

"Where are we going?"

"To take Mr. Toad's Wild Ride. You're going to love it."

Oddly enough, she did.

It was fast and foolish and certainly designed for the younger set, but Johanna found herself gasping and giggling as the car swerved and twisted through the tunnels. She'd barely put her foot on the ground again before Sam was dragging her off to the next line.

They rode down a mountain in a raft, and the final waterfall drop surprised a scream out of her. Wet and breathless, she didn't even protest when he pulled her along again. By the time they'd done Fantasyland to his satisfaction, she'd been spun, twirled, flown and floated. The Mad Hatter's Tea Party had left her giddy and weak-kneed and without the least notion that she was being educated.

He bought her mouse ears with her name stitched across the front, using her own hairpins to secure it even when she grumbled.

"Looks cute," he decided, then kissed her. She might not have known it, Sam thought, but she was more relaxed than he'd ever seen her. "I think you're ready for the Haunted Mansion."

"Does it spin?"

"No, it strikes terror into your heart. That's why you're going to hang on to me and make me feel brave." He swung an arm around her shoulders and began to walk. Johanna had already discovered he knew the park very well.

"You really do come here a lot, don't you?"

"When I first came to California I had two priorities. Get a job—an acting job—and go to Disneyland. Whenever my family comes out we always spend at least one day here."

Johanna looked around as they walked. There were families, so many families. Infants and toddlers pushed in strollers, children with sticky faces riding piggyback and pointing toward the next adventure.

"I guess it is an amazing place. Everything seems real while it's going on."

"It is real when it's going on." He stepped to the back of the line, undaunted by its length. After a moment's hesitation, he took a chance. "I was Pluto for six weeks."

"Pluto?"

"The dog, not the planet."

"I know who Pluto is," she murmured. Absently adjusting her hat, she frowned at him. "You actually worked here?"

"In a dog suit. A very hot dog suit—no pun intended. It paid my first month's rent."

"What exactly did you do?" The line shifted up.

"Marched in the parade, posed for pictures, waved and sweated a lot. I really wanted to be Captain Hook, because he gets to have sword fights and look evil, but Pluto was all that was open."

Johanna tried to imagine it, and nearly could. "I always thought he was cute."

"I was a terrific Pluto. Very lovable and loyal. I did cut it from my résumé after a while, but that was on Marv's suggestion."

"Marv? Oh, your agent?"

"He thought playing a six-foot dog was the wrong image to project."

While Johanna thought that one through, they were ushered inside. The spiel was camp and full of bad puns, but she couldn't help being pulled in. The pictures on the walls changed, the room shrank, the lights went out. There was no turning back.

By the time they were in their tram and starting on the tour she was, so to speak, entering into the spirit of things.

The producer in her couldn't fail to be impressed by the show. Holograms, music and elaborate props were blended to entertain, to raise goose pimples and nervous chuckles. Not so scary that the toddlers in the group would go home with nightmares, but not so tame that the adults felt cheated out of the price of a ticket,Johanna decided as she watched ghosts and spirits whirl around in a dilapidated, cobweb-draped dining room.

Sam had been right about one thing. It was real while it was going on. Not everything in life could be trusted to be the same.

She didn't have to be prodded any further, not to visit a pirate's den and dodge cannon fire, nor to take a cruise up the Amazon or a train ride through Indian territory. She watched mechanical bears perform, ate dripping ice cream and forgot she was a grown woman who had been to Paris and dined in an English manor but had never been to Disneyland.

By the time they started back to the car she was exhausted, but in the most pleasant way she could remember.

"I did not scream," she insisted, holding the small stuffed Pluto he'd bought her in a headlock.

"You never stopped screaming," Sam corrected. "From the minute that car started moving through Space Mountain until it stopped again. You've got excellent lungs."

"Everyone else was screaming." In truth, she hadn't a clue whether she'd screamed or not. The car had taken its first dive, and planets had raced toward her. Johanna had simply squeezed her eyes shut and held on.

"Want to go back and do it again?"

"No," she said definitely. "Once was quite enough."

Sam opened the car door but turned before she could climb in. "Don't you like thrills, Johanna?"

"Now and again."

"How about now?" He cupped her face in his hands. "And again later."

He kissed her as he'd wanted to do since he'd seen her studiously mopping her floor that morning. Her lips were warm, as he'd known they would be, but softer, incredibly softer, than he'd remembered. They hesitated. There was a sweetness in that, a sweetness that was its own allure.

So he lingered, longer than he'd intended. He wanted, more than was wise. When she started to back away, he gathered her closer and took, more than either of them had expected.

It wasn't supposed to be like this, Johanna told herself even as she stopped resisting both of them. She was supposed to be strong, in charge, reachable only when and if she chose to be. With him, he only had to touch… No, he only had to look and she began losing ground.

All her careful analysis that morning was blown to dust the minute his mouth was on hers.

I don't want this. Her mind tried to cling to that thought while her heart beat out steadily: But you do, yes, you do. She could almost feel herself separating into two parts, one aloof, one almost pitifully vulnerable. The most frightening thing was that this time she was more than afraid that vulnerability would be the stronger.

"I want to be alone with you, Johanna." He said it against her lips, then again against her cheek as he trailed kisses there. "Anywhere, anywhere at all as long as it's only you and me. I haven't been able to get you out of my system."

"I don't think you've been trying."

"You're wrong." He kissed her again, feeling her renewed resistance swerve toward passion. That was the most exciting, the most irresistible thing about her, the way she wanted, held back and wanted again. "I've actually given it a hell of a shot. I kept telling myself you're too complicated, too uptight, too driven." He felt her lips move into a frown and was seduced into nibbling on them. "Then I find ways to see you again."

"I'm not uptight."

He sensed her change of mood but could only be amused by it. Johanna, outraged, was fascinating. "Lady, half the time you're like a spring that's wound to the limit and just waiting to bust out. And I damn well intend to be there when you do."

"That's ridiculous. And don't call me lady." She snatched the keys from him, decided she'd do the driving this time.

"We'll see about that." He climbed into the car and nearly managed to stretch out his legs and get comfortable. "Going to give me a lift home?"

She was tempted, more than tempted, to order him out and strand him in the parking lot, right under Donald Duck's cheerful beak. Instead, she decided to give him the ride of his life. "Sure." Johanna put the car in gear.

She drove cautiously enough through the lot. It was, after all, full of pedestrians, many of them children. Things changed when she hit the freeway. She whipped around three cars, settled in the fast lane and rammed down on the gas pedal.

Drives like she's ready to bust, too, Sam thought, but said nothing. Her speedometer might have been hovering around ninety, but her hands were competent on the wheel. And she might, he thought, burn off that temper that had fired up when he'd called her uptight.

She hated it that he was right. That was the worst of it. She knew very well that she was full of nerves and hang-ups and insecurities. Didn't she spend most of her time fighting them off or blanketing them over? It didn't do her any good to hear Sam pinpoint it so casually.

When she'd made the conscious and very calculated decision to make love with a fellow college student, he, too, had called her uptight. Sexually. "Loosen up" had been his sage advice. She hadn't been able to, not with him, who she'd been fond of, nor with any of the men she'd developed careful relationships with. So she'd stopped trying.

She wasn't a man-hater. That would be absurd. She simply didn't want to be tied to one, emotionally or sexually. Her eyes had been opened young, and she'd never forgotten how those two tools could be used. So perhaps she was uptight, though she detested the word. Better that than loose enough to tumble for a pair of wonderful blue eyes or a lazy drawl.

Mad as hell, Sam thought. That was fine. He preferred strong emotion. As a matter of fact, he preferred any emotion at all when it came from Johanna. He didn't mind her being angry with him, because if she was angry she was thinking. About him. He wanted her to do a lot of that.

God knew he'd been thinking about her. Constantly. He'd been telling her no less than the truth when he'd said he'd tried to get her out of his system. When it hadn't worked, he'd decided to stop beating his head against the wall and see where the road would lead.

It was a bumpy ride, but he was enjoying every minute of it.

He was going to have her, sooner or later. Sooner, he hoped for the sake of his sanity. But for now he'd let her drive awhile.

When he saw she was going to miss the exit, he gestured. "You want to get off here."

Johanna switched lanes, aggressively challenging traffic, and breezed onto the ramp.

"How about dinner next week?" He said it casually, as though the interlude in the parking lot had been as make-believe as the rest of the day. When she said nothing, he fought back a grin and tossed his arm over the seat. "Wednesday's good for me. I can pick you up at your office."

"I'm busy next week."

"You've got to eat. Let's make it six."

She downshifted for a turn. "You're going to have to learn to take no for an answer."

"I don't think so. Take the left fork."

"I remember," she said between her teeth, though she didn't.

She drove in silence, slowing down only slightly when she passed through the gate of his ranch. Sam leaned over casually and tooted her horn. When she stopped in front of his house he sat there a moment, as though gathering his thoughts.

"Want to come in?"

"No."

"Want to fight?"

She would not be amused or charmed or soothed. "No."

"All right, we can fight some other time. Want to hear a theory of mine? Never mind," he said before she could answer. "Listen anyway. The way I figure it, there are three stages to a relationship. First you like somebody. Then, if things work out, you start to care for them. When the big guns hit, you fall in love with them."

She kept her hands on the wheel because they'd gone damp all at once. "That's very interesting. If only life worked that neatly."

"I've always thought it does—if you let it. Anyway, Johanna, I went past liking you last night and went straight into the second stage. A woman like you wants reasons for that kind of thing, but I haven't got a handle on them yet."

Her hands had stopped sweating and were now as cold as ice, though the heat was baking right through the windshield. "Sam, I said before I don't think this is a good idea. I still believe that."

"No, you still want to believe that." He waited patiently until she looked at him. "There's a difference, Johanna. A big one. I care for you, and I figured we'd do better if I let you know." He leaned over to kiss her. A very gentle threat. "You've got until Wednesday to think about it."

He got out of the car, then leaned in through the window. "Drive carefully, will you? You can always kick something when you get home if you're still mad."

CHAPTER
SEVEN

It had been a long day. In fact, it had been several long days. Johanna didn't mind. The pressure to solve problems and work through a few minor crises had kept her mind off her personal life.

Her lighting director had chosen Monday, taping day, to have an appendectomy. She sent flowers and wished him—not for totally altruistic reasons—a speedy recovery. John Jay, in the middle of contract negotiations, had decided to have laryngitis. Johanna had been forced to pamper and cajole—and make a few veiled threats—to work an instant and miraculous cure. Her assistant lighting man had proven to be competent and unruffled, even after three technical hitches. Still, the day had been lengthened by two hours.

Tuesday had stretched even further with meetings to discuss the photo sessions for the ads and the final preparations for the following week's contest. Security had been strengthened to guard that set of questions. A special safe had been purchased, and only she had the combination. Only she and Bethany knew which five questions had been sealed inside. Johanna began to feel like the head of the CIA.

A meeting with her father had been draining and difficult. They'd both been professional, executive producer to producer, as they'd discussed the show's status and plans for expansion. He'd absently mentioned an engagement party and told her his secretary would be in touch.

And, of course, because she considered it part of her job, Johanna watched *Trivia* every morning. It was just a nasty trick of fate that Sam's appearance ran this week. It was difficult enough not to think of him, and impossible when she was forced to watch him every day—long shots, close-ups. By Wednesday they had already received a stack of mail from delighted viewers.

Wednesday.

He'd given her until Wednesday to think about it. To think about him. Them. She just hadn't had the time, Johanna told herself as she turned up the volume and prepared to watch the day's segment. If she'd allowed herself to think about it she would have come up with a way, a polite and reasonable way, to get out of a dinner she hadn't even accepted.

The bright, bouncy opening theme came on, the

lights flashed. The two celebrity panelists walked through the arch, then paused for applause before they took their seats. Johanna struggled to look at the big picture, but she kept focusing on him.

Relaxed. He always looked so relaxed, so confident about who he was. That was something she couldn't help but admire about him. He was at ease and put his partner at ease while still maintaining that larger-than-life quality people expected from stars.

So he was good at his job, Johanna told herself as she paced back and forth during the commercial break. That didn't mean she was infatuated with him.

When the show came back on, she took her chair again, wishing she didn't need to have that very small and indirect contact with him.

It's my job, Johanna reminded herself. But she lost track of the game as she watched him. And she remembered, a bit too clearly, that after this segment had been taped she had had her first real conversation with him. She'd taken a dare, and had lost. Since that one miscalculation, nothing had been the same.

She wanted it to be the same. The quick panic surprised her, but she fought it back and tried to think logically. She did want it to be the same as it had been before, when her life had been focused on career and nudged by ambition, both heated and cooled by pride. There hadn't been any sleepless nights then. Tension and self-doubt, perhaps, but no sleepless nights.

And there hadn't been any rides down a mountain on a raft, either, her mind echoed.

She didn't need them. Sam could keep his thrills. All she required was peace of mind.

He was in the winner's circle, surrounded by lights and the audience's total support. Johanna remembered that the quick, cocky grin had been for her benefit. The minute the congratulatory applause began, she snapped off the set.

On impulse, she went to the phone. Rather than going through her secretary, Johanna dialed direct. Such minor precautions were a bit late, since her picture—with Sam—had already been in the paper, and the speculation about them as a couple had already begun. Johanna had decided there was no use adding to the gossip that was already buzzing around the office.

She was calm, she told herself even as she wound the phone cord around her fingers. She wasn't being stubborn or spiteful, but sensible.

A woman's voice answered. Hearing it gave Johanna all the justification she needed. A man like Sam would always have women around. And a man like that was precisely what she wanted to avoid.

"I'd like to speak with Mr. Weaver. This is Johanna Patterson calling."

"Sam's not in. I'd be happy to take a message." On the other end of the line, Mae was digging for the notepad she always carried in her apron pocket. "Patterson?" she repeated, then shifted the phone and grinned. "Sam's spoken about you. You're the one who does *Trivia Alert*."

Johanna frowned for a moment at the idea of Sam talking about her to one of his women. "Yes, I am. Would you mind—"

"I never miss it," Mae continued conversationally. "I always keep it on when I'm cleaning. Then I see if

Joe can answer any of the questions that night at dinner. Joe's my husband. I'm Mae Block."

So this was Mae, the one who shoveled out the dust and grew the snapdragons. Johanna's vision of a pretty morning visitor faded and left her more than a little ashamed. "I'm glad you like the show."

"Crazy about it," Mae assured her. "As a matter of fact, I just had it on. Got a real kick out of seeing our Sam on it. Thought he did real good, too. I even put it on the VCR so Joe could see it later. We're all just crazy about Sam. He speaks real kindly of you, too. Did you like your flowers?"

Having at last found a space in Mae's rapid-fire conversation for a word, Johanna managed to insert one. "Flowers?"

"Sam doesn't think I saw him snitch them."

"They were lovely." Despite all her resolutions, Johanna felt herself soften. "I hope you didn't mind."

"Plenty more where they came from. I figure flowers should be enjoyed, don't you?"

"Yes. Yes, I do. Mrs. Block—"

"Mae. Just Mae, honey."

"Mae, if you could tell Sam I called." Coward, her mind said all too clearly. Johanna closed herself off from it and continued. "And that—"

"Well, you can tell him yourself, honey, 'cause he just this minute walked in. Hold on now."

Before Johanna could babble an excuse, she heard Mae yelling. "Sam, that lady you've been mooning about's on the phone. And I'd like to know what you're thinking of wearing a white shirt when you're wrestling with horses. How you expect me to get out those stains is more than I can understand. Did you wipe your feet? I just washed that kitchen floor."

"Yes, ma'am. It's an old shirt," he added in a half apology Johanna recognized even over the wire.

"Old or not, it's a dust rag now. A boy your age oughta know better. Don't keep your lady waiting all day. I'll make you a sandwich."

"Thanks. Hello, Johanna."

Mae hadn't mentioned her name. *The lady you've been mooning about.* That was something Johanna would have to think about later. "I'm sorry to bother you in the middle of the day. You must be busy."

"Having my wrist slapped." He pulled out a bandanna and wiped the line of sweat from his temple. "I'm glad you called. I've been thinking about you."

"Yes, well…" Where were all the neat excuses she'd thought up? "About tonight."

"Yes?"

Very carefully she unwrapped the cord from around her fingers. "We'd left things a bit unstructured, and as it turns out, I have a late meeting. I can't be sure what time I'll wrap things up, so—"

"So why don't you drive out here when you're finished?" He recognized a lie when he heard one. "You should know the way by now."

"Yes, but it might run late. I don't want to mess up your evening."

"The only way you'd mess it up is not to come."

She hadn't a clue as to how to respond to that. "I never actually agreed to come." Her conscience insisted on reminding her she hadn't stuck by a refusal, either. "Why don't we make it some other time?"

"Johanna," he said, very patiently, "you don't want me to camp on your doorstep, do you?"

"I just think it would be better—"

"Safer."

Yes. "Better," she insisted.

"Whatever. If you don't show up by eight I'm coming after you. Take your choice."

Bristling wasn't nearly as effective over the phone. "I don't like ultimatums."

"That's a pity. I'll see you when you get here. Don't work too hard."

Johanna scowled at the dial tone, then dropped the phone on the hook. She wouldn't go. She would be damned if she did.

Of course, she went.

Only to prove that she wasn't a coward, Johanna assured herself. In any case, avoiding a situation didn't solve anything, it only postponed things. Loose ends were something she invariably tied up.

It was true that she enjoyed his company, so there was no reason to be out of sorts. Except for the fact that she'd been maneuvered again. No, he hadn't done the maneuvering, she corrected. She'd done that all by herself, thank you very much. If she hadn't wanted to go, she would never have called him to say she wasn't going to. Deep down she'd wanted to keep the engagement because she'd always had a need to face up to whatever could be faced.

She could certainly face Sam Weaver.

A simple dinner, she decided. Between friends. They could, cautiously, be called friends by this time. A little conversation never hurt, particularly between two people who were in the same business. Game shows or movies, it all came down to entertainment. She picked up speed a bit, and the plastic bags over this week's dry cleaning snapped and rustled on their hangers behind her.

At least this time she had her own transportation. She would leave when she was ready to leave. There was some security in that.

When she passed through the gates leading to the ranch, she promised herself that she would enjoy the evening for what it was. A simple dinner with a friend. She stopped her car in front of his house and stepped out, refusing to glance in the visor mirror. She wouldn't fuss with or freshen her makeup any more than she had fussed with her outfit. Her gray suit was stylish but certainly businesslike, as were the three hanging in the car. Her low-heeled pumps were comfortable, purchased as much for that as for fashion.

She glanced at her watch and was pleased with the time. Seven-thirty. Not so early that it would appear that she'd been cowed, nor so late that it made her look spiteful.

She looked as she had on that first day, Sam thought. Composed, coolheaded, subtly sexy. His reaction to her now was exactly the same as it had been then. Instant fascination. Stepping out on the porch, he smiled at her.

"Hi."

"Hello." She didn't want to be unnerved, not again, not the way she seemed to be every time she saw him. She answered his smile, though cautiously, and started up the steps. His next move was so unexpected that she had no chance to block it.

He cupped a hand around the base of her neck and kissed her, not passionately, not urgently, but with a casual intimacy that shot straight through her. Welcome home, it seemed to say, and left her speechless.

"I love the way you wear a suit, Johanna."

"I didn't have time to change."

"I'm glad." He glanced beyond her at the sound of a truck. With a half smile, he shaded his eyes. "You forgot to blow your horn," he told her.

"Everything all right here, Sam?" In the cab of a pickup was a man of about fifty with shoulders like cinder blocks.

"Everything's fine." Sam slipped an arm around Johanna's waist.

The man in the truck chuckled, then spun the wheel and made a U-turn. "I can see that. Night."

"That was Joe," Sam explained as they watched the truck cruise down the hard-packed road. "He and Mae keep an eye on the place. And me."

"So I see." It was entirely too easy, standing on the porch, his arm around her, as the sun lowered. Johanna didn't deliberately step away. The move was automatic. "Your housekeeper told me she watches *Trivia*."

She also said you were mooning over me. Johanna kept the fact that she'd overheard that little piece of information to herself. It was ridiculous, of course. Men like Sam Weaver didn't moon over anyone.

"Religiously," he murmured, studying her. She was nervous. He'd thought they'd passed that point, and he wasn't sure whether to be pleased or frustrated to discover otherwise. "In fact, Mae considers my, ah…performance so far this week the height of my career."

The smile came quickly. Her fingers relaxed their grip on the railing. "Emmy material, I'm sure."

"Is that a smirk?"

"I never smirk, and especially not about my show. I suppose I'll have to risk inflating your ego, but we've already gotten a tremendous amount of mail. 'Sam Weaver is the cutest thing on two legs,'" Johanna quoted, and was amused when he grimaced. "That was from a seventy-five-year-old woman in Tucson."

"Yeah." He took her hand and drew her inside. "When you've finished smirking—"

"I told you, I never smirk."

"Right, and when you're finished we'll see about dinner. I figured we'd barbecue, since I wasn't sure when you'd wind up that meeting."

"Meeting?" The lie had slipped away from her. Remembering, Johanna did something else she couldn't remember having done before. She blushed. Just a little, but enough. "Oh, well, it moved along faster than I'd expected."

"Lucky for both of us." He could have pinned her on it, Sam mused, but decided to let her escape. If he understood Johanna as well as he believed he was coming to understand her, she was already berating herself for the excuse, and for botching it. "I've got some swordfish. Why don't you pour yourself some wine and I'll heat up the grill?"

"All right." The bottle was already open. Johanna filled the two glasses he'd set on the kitchen counter as he breezed through the back door.

He'd known the meeting was nothing more than a weak excuse. She couldn't remember ever having been quite so transparent. Johanna sighed, sipped, then sighed again. He was letting it go so that she wouldn't be embarrassed. That only made it worse. The least she could do, she thought as she picked up his glass, was to be pleasant company for the rest of the evening.

The pool looked cool and delightfully inviting. Swimming had been a daily habit when she'd lived in her father's house. Now she couldn't seem to find time for the health club she'd conscientiously joined. She skirted around the pool to where Sam stood by the stone barbecue pit with two fish steaks on a platter, but she did glance at the water rather wistfully.

"You want to take a quick swim before dinner?" he asked.

It was tempting. Johanna found herself tempted too often when around him. "No, thanks."

"There's always after." He set the steaks on the grill, where they sizzled. Taking his glass from her, he clinked it lightly against hers, then drank. "Go ahead and sit down. These won't take long."

Instead, she wandered a short distance away, looking at his land, the tidy outbuildings, the isolation. He seemed so comfortable here, she thought, so much at home. He could be anybody, an ordinary person. But she remembered that she'd read about him just that morning.

"There's a very hot write-up in this week's *TV Guide* about *No Roses for Sarah*."

"I saw it." He saw, too, how the sun bounced off the water of the pool and onto her skin, making her seem like an illusion. The trim gray suit didn't make him think of offices or board meetings, but of quiet evenings after the day was over.

"*Variety* was equally enthusiastic. 'Gripping, not to be missed,' and so on." She smiled a little as she turned to him again. "What was the adjective used to describe you…" She trailed off as if she couldn't quite remember, though the exact quote had engraved itself on her brain. "'Weaver executes a'— Was it 'sterling performance'?"

Sam flipped the steaks, and they hissed. Smoke rose up, hot and sultry. "'Sizzling,'" he corrected, knowing when he was being strung along.

"Yes, sizzling." She paused to touch her tongue to her upper lip. "'A sizzling performance as a down-on-his-luck drifter who seduces Sarah and the audience with equal panache.' Panache," she repeated. "That one rolls around on the tongue, doesn't it?"

"I didn't realize you were such a smart aleck, Johanna."

She laughed and crossed over to him. "I'm also human. Nothing could drag me away from my set on Sunday night when the first part's aired."

"And Monday?"

"That'll depend, won't it?" She sipped her drink and sniffed appreciatively at the mesquite smoke. "On how *sizzling* you were on Sunday."

The grin was fast and crooked, as if he had no doubt where she would be at nine o'clock Monday night. "Keep an eye on these, will you? I'll be right back."

She'd keep an eye on them, but she hoped the steaks didn't do anything they weren't supposed to do until he got back. Alone, she stretched her arms and worked the muscles in her back. The late meeting had been a lie, but the long day hadn't. Wistfully she glanced at the pool again. It really was tempting.

If she were just anyone—if he were just anyone—she could share this meal with him, laugh a little over something that had happened during the day. Afterward, while the wine was still cool and the air still hot, they could slide into the water and relax together. Just two people who enjoyed each other and a quiet evening.

Later, when the moon came out, they might stay in the water, talking quietly, touching, easing gently into a more intimate form of relaxation. He would have music on again, and the candles on the table would burn down and drown in their own melted wax.

When something brushed against her legs, she jolted, sloshing wine over her hand. The fantasy had come through a bit too clearly, too compellingly, and that wasn't like her. Johanna turned away from the pool and the ideas it had had stirring inside her. With a hand to her heart, she looked down at a fat gray cat. He rubbed up against her calf again, sent her a long, shrewd look, then settled down to wash.

"Where did you come from?" Johanna wondered as she bent to scratch his ears.

"The barn," Sam told her, coming up from behind her. "Silas is one of the barn cats, and I'd guess he got a whiff of the fish and came down to see if he could charm any out of us."

She didn't look at Sam right away, concentrating on the cat instead. The daydream was still a bit too real. "I thought barn cats were fast and skinny."

Not when someone was always taking them down scraps, Sam thought ruefully as he set the bowl of pasta salad on the table and flipped the fish onto a platter.

"Silas can be pretty charming," he said, and pulled out a chair for Johanna.

"Silas is pretty huge."

"You don't like cats?"

"No, actually, I do. I've even thought of getting one myself. Why Silas?"

"Marner," Sam explained easily as he served her. "You know how he hoarded gold. Well, this Silas hoards mice."

"Oh."

He laughed at her expression and topped off her wine. "You wanted to know. I've been meaning to ask you," he said, thinking she deserved a change of subject, "when you go on nighttime."

"Two weeks." Johanna told herself she wasn't nervous, not nervous at all. "We tape in two weeks, actually, and go on in four."

"Adding more crew?"

"Some. For the most part it just means that we'll be taping two days a week instead of one. Interested in making another appearance?"

"I'm going to be a bit tied up for a while."

"The new movie." She relaxed a few more degrees. This was how her practical mind had imagined the evening. Shoptalk, nothing more. "When do you start?"

"Any day, theoretically. Realistically, in a week or two. After some preproduction and studio work here, we'll head east. They figure about three weeks on location in Maryland, in and around Baltimore."

"You must be anxious to begin."

"I always get lazy between pictures. Nothing like

a few 6:00 a.m. calls to get you back in gear. How's your fish?"

"It's wonderful." And once again, she'd all but cleared her plate without realizing it. "I bought a grill a few months ago, but I burned everything I put on it."

"A low flame," he said, and something in his voice made her skin tingle. "A careful eye." He took her hand, linking their fingers. "And patience."

"I—" He brought her hand to his lips, watching her over it as he kissed her fingers. "I'll have to give it another try."

"Your skin always smells as though you've walked through the rain. Even when you're not here I can't help thinking about that."

"We should—" Stop pretending, she thought. Acquiesce. Take what we want. "Go for a walk," she managed. "I'd like to see your pond again."

"All right." Patience, Sam reminded himself. But the flame wasn't as low as it had been. "Hold on a minute." He tossed a few scraps onto the grass before gathering up the dishes. She knew she should have offered her help, but she wanted, needed—badly needed—a moment alone.

She watched the cat saunter over to the fish with an arrogance that told her he'd been certain all along he'd get what he'd come for. Sam walked like that, Johanna thought, and suddenly cold, she rubbed her hands over her arms.

She wasn't afraid of him. She reminded herself of that to boost her confidence. But it was no less than the truth. She wasn't afraid of Sam: fear of herself, however, was another matter.

She was here because she wanted to be here. Wasn't it time to face that one fact? She'd already admitted that she hadn't come because he'd maneuvered her. She'd maneuvered herself, or that part of herself that was still determined to stand apart.

There was another part of herself, a part that was slowly taking charge, that knew exactly what she wanted. Who she wanted. That was a part that had already made an enormous mistake by falling in love with Sam.

Before she had a chance to deal with the enormity of that realization, he was back, carrying a plastic bag filled with crackers.

"They'll expect to be— Are you all right?"

She was pale, and her eyes were huge. If Sam hadn't known better he would have sworn someone had come along and given her a fast, unexpected backhand.

"I'm fine." Thank God her voice was steady. She still had that much under control. "Your pets keep you under their thumb, don't they?"

Her smile didn't quite reach her eyes, but he nodded. "It looks that way." He touched her face. She didn't flinch, but he felt the muscles of her jaw tense. "You look a little dazed, Johanna."

Terrified was the word. In love with him, her mind repeated. Good Lord, when, how and, most of all, *why?*

"It's probably the wine. I'll walk it off."

It had nothing to do with the wine, but he let it go. Taking her hand firmly in his, he started toward the path. "Next time you come, you're going to have to dress for this. As sensible as those shoes are, boots or sneakers are better for the hike."

Sensible. Frowning, Johanna looked down at her trim, low-heeled Italian pumps. Damn it, they were sensible. She managed to bite off the sigh. Sensible. Like her. "I told you I didn't have time to change."

"That's okay, I can always carry you."

"That won't be necessary."

There it was again, that low, cool tone. He didn't bother to fight back the smile as he steered her along.

The sun was nearly down, so the light was soft and pearly. There were wildflowers along the path that hadn't yet bloomed the last time they'd taken this walk. He imagined Johanna could name them for him if he asked, but he preferred to let them pop out of the ground anonymously.

He could smell the water now, and could just hear its faint lap against the high grass. Every time he'd walked there in the last few weeks he'd thought of her. The birds were quiet now, settling down for the night. Those that called the night their own had yet to stir. He liked the quiet of dusk, the aloneness of it, and wondered if she felt the same. He remembered how she'd knelt in front of a bank of flowers at sundown and figured that she did.

The water of the pond was darkening, like the sky. The shadows of the trees were long and dim across it. It still made her smile to see the ducks gliding over it, preening a bit in anticipation of an audience.

"I take it Silas and his companions don't bother them."

"Too much effort to come all the way out here and get wet when they've got the barn. Here." He handed her the bag. As she had before, Johanna laughed at the ducks' antics as she tossed the crackers to them.

"I guess no one spoils them like this when you're away."

"Mae does. She wouldn't admit it, though."

"Oh, I didn't see the drake close up before." She skimmed a cracker to him. "He's beautiful. And look how the babies have grown." She scattered crumbs on the water until the bag was empty. Without thinking, she tucked it into her pocket. "It's so nice here," she murmured. "Just the water, and the grass." And you, she thought. But she didn't look at him, not until his hand was on her cheek, gently urging her to.

It was just as it had been the first time. And yet it was nothing like it. This time she knew exactly how she would feel, how she would want, when he kissed her. She knew he would touch her hair before he drew her close. She knew her mind would cloud and her pulse would quicken.

She knew, but it still stunned her.

He felt as though he'd waited forever. It hadn't been merely weeks since he'd first seen her. She'd been under his skin, inside his heart, for as long as he could remember. A dream, a half-formed wish that had only taken one look at her to click solidly into place. It was so right. Somehow it was exactly right when his mouth found hers.

She still wasn't sure. He could feel the hesitation even as he felt the passion that drummed beneath it. But he was sure enough for both of them.

It was meant to be here, here where those first shock waves had passed through both of them. It was meant to be now, before night fell.

She tightened her grip on his shirt, holding on, holding back. In a moment, she knew, she wouldn't be able to think clearly. It would be wise to withdraw now, to leave things as they had been. But his lips coaxed her to stay. To trust.

She murmured, tensing up when she felt him slip the jacket from her shoulders. A step was being taken. Then he was soothing her, giving her time, plenty of time, but no choice at all. The buttons that ran down her back were loosened one by one in an agony of sweetness and promise. When she felt his fingers brush her skin, she shuddered at the contact and searched for the will to end it.

But his lips skimmed her throat as he peeled the blouse from her. She was helpless, but the sensation was no longer frightening.

Is this what it felt like to give in, at last, fully, completely give in to something not quite known but only sensed? Hadn't she waited for it, anticipated it, even while she'd struggled against it? Now the struggle was almost over.

He had to use every ounce of self-control not to rush her. He knew she needed time and care, even as his own needs balled like fists inside him. He'd already imagined what it would be like to touch her like this, to feel her tremble when he did. Her skirt slid down her hips. His hands followed it.

The sun had dropped away, but he could see her, her hair haloed around her face, her eyes wide and uncertain. He kissed her again, slowly, trailing his lips over her jaw as he shrugged out of his shirt. He saw her start to reach for him, then hesitate just short of contact. Taking her hand, he brought it, palm up, to his lips and felt her go limp.

He lowered her to the grass.

It was cool, soft and damp with early dew—a sensation Johanna knew she would remember always. He was over her, so she could only see his face, then only his eyes. She heard the first owl call before he bent to her. Then there was only him.

He touched. She shuddered, no longer from fear or from doubt, but from a pleasure so pure she could never have described it. He tasted. She floated, no longer helpless, but a willing partner. And when she reached for him, drew him closer, the world was shut off for both of them.

She was so soft, so generous. He wondered that he could still be surprised by how many facets there were to her. She'd opened to him now, as completely as he could have hoped.

If her touch was still shy, it was only more endearing. He wanted it to be sweet for her, memorable, and as special as he already knew it would be for him. Somewhere along the line she had stopped being a woman, however desirable, however fascinating, and had become his woman.

He took her, gently, higher.

When she moaned, desire thrummed in him, hard, demanding. He fought it back, wanting her to ride the wave as long as they could both stand it. Slowly, drawing out the process, he slipped her teddy down to her waist, then to her hips, letting the hunger build inside him.

Her fingers dug into the grass as he brushed his lips

over her. She could feel her skin tremble wherever he chose to linger. Then, abruptly, the pleasure rocketed up, beyond anything she'd dreamed possible. She cried out his name, her body arching up. Pleasure doubled back, and he was with her again. Now her fingers dug into his shoulders desperately.

Stars began to wink to life above them.

The breath was dragging in and out of his lungs when he filled her. Now he was helpless, his face buried in her hair, his body more her prisoner than she had ever been his. Need expanded and became the focus of his world, and then even that shattered, leaving only her.

CHAPTER EIGHT

He couldn't speak. At the moment Sam wasn't sure his mind would ever be able to direct that basic function again. He knew he should shift his weight from her but couldn't bear to break the bond.

Whatever else it had been—passion, desire, chemistry—it had forged a bond.

Overhead, the stars were still coming out. Johanna could see them now, but all she could think of was the way Sam's heart still raced against hers. She hadn't known she was capable of giving or receiving that kind of pleasure. Though the heat had eased, his body was still warm, a continuing contrast to the cool grass that waved around them. The water, pushed by the night breezes, lapped only a few feet away.

It had been a shock to realize she was capable of feeling anything this intensely, but more, she had seen his eyes, felt his body shudder, and had known for the first time in her life that she could give.

Hardly realizing she was doing so, she lifted a hand to stroke his hair. Sam was aware, even if she wasn't, that it was the first time she'd touched him without being backed into a corner. He closed his eyes and held on to that thought. What would once have been a small thing to him was now an enormous one. He'd slipped into the third phase, into love, almost painlessly.

"Johanna." When he could speak, her name was the first thing that formed. Because he wanted to see her, he found the strength to raise himself onto his elbows. Her hair was spread out on the grass that had bent under them. Her eyes were half-closed, but what he could see was still dazed with pleasure. "You're so lovely."

Her lips curved a bit, and she touched him again, her fingers on his face. "I didn't think this would happen. I didn't think it could."

"I imagined it, here, just like this." He lowered his head, just to brush his lips against hers. "But my fantasy didn't even come close to the real thing. Nothing ever has." He felt her withdraw at that, just a fraction, but enough that he felt compelled to take her face in his hand. "Nothing and no one, Johanna."

His eyes insisted that she believe him, and she wanted to, but there was still too much of a block within her to make that possible. "I've wanted you." At least she could be honest with both of them. "I can't think about what happens next."

"We're both going to have to. I've no intention of letting you go." She opened her mouth to protest, to make some excuse, and only managed to moan as she felt him harden inside her. "Not a chance," he murmured, before desire clouded his mind completely.

When she could think again, she tried to draw away. She was going to need time to put this in perspective, to work out the steps. The first was to be an adult, and not to expect.

They had shared something. Perhaps it hadn't been casual for her, but she'd always understood that every relationship had its limitations. Better to remember that now and face it from the outset. She cared, too much for her own good, but she still knew better than to cuddle up at his side and start thinking about tomorrows.

"It's late." She pulled her hands through her hair as she sat up. "I have to go."

He'd have been surprised if he could have moved again for eight hours. "Go where?"

"I have to go home." She reached for her teddy but missed by an inch when his hand braceleted her wrist.

"If you expect me to let you go anywhere tonight, you're crazy."

"I don't know what you're talking about." Her voice was amused as she tugged on her hand. "In the first place, it's not a matter of you *letting* me go anywhere." After picking up her teddy, she shook it out. "And I can hardly sleep in the grass all night."

"You're absolutely right." If she hadn't been so relaxed, she would have realized he'd given in too easily. "Here, put on my shirt. It'll be easier for you to dress inside."

Because it made sense, Johanna allowed him to bundle her into it. It carried his scent. Unconsciously she rubbed her cheek against the collar as Sam pulled on his jeans.

"Let me give you a hand with those." Sam took her now-folded clothes and draped them over his arm. "Better let me go first. There isn't much light tonight."

Johanna followed him down the path, hoping she seemed as casual and at ease as he. What had happened by the pond, weeks ago and now tonight, had been beautiful. She didn't want to lose the importance of it. But she didn't want to exaggerate its importance, either.

Nothing and no one else.

No, she'd be a fool to believe it—to hope for it. He might have meant it at the moment he'd said it. She could believe that because she'd come to understand that Sam wasn't a man for lies, even pretty ones. She could believe, too, that he cared for her—again, for the moment.

Intense feelings rarely lasted, and all the hopes and promises built on those feelings eventually crumbled. So she didn't allow herself to hope and refused to make promises.

They still had a long way to go, Sam mused. She wasn't ready to take what he'd discovered he was ready to give. The trouble was, now that he was in love with her he wouldn't be able to be so patient. Johanna was just going to have to keep pace.

As they stepped onto the terrace, he set her clothes

neatly on the table. A frown formed between her brows as he casually stripped off his jeans.

"What are you doing?"

He stood before her, undeniably magnificent in the light of the moon. With a smile that warned her an instant too late, he hauled her into his arms.

"It's what *we're* doing," he said simply, and jumped into the pool.

The water was several degrees warmer than the night air, but it was still a shock. Before it closed over her head, she had time for one surprised shriek. Her legs tangled with his as the plunge separated them and the shirt billowed up around her head. Then her feet touched bottom, and instinctively she pushed upward. Gasping, she surfaced, blinking water from her eyes.

"Damn it!" She drew her arm through the water, hand fisted, and shot a spray into his grinning face.

"Nothing like a midnight swim, is there, Jo-Jo?"

"Don't call me that. You must be out of your mind."

"Only about you," he told her, then sent an unlovely splash in her direction.

Johanna dodged it, barely, telling herself she wasn't amused. "What the hell would you have done if I couldn't swim?"

"Saved you." He trod water with little effort. "I was born to be a hero."

"Jerk," she corrected. She turned, and in two strokes had reached the side. Before she could haul herself out, Sam caught her by the waist.

"When you stop being mad, you'll admit you like it." He nuzzled the back of her neck. "Want to race?"

"What I want to do is—" She turned—another miscalculation. His hands slid up her wet skin to her breasts as he bent his lips to her throat.

"Me too," he murmured.

She lifted a hand to his shoulder where it skimmed over cool skin just beginning to heat. "Sam, I can't."

"That's okay. I can." He slid into her.

Johanna woke with a faint grumble and tried to roll over. It took her several confusing seconds to realize that Sam's arm had her pinned. Lying still, she turned her head cautiously to look at him.

He slept more on her pillow than on his own. No, they were both his pillows, Johanna reminded herself. His bed, his house. Would he think her a fool or a freak if she told him this was the first time she'd ever woken up in a man's bed? It didn't matter; she wouldn't tell him. How could she tell him he was the first man she'd cared for enough, trusted enough, to share that private vulnerability called sleep?

She still wasn't quite sure how he'd managed to nudge her into it. One minute she'd been standing, naked and dripping, by the side of the pool, and the next... They hadn't even made love there, but had simply fallen into bed much like two exhausted children.

He'd made her laugh, too, and he'd given her, all unknowing, the sweet daydream of her own making.

Now it was morning and she had to remind herself again that she was an adult. They had wanted each other, enjoyed each other. It was important not to add complications to that simple formula. There wouldn't be regret. Regret usually meant blame, and she didn't want that, either. Wisely or not, she'd made a decision.

The decision had taken her into intimacy with Sam. She wouldn't use the word *affair*.

Now that it was done, she had to be realistic. This intensity, this flash of feeling, would fade, and when that happened, she'd be hurt. It couldn't be prevented, only prepared for.

Her emotions had already deepened beyond her control, but she still had her strength and her sense. No strings. He'd said it. She'd meant it.

Despite that, she lifted a fingertip to brush the hair from his forehead.

Oh, God, I'm in love with him, I'm so ridiculously in love with him, and I'm bound to make a fool of myself.

When he opened his eyes, those dark, heavy-lidded eyes, she didn't give a damn.

"Hi."

She lowered her hand, flustered because he'd caught her petting him. "Good morning."

It was there, even after their incredible night together. The trace of shyness he found so appealing. So exciting. Because he didn't want to give her time to layer it over with composure, he rolled on top of her.

"Sam—"

"It occurs to me," he began as he drew longer, lazier kisses from her, "that we never made love in bed." He ran his hand down her side, from shoulder to hip, from hip to thigh. "I'm feeling traditional this morning."

She didn't have time to analyze what she was feeling. Even as she tried to say his name again, her breath caught. This morning he wasn't so patient—or perhaps she, knowing what could be, was more sensitive.

She curled around him and let herself go.

* * *

Time had gotten away from her. Everything had gotten away from her, Johanna corrected as she stepped out of the shower and began to towel off quickly. If she threw on her clothes, let her hair air-dry on the way to work and pushed the speed limit, she might just make it.

She grabbed a few basic cosmetics out of her purse. The effort would be sketchy, but it was all she could afford. In the bedroom she ripped the plastic off the first suit Sam had brought up from her car. Yesterday's blouse would have to work with it. Cursing herself for not having planned properly, she zipped the skirt and ran down the hall carrying her shoes.

"Where's the fire?" Sam asked her as she rested a hand against the wall and struggled into her shoes.

"I'm running late."

He lifted a brow. "Do you get demerits for being tardy?"

"I'm never late."

"Good, then you can afford to be. Have some coffee."

She took the cup he offered, grateful. "Thanks. I really have to run."

"You haven't eaten anything."

"I never eat breakfast."

"Today you do." He had her arm. To prevent the contents of the cup sloshing all over her freshly laundered suit, she kept up with him. "Five minutes, Johanna. Catch your breath, drink your coffee. If you argue, it'll take ten."

She swore, but downed more coffee as he pulled her into the kitchen. "Sam, you're the one who's on vacation, not me. I've got a full day scheduled that might, if I'm lucky, end before six."

"All the more reason you should have a decent breakfast." He couldn't remember ever having felt better in the morning, more alive or full of energy. Briefly he wished he was in the middle of filming so that he could pour some of that energy into a part. "Sit. I'll fix you some eggs."

Because her temper was beginning to fray, she drank more coffee. "I appreciate it, really I do, but I don't have time. We're shooting ads today for the home viewers' contest, and I'm the only one who can handle John Jay."

"A dubious talent." The English muffin he'd dropped in the toaster popped up. "You can at least eat this."

Annoyed, she snatched it from him, ignored the butter and jam on the table and bit into it. "There," she said, and swallowed. "Satisfied?"

Her hair was still dripping around her face, and she'd forgotten her lipstick. Eyes still shadowed from the long night glared at him. He grinned and flicked a crumb off her chin. "I love you, Johanna."

If he'd drawn back and planted his fist on her chin she would have been no less shocked. She stared at him as the muffin slipped out of her boneless fingers onto the table. Her step back was instinctive, defensive. Sam lifted his brow at it, but that was all.

"Don't say that to me," she managed at length. "I don't need to hear that. I don't want to hear it."

She needed to hear it all right, he thought. She might not have wanted to, but she needed to. He was going to see that she did, at regular intervals, but right now she'd gone pale again. "All right," he said slowly. "It doesn't change the facts one way or the other."

"I—I have to go." She ransacked her purse almost desperately for her keys. "I'm really running late." What was she supposed to say? What was supposed to be said on the morning after the night? With her keys clutched in her hand, she looked up. "Goodbye."

"I'll walk you out." His arm went around her shoulders. She tried not to tense. She tried not to lean against him. She could feel the tug-of-war as they walked. "There's something I'd like to tell you, Johanna."

"Please, it isn't necessary. We agreed even before— before last night—that there wouldn't be any promises."

"Did we?" Damned if he remembered that, but if he had agreed, that was one agreement that would have to be broken. He pushed the front door open and stepped onto the porch before turning her to him. "We'll have to talk about that."

"All right." She would have agreed to almost anything if it had meant he'd let her go. Because she wanted to stay. More than she'd ever wanted anything, she wanted to toss her keys over her shoulder, throw herself into his arms and stay as long as he'd have her.

"In the meantime, I want you to know that I've never had another woman in that bed." He saw the flash of doubt in her eyes before she was able to mask it. And before he could stop himself, he'd hauled her up by the lapels. "Damn it, a man gets tired of having everything he says dissected in that brain of yours. I didn't say there haven't been other women, Johanna, but there's never been another woman here. Because here's special to me. It's important. And so are you." He let her go. "Chew on that for a while."

* * *

Johanna thumbed another antacid tablet from the roll. She'd told Sam no less than the truth when she'd said she was the only one who could handle John Jay. It just so happened that today she wasn't doing a good job of it. The two-hour photo session had stretched into three, and tempers were fraying. If she didn't have the crew, equipment and two cars out of the studio in another forty-five minutes she was going to have the producer of *Noon with Nina* on her back.

Resigned, Johanna chewed the antacid and prayed it did its job better than she was doing hers. She signaled for a halt and hoped the five-minute break would keep the photographer from strangling her host.

"John Jay." She knew the game. Johanna pasted a smile on her face as she crossed to him. "Can I have a minute?" Her voice was calm, her touch light and friendly, as she took his arm to guide him to a corner. "Sessions like this are so annoying, aren't they?"

He literally pounced on the sympathy. "You have no idea, Johanna. You know I want what's best for the show, darling, but that man…" He glanced over at the photographer with loathing. "He has no conception of mood or image."

"That man" was one of the tops in his business and was being paid by the incredibly expensive hour. Johanna bit off an oath in time to have it slip out as a sigh. "I know, but unfortunately we have to work with him. We're running behind schedule, and the last thing I want is to have him take shots of the cars only." She let the threat hang until she was certain it had sunk in. "After all, there are three stars here. The cars, the show itself and, of course, you. The teasers went beautifully, by the way."

"I was fresh." He fussed with the knot of his tie.

"I understand perfectly. But I have to ask you to keep the energy up for just a few more minutes. That suit's very becoming, John Jay."

"It is, isn't it?" He held out an arm, turning it over to study the sleeve.

"These shots are going to make quite a statement." If she didn't strangle him herself first. "All I want you to do is stand between those two cars and flash the smile America loves."

"For you, darling." He squeezed her hand, ready to sacrifice himself to the masses. "You know, you're looking a little dragged-out."

Her smile didn't fade, only froze. "It's lucky I'm not having my picture taken."

"It certainly is," he agreed, patting Johanna's head. He already knew his producer could grow fangs if he patted her elsewhere. "You have to try to relax more, Johanna, and take those vitamins I told you about. God knows I couldn't get through the day without them." He watched the photographer come back on the set. With a sniff, John Jay signaled for makeup. "Johanna, there's a rumor running rampant that you're seeing Sam Weaver."

"Is there?" Johanna ground her teeth as John Jay got a dusting of powder. "It's amazing how these things get started."

"What a town." Satisfied that he was perfect, John Jay strode over to do his duty.

It took only twenty minutes more. The moment she'd

sent her host on his way, Johanna apologized to the photographer, offered him and his assistant lunch on her and handed out tickets to Monday night's taping.

By the time she drove from the studio in Burbank back to her offices in Century City, she was two hours behind schedule and had consumed almost half the roll of antacids in her pocket.

"You've got a half-dozen messages," Bethany told her the moment she walked in. "Only two of which require answers yesterday. I contacted Tom Bradley's agent. He's interested in doing the pilot."

"Good. Let's set it up." In her office, Johanna dropped her briefcase, accepted the cup of coffee Beth was already offering and sat on the edge of her desk. "I've thought of twenty-seven ways to successfully murder John Jay Johnson."

"Would you like me to type them up?"

"Not yet. I want to wait until I have an even thirty." Johanna sipped her coffee and wished for five minutes, five full minutes to be completely alone, so that she could take her shoes off, put her feet up and close her eyes. "Bradley has a reputation as being very professional."

"A veteran. Did his first show in '72, when he was still wet behind the ears. It ran for five years, and he slid right into the old classic *Word Bingo*. That was on the air from '77 to '85. Pretty amazing. He retired as sort of the guru of game shows, but his face is still recognizable from occasional appearances on other daytime shows and grand-marshaling parades. Luring him back to the fold would be no small accomplishment."

She stopped because Johanna was drinking coffee

and staring out the window. There were shadows under her eyes, Bethany noted, and a definite look of melancholy in them. "Johanna, you look terrible."

Taken aback, Johanna set her coffee aside. "So I've been told."

"Is everything all right?"

"Everything's fine." Except that Sam said he was in love with her and she was so terrified she wanted to get in her car and keep driving. She drew out her roll of tablets.

Frowning, Beth eyed it. "Was that a new roll this morning?"

"It was, before I spent most of it with John Jay."

"Have any lunch?"

"Don't ask."

"Johanna, why don't you take the rest of the day off, go home, take a nap, watch the soaps?"

With a small smile, Johanna rose to move behind her desk. "I've got to answer those questions yesterday. Beth, let's see if we can set that pilot up for the week after next. Be sure to notify Patterson Productions."

Bethany shrugged and stood. "You're the boss," she said, and set the stack of messages on Johanna's desk.

Absolutely true, Johanna thought as Bethany closed the door behind her. She was the boss. Johanna rubbed at the headache behind her temple and wondered why she felt as though someone else were pulling the strings.

He didn't know what he was doing there, sitting on her front steps like a lovesick teenager. Because he was lovesick, Sam told himself as he crossed his booted ankles.

He hadn't felt this stupid about a woman since he'd fallen like a ton of bricks for Mary Alice Reeder. She'd been an older woman, sophisticated, wise and like most sixteen-year-old girls, not very interested in a fourteen-year-old pest. But he'd loved pretty little Mary Alice with a kind of worshipful devotion that had lasted nearly nine months.

Calf love, his mother had called it, not unkindly.

Since then he'd fallen into the second stage, the care-for stage, with a number of women. But he hadn't loved anyone else since Mary Alice Reeder. Until Johanna.

He almost wished he could go back to that calf love. However painful it was, it passed, and it left a man with sweet and rather filmy memories. Hearts and initials carved surreptitiously in a tree trunk, daydreams that always ended with him saving his girl from some horrendous disaster that opened her eyes to his charm and bravery.

Sam laughed at himself and looked at a spiky blue flower that was just beginning to bloom in Johanna's garden. Times changed. Mary Alice had slipped through his shaky fingers. But he wasn't fourteen anymore, and Johanna, like it or not, was going nowhere.

He wanted her. Just sitting there in front of her quiet, empty house, with a basket beside him and her flowers sleeping in the evening sun, he wanted her. For good. It wasn't a decision he'd made with a snap of his fingers, though she might think so. It was something that had happened to him, and not entirely in a way he liked. The only plans he'd counted on, the only pressure he'd expected, had been career-oriented.

If he'd had his choice, he would have cruised along

for another few months, a year. Ten years. Time didn't have a damn thing to do with it. He'd looked at her, he'd touched her, and the decision had been made for him.

Hadn't he sat right here not so long before and told her they should get to know each other better? Companions, with no strings. He'd meant it, every bit as honestly as he'd meant it when he'd told her he loved her.

She'd accepted the first—warily, but she had accepted it. The second had been met with pure panic.

What was it that made Johanna so skittish? Another man? She'd never mentioned one, never even hinted at one. Unless he was completely obtuse, the woman he'd made love with the night before had been almost frighteningly innocent. If she'd been hurt, he felt it must be buried deep in the past, and it was time for her to let it go.

Time. He didn't have much of that, he thought as he lifted the lid of the basket to check on his gift. Any day he could get the call that would send him three thousand miles away. It would be weeks before he could be with her again. He could handle that. He thought he could handle that, but only if she gave him something to take with him.

When he heard the car he set the lid carefully back in place. Lovesick, he thought as his stomach knotted and his nerves began to jangle. It was a very apt phrase.

Johanna pulled in behind his car and wondered what the hell she was going to do. She'd been so sure she would be able to come home, close herself in, maybe dive into bed and sleep for hours without thinking at all. But he was here, invading her privacy, stealing away her quiet hours. The worst of it was, she was glad, so glad to see him.

"You put in a long day." He rose but didn't cross to her.

"A lot of things are coming to a head at once."

He waited until she stood in front of him. "I know what you mean." He touched her then, just a light stroke down her cheek. "You look tired."

"So I've been informed, with annoying regularity."

"Are you going to let me come in?"

"All right." He hadn't kissed her. Johanna had expected it this time, had been prepared for it. As she turned toward the house she suspected that was exactly why he hadn't done it. She spotted the wicker basket and paused as he scooped it up. "What did you do, bring sandwiches in case I was late?"

"Not exactly." He followed her inside. It was precisely as it had been the last time, neat, homey, smelling faintly of potpourri and fresh flowers. They were peonies this time, fat red blooms in a dark blue jar.

Johanna started to slip out of her shoes, caught herself and set down her briefcase.

"Can I get you a drink?"

"Why don't you sit down and I'll fix you one?" He set the basket down next to the jar of flowers. "I'm the one on vacation, remember?"

"I usually just get some coffee, but—"

"Fine. I'll get it."

"But—"

"Relax, Johanna. It'll just take a minute."

He strode off as she stood where she was. As far as she could remember, no one had ever cut her off in the middle of so many sentences. Well, he'd invited himself, she decided. He could heat up the coffee as well as she. And she did want to sit down, for just a minute.

She chose the corner of the sofa and thought she might rest her eyes until she heard Sam coming back. Johanna stifled a yawn, shut her eyes and was asleep in seconds.

She awoke the same way, instantly. Somehow she'd snuggled down and had pulled an afghan up to her chin. Sitting up, Johanna dragged her hands through her hair just before she spotted Sam sitting across from her drinking coffee.

"I'm sorry." She cleared the huskiness out of her voice. "I must have dozed off."

She'd slept like a rock for half an hour. He'd tucked her up himself. "How do you feel?"

"Embarrassed."

He smiled and rose to go to the coffeepot he'd set on a warmer. "Want this now?"

"Yes, thanks."

"You didn't get much sleep last night."

"No." She took the coffee, studying the little painted cup as though it fascinated her. "Neither did you."

"I didn't put in a ten-hour day." He sat beside her. She was up like a spring.

"I'm starving," she said quickly. "There isn't much out in the kitchen, but I can put together a couple of sandwiches."

"I'll give you a hand."

Even as he rose, she was shrugging out of her jacket. "That's all right, it's no trouble." Nervous, she turned the jacket over, spilling out the contents of the pockets.

Sam bent over and picked up loose change, a hairpin and what was left of the roll of antacids.

"What do you need these for?"

"Survival." Taking everything from him, she set them on the table.

"You put yourself under too much pressure. How many of these do you take?"

"For heaven's sake, Sam, they're more candy than medicine."

Her defensive tone had his eyes narrowing. Too many, he decided. "I'm entitled to worry about you." When she started to shake her head, he cupped her chin in his hand. "Yes, I am. I love you, Johanna, whether you can deal with it yet or not."

"You're pushing me too fast."

"I haven't even started to push yet."

With her face still caught in his hand, he kissed her. His lips demanded response, nothing timid, nothing cool. She could taste the trace of anger on them, the hint of frustration. Desire, kicked into high gear by other emotions, held sway. If it had been possible, she would have pulled back, ended it then and there. But it wasn't possible.

She touched a hand to his cheek, not even aware that she sought to soothe. As the kiss deepened, she slid her hand up into his hair. His name was like a sigh from her lips to his. Then she was locked close.

It was the whirlwind again, fast and furious. This time it was she who tugged at his shirt, wanting that contact, that intimate, secret feel of flesh against flesh. Her need was a springboard for his. Tangled, groping at buttons, they tumbled onto the couch.

Even last night, in that first burgeoning passion, she hadn't been like this. She trembled as she had trembled before, but now it was anticipation, even impatience, that shivered through her. To be swept away wasn't what she looked for now; to be taken wasn't enough. It had only taken one night for her to realize her own power. Now she was driven to test it again.

He struggled to keep his hands gentle as the insistence of hers had desire clawing at him. Her mouth, open and hungry, sought the taste of him, chest, shoulders, throat, while she tugged at the snap of his jeans and sent his stomach muscles dancing.

"Johanna." As much for her preservation as his own, he tried to slow the pace. Then her mouth was back on his, silencing him, ripping the last shreds of control.

The last light of day streamed through the windows of a room scented by flowers in a house tucked almost secretly in the hills. As long as he lived he would think of her that way—in soft light, in fresh scents, alone.

She hadn't known she could be like this, so full of need, so desperate to be filled. Heedless, daring, reckless. She felt the teddy he'd slipped so carefully from her the night before tear as he yanked aside the barrier.

Then she captured him, drawing him in, arching high as pleasure arrowed into her. Fast, then faster still, she drove them both in a race for that final dazzling release.

He held on to her, even after her body went lax, after his own emptied. Her shyness had delighted him, lured him, but this Johanna, the one who could flash with white heat, could make him a slave. He wasn't certain what he'd done, he only remembered the grasping, titanic lunge into delirium.

"Did I hurt you?" he murmured.

"No." She was too stunned by her own behavior to notice any bruises. "Did I hurt you?"

He grinned against her throat. "I didn't feel a thing." He tried to shift her to a more comfortable position and spotted the remains of her teddy on the floor. "I owe you some lingerie," he murmured as he lifted it up.

Johanna studied the torn strap and rent seam. Abruptly she began to laugh. She felt like that, torn open, and God only knew what would pour through the holes. "I've never attacked a man before," she managed.

"You can practice on me anytime. Here." He picked up his shirt and slipped it over her shoulders. "I always seem to be lending you a shirt. Johanna, I want you to tell me how you feel. I need you to."

Slowly, hoping to gather up some of her scattered senses, she buttoned the shirt. "There are reasons... I can't talk about them, Sam, but there are reasons why I don't want things to get serious."

"Things already are serious."

He was right. She knew he was right even before she looked into his eyes and felt it. "How serious?"

"I think you know. But I'm willing to spell it out for you again."

She wasn't being fair. It was so important, and sometimes so impossible, to be fair. There was too much she couldn't tell him, she thought. Too much he'd never be able to understand even if she could. "I need time."

"I've got a couple of hours."

"Please."

"All right." It wasn't easy, but he promised himself he'd give her time, even though he felt it slipping away.

He tugged on his jeans, then remembered the basket. "I almost forgot. I brought you a present." He plucked up the basket and set it in her lap.

He wasn't going to push. She shot him a quick look of gratitude, then added a smile. "What, a picnic?" She flipped back the lid, but instead of cold chicken she saw a small dozing kitten. Johanna drew her out and was instantly in love. "Oh, Sam! She's adorable." The kitten mewed sleepily as she rubbed its rust-colored fur against her cheek.

"Blanche had a litter last month." He tickled the kitten's ears.

"Blanche? As in Dubois?"

"Now you're catching on. She's sort of a faded Southern belle who likes to pit the toms against each other. This one's weaned, and there's enough cat food in the basket to get you through about a week."

The kitten climbed down the front of her skirt and began to fight with one of the buttons. "Thank you." Johanna turned to him as he stroked the kitten's head. For the first time, she threw her arms around Sam's neck and hugged him.

CHAPTER NINE

He knew he shouldn't be nervous. It was an excellent production, with a quality script, top-notch casting and a talented director. He'd already seen the rushes, as well as a preview of the press screening. He knew he'd done a good job. But still he paced and watched the clock and wished like hell it was nine.

No, he wished it was eleven and the damn thing was over.

It was worse because Johanna was engrossed in the script Max Heddison had sent him. So Sam was left to worry, nurse the brandy he had no desire for and pace her living room. Even the redheaded kitten, which Johanna had christened Lucy, was too busy to bother with him. She was involved with wrestling a ball of yarn under Johanna's feet.

Sam made himself sit, poked at the Sunday paper, then was up again.

"You could take a walk outside for a change of scenery," Johanna suggested from across the room.

"She speaks! Johanna, why don't we go for a ride?"

"I have to finish this. Sam, Michael's a wonderful part for you, a really wonderful part."

He'd already decided that, but it was Luke, the character who would be exposed to millions of eyes in a matter of thirty minutes, who worried him. If he took on Michael, that would be another worry at another time. "Yeah. Johanna, it's lousy for your eyes to hold papers that close."

She moved them back automatically. In less than a minute she had her nose against them again. "This is wonderful, really wonderful. You're going to take it, aren't you?"

"For a chance to work with Max Heddison, I'd take it if it was garbage."

"Then you're lucky it shines. God, this scene here, the one on Christmas Eve, just leaves you limp."

He stopped pacing long enough to glance at her again. She was rereading it as avidly as she'd read it the first time. And the papers were an inch from her face.

"You keep that up, you're going to need glasses." He saw the frown come and go and was distracted enough to smile. "Unless you already do."

Without bothering to glance up, she turned a page. "Shut up, Sam, you're breaking my concentration."

Instead, he pulled the script away and held it at a reasonable distance. "Read me some dialogue."

"You already know what it says." She made a grab for the script, but he inched it away.

"You can't, can you? Where are your glasses, Johanna?"

"I don't need glasses."

"Then read me some dialogue."

She squinted, but the words ran together. "My eyes are just tired."

"Like hell." He set the script down to take her hands. "Don't tell me my sensible Johanna's too vain to wear reading glasses."

"I'm not vain, and I don't need glasses."

"You'd look cute in them." When she pulled her hands away, he made two circles out of his index fingers and thumbs and held them over her eyes. "Studiously sexy. Dark frames—yes, that would be best. Very conservative. I'd love to take you to bed while you were wearing them."

"I never wear them."

"Ah, but you do have them. Where?"

She made a grab for the script, but he blocked her. "You're just trying to distract yourself."

"You're right. Johanna, I'm dying in here."

She softened enough to touch his face. It was something she still did rarely. Automatically he lifted his hand to her wrist and held it there. "The reviews couldn't have been better, Sam. America waits for nine o'clock with bated breath."

"And America might be snoring by nine-fifteen."

"Not a chance." Reaching over, she picked up the remote to turn on the set. "Sit down. We'll watch something else until it starts."

He eased into the chair with her, shifting her until she stretched across his lap. "I'd rather nibble on your ear until it starts."

"Then we'll miss the first scene." Content, she rested her head against his shoulder.

It had been an odd weekend, she thought. He'd stayed with her. After her first unease, they'd fallen into a simple routine that was no routine at all. Lovemaking, sleep, walks, the little chores a house required, even a trip to the market to fuss over fresh vegetables.

She hadn't felt like a producer for forty-eight hours, nor had she thought of Sam as an actor. Or a celebrity. He'd been her lover—or, as he had once put it, her companion. How lovely life would be if it could be that simple. It had been difficult, even for these short two days, to pretend it could be. It had been much less difficult to wish.

She'd changed his life. He didn't know how to explain it, or how to put it into words she might understand, but change it she had. He'd known that for certain when he'd gotten the script.

Max Heddison had been as good as his word. Sam had felt like a first-year drama student being offered the lead in a summer-stock production. It had come through Marv, of course, along with Marv's opinion about potential, the old school and the new, a million five plus percentages. Sam had taken it all in. It was never wise to forget that show business remained a business. Then he had devoured the script.

There was a part of him, a part he hoped would always be there, that could break out in a sweat at the chance to take on a new role. The character of Michael was complex, confused, desperately trying to unravel the mystery of his much-loved, much-detested father. He could already see Max Heddison in that role. Slowly, trying to see the script as a whole, as well as a vehicle, he'd read it again.

And he'd known he wanted to do it. Had to do it.

If Marv could get a million five, fine and dandy. If he could get peanuts and a keg of beer, that was all right, too. But rather than picking up the phone and calling his agent with a go-ahead, he'd bundled up the script and taken it to Johanna.

He'd needed her to read it. He'd needed her opinion, though throughout his career he'd always gone on his own gut instinct. Agent or not, the final decision had always been his. Now that had changed.

In a matter of weeks she'd become entwined with his life, his thoughts, his motives. Though he'd never thought of himself as a solitary person, he'd stopped being alone. She was there now, to share with—the big things, like the script, and the small things, like a new litter of kittens. It might have been true that she still held back from him, but in the last two days he'd seen her relax. Degree by degree, certainly, but he'd been able to see the change. That morning she'd seemed almost used to waking beside him.

He was giving her time, Sam thought as he brushed his lips over her hair. But he was also making his moves.

"Here come the teasers," Johanna murmured, and he was jerked back to the present. His stomach clenched. He swore at himself, but it tightened anyway, as it did whenever he prepared to watch himself on-screen. He flashed on, wearing only faded jeans, a battered panama and a grin, while the voice-over promised the sultry and the shocking.

"It is a nice chest." She smiled and kissed him on the cheek.

"They spent half the time spraying it so it'd have that nice jungle-fatigue shine. Do women really pant over a sweaty chest?"

"You bet," she told him, and settled down to watch the opening credits.

She was drawn in before the first five minutes were over. Luke drifted into town with two dollars in his pocket, a reputation on his back and an eye for the ladies. She knew it was Sam, pulling bits and pieces of his art together to meld with the writer's, but it rang true. You could almost smell the sweat and boredom of the sleepy little town in Georgia.

During the first commercial he slid down to the floor to give her the chair. He didn't want to ask her now, didn't want to break the rhythm. But he rested a hand on her calf.

For two hours they said nothing. She rose once and came back with cold drinks, but they didn't exchange words. On screen she watched the man she'd slept with, the man she'd loved, seduce another woman. She watched him talk himself out of one fight and raise his fists for another. He got drunk. He bled. He lied.

But she'd stopped thinking of him as Sam. The man she watched was Luke. She felt the slight pressure of Sam's fingers against her leg and kept her eyes on Luke.

He was irresistible. He was unforgivable.

When the segment ended, it left her hanging and Sarah's roses dying in the bowl.

Sam still said nothing. His instincts told him it was good. It was better than good. It was the best he'd ever done. Everything had fallen into place—the performances, the atmosphere, those lazy two-edged words that had first caught his imagination and his ambition. But he wanted to hear it from her.

Rising, he shifted to sit on the arm of her chair. Johanna, his Johanna, was still frowning at the screen. "How could he do that to her?" she demanded. "How could he use her that way?"

Sam waited a moment, still careful. "He's a user. It's all he knows."

"But she trusts him. She knows he's lied and cheated, but she still trusts him. And he's—"

"What?"

"He's a bastard, but— Damn, there's something compelling about him, something likable. You want to believe he could change, that she could change him." Unsettled, moved, she looked up at him. "What are you grinning at?"

"It worked." He hauled her up and kissed her. "It worked, Johanna."

She backed up enough to breathe. "I didn't tell you how good I thought you were."

"You just did." He kissed her again, then began tugging up her shirt.

"Sam—"

"I suddenly find myself with all this energy—incredible energy. Let me show you." He slid back into the chair, taking her with him.

"Wait a minute." She laughed, then moaned when his hands began to wander. "Sam, give me a minute."

"I've got hours for you. Hours and hours."

"Sam." With one laughing shove, she held him off. "I want to talk to you."

"Is it going to take long?" He tugged at the waistband of her slacks.

"No." To stop him, she framed his face with her hands. "I want to tell you how really exceptional you were. I pretended once that I didn't pay attention to your films, but I have. And you were never better than tonight."

"Thanks. It means a lot coming from you."

She took a deep breath, managing to push herself out of the chair. "You put a lot into that part."

She was leading somewhere. Though he wasn't sure he'd like the destination, he let her take the lead. "A part's not worth anything unless you do. Nothing is."

No, nothing was. "I, ah...I almost forget, when we're like this, who you are. These past few weeks, here, at the ranch, it hasn't been like being with Sam Weaver in capital letters."

Puzzled, he rose with her. "Johanna, you're not going to try to tell me you're intimidated by actors? You've been around the business all your life."

"All my life," she murmured. She didn't want to love him. She didn't want to love anyone, but most particularly not an actor, a movie star, a household name. The trouble was, she already did. "It's not a matter of being intimidated, it's just that it's been easy to forget you're not just an ordinary man who I ran into and grew fond of."

"Fond of," he repeated, drawing out the phrase. "Well, we're improving." He had her by the shoulders. That lazy drawl of a voice could fool you into forgetting how quick he was. "I don't know what the hell this is about, but we'll get to it in a minute. Right now, I want you to look at me. Really look at me, Johanna," he repeated, adding a little shake. "And tell me if you're in love with me."

"I never said—"

"No one knows better than I what you've never said." He drew her a little closer, insisting that her eyes stay on his. "I want to hear it now, and it has nothing to do with how I make my living, what the critics say or how much I'm worth at the box office. Do you love me?"

She started to shake her head but simply couldn't force it to move. How could she lie when he was looking at her, when he was touching her? She drew a deep breath to be certain her voice was calm. "Yes."

He wanted to take her then, just gather her close and hold on. But he knew that not only did he have to hear the words, she had to say them. "Yes, what?"

"Yes, I love you."

He looked at her for a long time. She was trembling a little, so he lowered his head and pressed his lips to her forehead. He didn't know why it was so difficult for her to say.

Not yet. But he was determined to find out.

"That should make things easier."

"But it doesn't," she murmured. "It doesn't change anything."

"We'll talk about it. Let's sit down."

She nodded. She didn't know what there was to say,

but there had to be something. Trying to make it seem normal, she started to the front door to lock up for the night. Then she heard the quick report on the evening news.

"Sources report that Carl W. Patterson, respected producer, has suffered a heart attack this evening. Paramedics were summoned to his Beverly Hills estate, which he shares with his fiancée, Toni DuMonde. His condition at this hour remains critical."

"Johanna." Sam laid a hand on her arm. She hadn't gasped or cried out. There were no tears in her eyes. She had simply stopped in her tracks as though she'd run into a wall. "Get your purse. I'll take you to the hospital."

"What?"

"I'll drive you." He switched off the set and went to get her bag himself. "Come on."

She only nodded and let him lead her out.

No one had called her. The oddness of it struck Sam as they rode the elevator up to Cardiac Care. Her father had had a heart attack, and she hadn't been notified.

The year before, when his mother had broken her ankle in a nasty fall on the ice, he'd received three calls in a matter of hours. One from his sister, another from his father and the last from his mother, telling him that his sister and father were fussbudgets.

Nonetheless the ankle had worried him enough to have him do some quick scheduling adjustments so that he could make the trip back east. He'd only had thirty-six hours to spare, but it had been time enough to see his mother for himself, sign her cast and put his mind at rest.

And a broken ankle was a far cry from a heart attack.

Johanna was Patterson's only child, yet she'd had to hear about her father's illness on the eleven-o'clock news. Even if they weren't close, as he'd already deduced, they were family. In Sam's experience, families stuck together in times of crisis.

She'd barely said a word since they'd left the house. He'd tried to comfort her, to offer both hope and support, but she hadn't responded. It seemed to him that she was just going through the motions, pale, a little dazed, but with the automatic control that had slipped effortlessly back into place. He watched her approach the nurses' station. Her hands were steady, her voice was calm and unwavering when she spoke.

"Carl Patterson was admitted this evening. They told me downstairs he's in CCU."

The nurse—sturdy, mid-forties and used to the night shift—barely glanced up. "I'm sorry, we're not permitted to give out patient information."

"He's my father," Johanna said flatly.

The nurse looked up. Reporters and the curious used all kinds of ploys to glean information on the famous. She'd already discouraged a few of them that evening. The woman on the other side of the counter didn't look like a reporter—the nurse prided herself on having a nose for them—but she hadn't been told to expect family, either. Recognizing doubt, Johanna drew out her wallet and identification.

"I'd like to see him, if that's possible, and speak with his doctor."

The nurse felt a stirring of sympathy. Her gaze shifted and locked on Sam. She recognized him, and though seeing him face-to-face would give her something to tell her husband when they passed over the breakfast table, she wasn't overly impressed. After twenty years of nursing in Beverly Hills she was accustomed to seeing celebrities, often naked, sick and vulnerable. But she did remember reading that Sam Weaver was having a fling with Carl Patterson's daughter.

"I'll be happy to page the doctor for you, Miss Patterson. There's a waiting room down the hall and to the left. Miss Dumonde is already there."

"Thank you." She turned and started down, refusing to think past the moment, refusing to think past the action required to get beyond that moment. She heard a bell ding quietly, almost secretively, then the soft slap of crepe-soled shoes.

The panic was gone, that first thunder of panic that had filled her head when she'd heard the news report. Replacing it was the knowledge that she had to put one foot in front of the other and do whatever needed to be done. She was used to doing such things alone.

"Sam, I have no idea how long this might take. Why don't you go home? I can take a cab back when I'm ready."

"Don't be ridiculous," was all he said.

It was enough, more than enough to cause her breath to hitch. She wanted to turn to him, to press her face against his chest. She wanted to be held, to be passive, to let him handle whatever had to be done. Instead, she turned into the waiting room.

"Sam!" Toni's eyes, already damp, spilled over. She

sprang out of her chair and launched herself into his arms. "Oh, Sam, I'm so glad you're here. I've been so frightened. It's a nightmare. I'm just sick with worry, Sam. I don't know what I'll do if Carl dies."

"Pull yourself together." Sam led her back to a chair, then lit one of the cigarettes she'd spilled from a pack onto the table. He stuck it between her fingers. "What did the doctor say?"

"I don't know. He was so technical and grim faced." She held out a hand to a blond man in a dinner jacket. "I never would have survived this without Jack. He's been a wall, an absolute wall. Hello, Johanna." She sniffled into a lacy handkerchief.

"Sam." Jack Vandear nodded as he patted Toni's hand. He'd directed two of Patterson's productions and had run into Sam at least a half-dozen times on the party circuit. "It's been a rough night."

"So we heard. This is Patterson's daughter."

"Oh." Jack rose and offered a hand.

"I'd like to know what happened."

"It was horrible." Toni looked up at Johanna through an attractive veil of tears. "Just horrible."

Jack sent her a look that was three parts impatient, one part sympathetic. He hadn't minded comforting her, but the truth was, he'd come for Carl. It went through his mind that with Sam here, the soggy-eyed Toni could be passed along.

"We were having a small dinner party. Carl looked a bit tired, but I took it to mean he'd been working too hard, as usual. Then it seemed he couldn't get his breath. He collapsed into a chair. He complained of pain in his chest and his arm. We called the paramedics."

He started to skim over the rest, then decided Johanna looked strong enough to handle it. "They had to bring him back once." At that Toni put up a low, heartbreaking sob and was ignored. "The doctor said it was a massive coronary. They've been working to stabilize him."

Her legs were shaking. She could keep her hands steady and her face impassive, but she couldn't stop her legs from trembling. Massive coronary. Darlene, her father's wry and witty third wife, would have said that Carl W. Patterson never did anything halfway.

"Did they tell you his chances?"

"They haven't told us much of anything."

"We've been waiting forever." Toni dabbed at her eyes again, then drew on her cigarette. In her own way, she was fond of Carl. She wanted to marry him even though she knew that divorce would be at the end of the rainbow. Divorce was easy. Death was another matter. "The press was here five minutes after we were. I knew how much Carl would hate having them report this."

Johanna sat and for the first time looked, really looked, at her father's fiancée. Whatever she was, the woman obviously knew Carl. The heart attack was a weakness, and he would detest having it made public knowledge. "I'll handle the press," she said tonelessly. "It might be best if you, both of you," she said, including Jack, "told them as little as possible. Have you seen him?"

"Not since they took him in." Toni took another drag as she looked out into the corridor. "I hate hospitals." After crushing out the cigarette, she began to pleat the handkerchief. The silver sequins on her evening dress sparkled opulently in the dim waiting room. "We were supposed to go to Monaco next week. Carl had some business there, but for the most part it was to be a kind of prehoneymoon. He seemed so...well, so virile." The tears started again when the doctor came into the waiting room.

"Miss DuMonde."

She was up and clutching at both his hands, the picture of the distressed lover barely holding back hysteria. It surprised her to discover it was only half an act. "He's all right. Tell me Carl's all right."

"His condition's stabilized. We're running tests to determine the extent of the damage. He's a strong man, Miss DuMonde, and overall his health seems excellent."

He looked tired, Johanna thought as she studied the doctor. Unbearably tired, but she recognized the truth. She rose as he glanced her way.

"You're Mr. Patterson's daughter?"

"I'm Johanna Patterson. How serious is his condition?"

"I have to tell you it's very serious. However, he's getting the best care possible."

"I'd like to see him."

"For a few moments. Miss DuMonde?"

"He wouldn't want me to see him this way. He'd hate it."

Because Johanna could only agree, she ignored the little stab of resentment and followed the doctor out. "He's sedated," she was told. "And he's being monitored very closely. The next twenty-four hours will tell the tale, but your father's relatively young, Miss Patterson. An incident like this is often a warning, to slow down, to take a hard look at your own mortality."

It had to be said, just once out loud, though she knew she would get no absolutes. "Is he going to die?"

"Not if we can help it." The doctor pushed open a glass door.

There was her father. She'd lived in his house, eaten his food, obeyed his rules. And she barely knew him. The machines that eased his breathing and monitored his vital signs hummed. His eyes were shut, his face pasty under his tan. He looked old. It occurred to her that she'd never thought of him as old, even when she'd been a child. He'd always been handsome, ageless, virile.

She remembered Toni using that word. Virile. That was so important to Carl. He'd often been described as a man's man—salty tongued, strong shouldered, reckless with women. He'd always been impatient with weaknesses, excuses, illnesses. Perhaps that was why, when he'd reached the middle of his life, the women he'd brought into it had become younger and younger.

He was a hard man, even a cold one, but he'd always been full of life. There was a genius in him, a genius she'd admired as much as she'd feared it. He was an honest man, a man of his word, but never one to give an inch more than he chose.

She touched him once, just a hand over his. It was a gesture she would never have considered making had he been awake.

"Will it happen again?"

"He has an excellent chance of full recovery, if he throws away the cigars, watches his alcohol intake and cuts back on his schedule. There's his diet, of course," the doctor went on, but Johanna was already shaking her head.

"I can't imagine him doing any of those things."

"People often do what others can't imagine after they end up in CCU. It'll be his choice, of course, but he's not a stupid man."

"No, he's not." She removed her hand. "We'll need a press release. I can take care of that. When will he be awake?"

"You should be able to talk to him in the morning."

"I'd appreciate a call if there's any change before then. I'll leave my number at the nurses' station."

"I should be able to tell you more in the morning." The doctor pushed open the door again. "You'd do well to get some rest yourself. A recovering cardiac patient can be wearing."

"Thank you." Alone, she started back down the hall. In self-defense, she blocked out the image of her father in the hospital bed. The moment she walked back in, Toni was up and grabbing both her hands.

"How is he, Johanna? Tell me the truth, tell me everything."

"He's resting. The doctor's very optimistic."

"Thank God."

"Carl will have to make some adjustments—diet, work load, that sort of thing. You'll be able to see him tomorrow."

"Oh, I must look a wreck." The need to check was so ingrained that Toni was already reaching for her compact. "I'll have to take care of that by tomorrow. I wouldn't want him to see me with my eyes all red and my hair a fright."

Again, because it was true, Johanna held back her sarcasm. "He won't wake up until tomorrow, according to the doctor. I'm going to handle the press—through a hospital spokesman, I think—and make certain his publicist has time to work up a statement. It might be a day or two before he's able to make those decisions for himself."

She wavered there a moment, trying to imagine her father unable to make any decision. "The important thing for you to do is to keep him calm. Go home and get some rest. They'll call if there's any change before morning."

"How about you?" Sam asked her when Jack had taken Toni down the corridor. "Are you all right?"

"Yes, I'm fine."

Wanting to judge for himself, he took her chin in his hand. There was something about the eyes, he thought. More than shock, certainly different than grief. Big secrets, he decided. Big fears. "Talk to me, Johanna."

"I've told you everything."

"About your father's condition." Though she tried to draw away, he held on. "I want to know about yours."

"I'm a little tired. I'd like to go home."

"Okay." Better, he thought, that they hash this, whatever it was, out at home. "We'll go back. But I'm staying with you."

"Sam, there's no need."

"There's every need. Let's go home."

CHAPTER
TEN

It was after one a.m. when they arrived at Johanna's house, but she went straight to the phone. With a pen in one hand, she began to flip through her address book. "It shouldn't take long for me to set this up," she told Sam, "but you don't have to wait up."

"I'll wait." There were things that had to be said, and he wanted them said before she had a chance to build the barricades again. Though she looked steady, perhaps too steady, he was coming to understand her. Still, he left her alone as she began to dial.

There was little enough she could do. She was certain her father would tolerate only the slightest interference from her, but he would want his people informed. Johanna fed information to his publicist, then hashed out a simple, straightforward press release.

While she was calming her father's assistant and making sure that the daily business of Patterson Productions would run as smoothly as possible, Sam handed her a mug. Grateful, Johanna sipped, expecting coffee. Instead she tasted the soothing herbal tea she'd bought on impulse and brewed occasionally after a particularly long day.

"I'll be able to tell you more tomorrow, Whitfield. No, whatever can't be handled by you or another member of the staff will have to be canceled. That would appear to be your problem, wouldn't it?"

Across the room, Sam had no choice but to smile at her tone. As producers went, he'd never heard better.

"Where's Loman? Well, call him back." She made a quick notation on a pad. "Yes, that's right, but I'm sure he'll be giving you instructions himself in a couple of days. You'll have to check with the doctor on that, but I don't think you'll be able to discuss that or anything else with Carl for at least forty-eight hours." Her voice changed, went frigid. "That's not really the issue here, Whitfield. You'll have to consider Carl unavailable until further notice. No, I won't take the responsibility, you will. That's what you're paid for."

She hung up, incensed by the man's insensitivity. "Idiot," she muttered as she picked up her tea again. "His main concern is that Carl insisted on supervising the editing of *Fields of Fire*, and the heart attack is going to put the project behind schedule."

"Are you finished?"

Still frowning, she skimmed down her notes. "I don't think there's any more I can do."

"Come and sit down." He waited until she'd joined him on the sofa, then poured more tea into her cup from the pot he'd brewed. Sensing tension even before he touched her, Sam began to massage her shoulders. "It's hard, only being able to wait."

"Yes."

"You handle yourself well, Johanna."

She sipped tea and stared straight ahead. "I had a good teacher."

"Tell me about your father."

"I told you everything the doctor told me."

"I don't mean that." She was tensing up again, even as he massaged the muscles. "Tell me about him, about you and him."

"There's really nothing to tell. We've never been particularly close."

"Because of your mother?"

She went stiff at that. "What does my mother have to do with it?"

"I don't know. You tell me." He'd been shooting in the dark, but he wasn't surprised that he'd hit the target. "Johanna, you don't have to be a gossip buff to know that your parents divorced when you were, what—four?"

"I'd just turned five." It still hurt. No matter how often she told herself it was foolish, even unhealthy, the child's pain and confusion leaked into the woman. "That's history, Sam."

He didn't think so. Instinct told him it was as much a part of the present as he was. "She went back to England," he prompted. "And your father retained custody of you."

"He didn't have much choice." The bitterness leaked out. She made a conscientious and difficult effort to bury it again. "It really isn't relevant."

"I'm not Whitfield, Johanna," he murmured. "Humor me."

She was silent for so long he decided to try another tactic. Then she sighed and began. "My mother went back to England to try to pick up the stage career she felt she'd sacrificed when she'd married. I didn't have a place there."

"You must have missed her."

"I got over it."

He didn't think so. "I don't suppose divorce is ever easy on a kid, but it's got to be worse when one of the parents ends up several thousand miles away."

"It was better that way, for everyone. They always fought terribly. Neither of them were happy with their marriage or…" She trailed off before she could say what was in her mind. *Me. Neither of them wanted me.* "With the situation," she finished.

"You'd have been pretty young to have known that." He'd begun to get a picture of five-year-old Johanna, dealing with the inexplicable ups and downs of a rocky marriage.

"You don't have to be very old to recognize turmoil. In any case, my mother explained it to me. She sent me a telegram from the airport." Her tea had gone cold, but she sipped automatically.

A telegram's just like a letter, the pretty young maid had told Johanna. If the maid hadn't been new, the telegram would have been handed over to Carl and disposed of. But the maid had been avid to know the contents, and more than willing to help Johanna struggle over the words.

> My darling girl. I'm devastated to leave you like this, but I have no choice. My situation, my life, has become desperate. Believe me, I have tried, but I've come to understand that divorce and a complete separation from what was, is the only way I can survive. I despise myself for leaving you in your father's hands, but for now mine are too frail to hold on to you. One day you'll understand and forgive. Love. Mother.

She remembered it still, word for word, though at the time all she had understood was that her mother was leaving her because she wasn't happy.

Sam was staring at her, amazed that she could be so matter-of-fact. "She sent you a telegram?"

"Yes. I wasn't old enough to fully understand, but I caught the drift. She was miserably unhappy and desperate to find a way out."

Bitch. The word rose up in his throat, hotly, and he had to swallow it. He couldn't imagine anyone being so self-absorbed and selfish as to say goodbye to her only child by telegram. He tried to remember that Johanna had told him how her mother had taken her to feed the ducks, but he couldn't equate the two acts with the same woman.

"It must have been rough on you." He put his arm

around her, as if he could find a way to protect her from what had already happened.

"Children are resilient." She rose, knowing that if he offered comfort she would break. She hadn't broken in over twenty years. "She did what she had to do, but I don't think she was ever happy. She died about ten years ago."

Suicide. He swore at himself for not remembering it before. Glenna Howard, Johanna's unhappy mother, had never quite achieved the sparkling comeback she'd sought. Disappointment had been eased by pills and alcohol until she'd taken a deliberate overdose of both.

"I'm sorry, Johanna. Losing her twice. It must have been hell for you."

"I never knew her that well." She reached for her tea again, for something to keep her hands busy. "And it was a long time ago."

He went to her, though she turned away. Patient but determined, he drew her back. "I don't think things like that ever stop hurting. Don't back off from me, Johanna."

"There's no use dredging all this up."

"I think there is." He took her shoulders, firmly enough to let her know he wasn't easing off. "I've wondered all along why you held off. I thought at first it was because you'd had a bad experience with another man. But it goes back farther than that, and deeper."

She looked at him then, her face set but her eyes desperate. She'd said too much, more than she'd ever said before. In saying it, the memories became all too clear. "I'm not my mother."

"No." He lifted a hand to brush at her hair. "No, you're not. And you're not your father either."

"I don't even know if he *is* my father."

The moment it was said, she went white. The hands she had fisted unballed and went limp. Not once in all of her life had she said it out loud. The knowledge had been there, locked tight but never completely silent. Now she heard her words echo back to her and was afraid, terribly afraid, she'd be ill.

"Johanna, what are you talking about?"

His voice was calm and quiet, but it shot like a bullet through her shock. "Nothing, nothing. I'm upset. I'm tired. Tomorrow's going to be a difficult day, Sam. I need to sleep."

"We both know you're too wired to sleep." He could feel the violent shudders begin as he held her there. "And you will be until you get the rest of it out. Tell me about your father, Johanna. About Carl."

"Will you leave me alone?" There were tears in her voice that only frightened her more. She could feel the walls cracking, the foundation giving way, but didn't have the strength to shore it up again. "For God's sake, can't you see I've had all I can manage? I don't want to talk about my mother. I don't want to talk about him. He could be dying." The tears spilled out, and she knew she'd lost. "He could be dying, and I should feel something. But I don't. I don't even know who he is. I don't know who I am."

She fought him, pushing away as he gathered her to him, swearing at him as he held her there. Then she collapsed in a storm of weeping.

He didn't offer comforting words. He hadn't a clue

which ones to choose. Instead, he lifted her into his arms. With her sobs muffled against his throat, he sat down, cradling her to him. Sam stroked her hair and let her purge herself. He hadn't known it was possible to hold that many tears inside.

She felt ill. Her throat and eyes burned, her stomach heaved. Even when the tears were over, the raw, sick feeling remained. Her strength had been sapped, as if someone had pulled a plug and let it drain away. She didn't object when Sam shifted her, nor when he rose. He was going away. It was something she accepted even as her own battered heart suffered another crack.

Then he was sitting beside her again, placing a snifter in her hands. "It might help some," he murmured. "Take it slow."

If there'd been any left, more tears would have fallen. She nodded, took a sip of brandy and let it coat the raw wounds.

"I was always in awe of him," Johanna began without looking up. "I don't know even now if I loved him as a child, but he was always the largest and most important figure in my life. After my mother left—" she paused to sip again "—after my mother left I was terrified that he'd leave, too, or send me away. I didn't understand then how important it was to him to keep his private affairs private. The public could accept and be entertained by his romances and marriages, but if he'd shipped off his only child without a blink, they'd have taken a different view. No one forgot that he'd been married to Glenna Howard and that she'd had his child. No one except him."

How could she explain how lost she had been? How

confusing it had been to see her father entertain other women as though her mother had never existed.

"When he married again it was horrible. There was a big, splashy wedding, lots of photographers, microphones, strangers. They dressed me up and told me to smile. I hated it—the stares and innuendos about my mother. The whispers about her. He could ignore it. He'd always had that kind of presence, but all I could think was that my mother was being replaced with someone I didn't even know. And I had to smile."

Insensitive, selfish idiots. Even as he thought it, he tightened his arms around her. "Wasn't there anyone else...any family?"

"His parents had died years before. I remember hearing or being told somewhere along the line that he'd been raised by his grandmother. By that time she was gone, too. I'd never met her. I had what you'd call a governess, who would have literally died for my father. Women react that way to him," she said wearily. "Nothing could have stopped it—my being in the wedding was important. Impressions, photo opportunities, that kind of thing. After it was over, I didn't see him again for three months. He was spending a lot of time in Italy."

"You stayed behind."

"I was in school." She pulled a hand through her hair, then clasped them in her lap. "It was perfectly legitimate for him to leave me behind with my tutors and instructors. In any case, his second wife had little tolerance for children. Few of his liaisons did."

Because she could feel his sympathy reaching out to her, she shook her head. "I was happier here. I spent a lot of time with the Heddisons. They were wonderful to me."

"I'm glad for that." He drew her hand into his. "Go on."

"It was after his second divorce, when he was involved with…it doesn't matter who. Anyway, I was out of school and feeling sorry for myself. I went up to his room. I don't even know why, except to be there, to see if I could solve the mystery of my father. I solved it.

"I'd always felt inadequate, awkward around him. There seemed to be something lacking in me that kept him from loving me the way that he should. He had this wonderful old desk in his room, one with all these fascinating cubbyholes and compartments. He was away again, so I didn't have to worry about him catching me poking around. I found letters. Some of them were from his women, and I was old enough to be embarrassed, so I put them away again. Then I found one from my mother. An old one, one she'd written right after she'd gone back to England. Holding it was like seeing her again. Sometimes I hadn't been able to bring the picture of her into my head, but the minute I had that letter, I saw her exactly as she'd been. God, she was beautiful, so fragile and haunted. I could even hear her voice, that trained, extraordinary voice. I'd loved her so much."

He took the snifter from her and set it on the table. "You read the letter?"

"I wish to God I hadn't." She squeezed her eyes shut for a moment, but it was now, as it had been then, too late to turn back. "I was so hungry for anything she'd touched, any part of her, that I didn't even realize at first when I was reading. She must have been furious when she wrote it. It came across, the anger, the bitterness, the need to punish. I'd known, even as a child, that their marriage hadn't been smooth. But until I'd read the letter I'd had no idea how much hate had been built up between them."

"People say things they don't mean, or at least things that shouldn't be said under those kind of circumstances."

"Well, she's gone, has been gone, and there's no way of knowing if she meant what she'd said. No way for me to know, no way for my father—for Carl to know."

Her mouth was dry, but she no longer wanted the brandy. Johanna pressed her lips together and continued. "She brought up every hurt, every broken promise, every real or imagined infidelity. Then she brought out the big guns. Leaving me with him was the biggest payback she could think of. She was saddling him with a child who wasn't even his own. Not that he could ever prove it, or that she would ever tell him who had fathered the child he'd given a name to. There was, of course, the possibility that the child was his, but… She wished him a lifetime of hell wondering. And because I read the letter, she gave me the same."

Sam stared out the darkened window for a long time. The rage was so keen, so close to the surface, he was afraid to speak. She'd been a child, innocent, helpless. And no one had given a damn.

"Did you ever speak to him about it?"

"No, there was no reason to. He didn't change toward me. I was well tended, well educated and allowed to pursue my own interests as long as I didn't embarrass him."

"They didn't deserve you. Either of them."

"It doesn't matter," she said wearily. "I'm not a child anymore." Nor had she been from the moment she'd read the letter.

"It matters to me." He cupped her face in his hands. "You matter to me, Johanna."

"I never meant to tell you, or anyone. But now that I have, you must understand why I can't let what's between us go too far."

"No."

"Sam—"

"What I understand is that you had a lousy childhood, and that things went on around you that no kid should ever be a part of. And I understand that there're bound to be scars."

"Scars?" She gave a quick, brittle laugh as she rose. "Don't you see, my mother was ill. Oh, it was kept quiet, out of the press, but I managed to dig it up. She was in and out of sanitariums the last few years of her life. Manic depression, instability, alcohol addiction. And the drugs…" Johanna pressed her fingers to her eyes and struggled to get a grip on herself. "She didn't raise me, and I can't be sure who my father is, but she was my mother. I can't forget that, or what I may have inherited from her."

He rose slowly. His first instinct was to tread carefully, but then he realized it was the wrong one. She needed to be brought up short, and quickly. "It's not like you to be melodramatic, Johanna."

His words had exactly the effect he'd hoped for. Anger flashed into her eyes and whipped color back into her cheeks. "How dare you say that to me?"

"How dare you stand there and make up insufficient excuses why you can't commit to me?"

"They're not excuses, they're facts."

"I don't give a damn who your mother was, or your father. I'm in love with you, Johanna. Sooner or later you're going to have to swallow it and take the next step."

"I've told you all along that it couldn't lead anywhere. Now I'm telling you why. And that's only half of it. My half."

"There's more?" He hooked his thumbs in his pockets and rocked back on his heels. "Okay, give me the rest."

"You're an actor."

"Right the first time, but you're not going to set any bells ringing with that answer."

"I've been around actors all of my life," she continued, searching for patience. "I understand the strain and demands of the job, the impossibility, especially for a talented actor, of maintaining a private life that keeps anything truly private. And I know that even with the best of intentions and effort relationships suffer. If I believed in marriage—which I don't—I still wouldn't believe in marriage to an actor."

"I see." It was difficult enough not to be angry with her, and it was impossible not to be furious with the people who had had the major hand in forming her beliefs. "Then you're saying that because I'm an actor—worse yet, a good one—I'm too big a risk."

"I'm saying that what there is between us can't go any further." She stopped, wanting to be strong. "And that if you don't want to see me again, I'll understand."

"Will you?" For a moment he studied her, as though he were considering it. A few steps away, Johanna prepared herself. She'd known it would hurt when it ended, but even her worst fears hadn't come close to this. When he crossed to her, she made herself look in his eyes. She could read nothing in them.

"You're an idiot, Johanna." He yanked her against him so hard that her breath whistled out in surprise. "Do you think I can turn my feelings for you on and off? Damn it, you do, don't you? I can see it in your face. Well, I'm not going to step neatly out of your life, and if you think you can push me out, you're going to be disappointed."

"I don't want you to go." Tears clouded her eyes, though she'd thought she was through with them. "I just don't think—"

"Then don't think." He swept her up into his arms. "You do too much thinking."

She didn't protest when he carried her upstairs. She was through with arguing, with excuses, with reasons. Perhaps it was a weakness to want to be taken care of, but she couldn't find the strength to stand on her own tonight. She didn't want to think. He was right about that. She didn't want to think at all for whatever hours of the night were left. For once, feelings took no effort and she could let them dominate.

She needed him. If she hadn't been so drained it would have frightened her to realize it.

The bedroom was dark, but he didn't turn on the light. The fragrances from her garden were carried up and through the windows on the night air. In silence he laid her on the bed and sat beside her.

There was too much to say to speak at all just yet. He'd once thought her cool, tough and self-sufficient. That woman had attracted and intrigued him. Intrigued him enough, Sam thought, to have caused him to dig deeper. The more he knew about her, the more layers he'd discovered.

She was tough, in the best sense of the word. She'd taken the blows, the disappointments, and had worked her way through them. Some people, he knew, would have buckled under, found a crutch or given up. But Johanna, his Johanna, had carved a place for herself and had made it work.

Underneath the toughness he'd found passion. He'd sensed and now was certain that it had gone untapped. Whether it was fate, blind luck or timing, he'd found the key that had released it. He wouldn't allow it to be locked again, or to be opened by anyone but himself.

Beneath the passion was a touching shyness. A sweetness that was a miracle in itself, considering her childhood and the disillusionments she'd faced so early in life.

Now, beneath all the rest, he'd found a core of fragility. He was determined to protect that vulnerability. And it was to the fragile Johanna that he would make love tonight.

In kindness as much as love. In compassion, as well as desire.

Softly, his touch barely a whisper, he brushed her hair away from her face. There were tears still drying on her cheeks. With his fingertips, he wiped them away. He wouldn't be able to prevent more from being shed, but he would do whatever he could to see that she didn't shed them alone.

He kissed her once, then twice, where the tears had lain. Then he kissed her again, tenderly. Night shadows shifted across her face, but he could see her eyes, half closed with fatigue but very aware, as she watched him.

"Do you want to sleep?" he asked her.

"No." She put her hand over his. "No, I don't want to sleep. And I don't want you to go."

"Then relax." He brought her hand to his lips. His eyes, so dark and intense, seemed to absorb everything she was. "And let me love you."

It was just that easy.

She hadn't known love could be soothing. He hadn't shown her that before. Tonight, when her emotions were raw and her self-esteem at its lowest ebb, he showed her another side of desire. A desire to please, and one to nurture. A desire to have, and one to heal. He touched her as though she alone mattered.

He drew off her shirt so that the material trailed over her skin before it was discarded, but he didn't take what she would have given. With his eyes on hers, he removed his own. When she reached for him, he took her hands, pressing them both to his lips.

He undressed her slowly, carefully, as though she were asleep and he didn't want to disturb her. The tenderness of it brought its own strange ache. Though she was naked and totally open to him, he contented himself with long, lazy kisses and the feel of her hair under his hands.

Her skin looked so white against the dark spread. He ran his hand down her arm, watching the movement. The moon had waned to a thin crescent, shedding little light, but he already knew her so well. Still, he traced her face with his fingertip, outlining her features for his own pleasure.

He'd never treated her like this before. Johanna closed her eyes as she began to drift into contentment. Even through passion and hunger, he'd always shown her an unexpected sweetness. But this…this was what it meant to be cherished. This was the way promises were given when they were meant to be kept. It made her eyes swim and her heart break, just a little, at the beauty of it.

He felt stronger somehow, being gentle. He'd never wanted her more than he did at this moment, and yet he had never felt less need to rush. The passion was there, and growing, but it was filled with a need to comfort.

Time passed unnoticed, unheeded. In the darkest hours of the morning, he led her gently higher.

The rhythm of her heart beat under his lips, fast, unsteady, but not yet desperate. Her arms were around him, holding him close, but there was no urgent press of fingers. She moved with him, willing to let him set the pace, grateful that he had understood, even if she hadn't, that she needed care.

Had she ever noticed how strong he was? How the muscles of his back and shoulders flexed and rippled with his movements? She'd touched him before, held him just like this, but each time she had she'd been driven close to the edge. Now the ride was quiet and unhurried, like floating on a raft on a still lake.

Inspired by love, she sought to give him the same gentleness he showed her. Her touch was easy, her demands few. She heard in the murmur of her name that he felt as she did. They might never come together so perfectly, so unselfishly, again.

Her sigh was quiet as she opened for him. They merged without heat but with much warmth.

Later, much later, she lay beside him, sleepless as the sky began to lighten.

CHAPTER ELEVEN

He could have strangled her. When Sam woke, he found himself alone in bed and the house empty. In the bath, her still-damp towel hung tidily over the rail. The room carried, very faintly, the scent of her. The clothes he'd removed from her the night before had been put away. Downstairs, he saw that her briefcase was gone and the flowers freshened. Her phone machine had been cleared of messages and reset.

In crisis or in control, Johanna was always organized.

He was sure he would strangle her.

In the kitchen he found the glasses they'd used the night before conscientiously rinsed and draining.

Propped against the coffeepot was a note in Johanna's neat handwriting. *I didn't want to wake you. I needed to get to the hospital early, then to the studio. The coffee's fresh.*

She'd written something else, crossed it out, then signed the note simply *Johanna.*

His mother could have written it, Sam thought as he skimmed it a second time. Only she might have added, *Leave the kitchen the way you found it.* Damn it, Johanna.

He stood in the kitchen dressed only in jeans and tossed her note onto the counter. No one would ever accuse Johanna of not having her feet firmly on the ground. But there were times when it was better, even necessary, to keep them planted beside someone else's. She still needed to accept that he was that someone else. He'd been sure he'd gotten through, but he'd forgotten how incredibly stubborn she could be.

Absently he bent down and picked up the kitten, who was doing figure eights between his legs. She wasn't hungry. Johanna had left Lucy well taken care of, with a full dish in the corner. She only wanted some affection. Most creatures did, Sam mused as he stroked her fur. Apparently that wasn't enough to make Johanna purr and settle trustingly in his arms.

It looked as if he still had a fight on his hands. Sam gave the kitten's ears a last scratch before he set her down again. He could be hardheaded, as well.

She was thinking of him. Sam would have been amazed if he had known how hard and long she'd struggled over those few brief lines she'd left him. She'd

wanted to thank him for being with her and to tell him
how much it had meant to her that he'd been kind and
understanding when she'd been down for the count.
She'd wanted to tell him that she loved him in a way she
had never before and would never again love. But the
words had seemed so empty and inadequate on paper.

It was hard to need someone, really need him, when
you'd spent your entire life making certain you could
handle anything and everything on your own. How
would he have felt if he'd known how close she'd come
to waking him and asking him to come with her because she'd been dreading the thought of facing this
day alone? She couldn't ask, any more than she could
forget that she now had no secrets from him, physically or emotionally. Dealing with this day alone was
imperative if she was ever to face another without him.

The nurse on duty this morning was younger and
more approachable than the one the night before. She
told Johanna that her father was resting comfortably,
then asked her to have a seat until Dr. Merritt could
be located.

Johanna chose the waiting room because the cor-
ridors seemed so public. She'd managed to evade the
reporters outside but didn't want to take any chances
on having to deal with any who'd been clever enough
to sneak in.

Inside, an elderly woman and a boy of about twenty
sat half dozing on a sofa, hands linked. On the wall-
mounted television a morning show flashed cheerfully,
showing a demonstration of gourmet cooking. Johanna
moved to a table where twin pots of coffee and hot water
sat on warmers. She bypassed the tea bags, ignored the

little bags of powdered cream and sugar and poured a cup black. As she took the first sip, she heard the break for local news.

Carl W. Patterson was the top story. Dispassionately she listened to the newscaster recite the press release she and the publicist had written over the phone the night before. It gave a great deal more information on Carl's career than it did on his illness, and she knew Carl would have given it his nod of approval. The report ended by saying that Toni DuMonde, Patterson's house-mate and fiancée, could not be reached for comment.

At least the woman wasn't a fool, Johanna thought as she chose a seat. There were some, she knew, who would have spilled their guts to the press and enjoyed the melodrama. And if Toni had, Johanna imagined, Carl would have cut whatever strings tied them together as soon as he was able.

"Miss Patterson?"

Johanna rose automatically. The moment she saw the doctor, her calm fled. The nurse had said Carl was rest-ing comfortably, but that was hospital talk. She fought back the touch of fear and offered her hand.

"Dr. Merritt, I hope I'm not too early." Or too late.

"No, as a matter of fact your father's awake and sta-ble. As a matter of precaution we'll keep him in CCU for another twenty-four hours. If he continues to prog-ress, he can be moved to a private room."

"The prognosis?"

"The prognosis is good, if he cooperates. A lighter work load is essential. How much influence do you have over him?"

Her smile was almost amused. "None at all."

"Well, then, he might find himself confined to the hospital a day or two longer than he's counting on." Merritt took off his glasses to polish the lenses on the hem of his coat. "As I explained to you last night, certain adjustments will have to be made. Mr. Patterson will have to realize that, like the rest of us, he has certain limitations."

"I understand. And I wish you the best of luck explaining the same to him."

"I've already spoken to him briefly." Merritt slid the glasses back on his nose. He gave Johanna a smile that was gone almost before it formed. "At the moment, it's more important to reassure him. We'll speak about future care soon enough. He's asked to see Miss Du-Monde and someone named Whitfield. It may be good for him to see his fiancée, but—"

"Don't worry about Whitfield. I'll handle it."

Merritt only nodded. He'd already decided Patterson's daughter had a good head on her shoulders. "Your father's a fortunate man. If he's sensible, there isn't any reason why he shouldn't lead a full and productive life."

"Can I see him?"

"Fifteen minutes only. He needs calm and quiet."

She was both as she walked into the small curtained-off room in CCU. Her father was as he'd been the night before, eyes closed, wired to machines. But his color was better. She stood by the bed, studying him, until his eyes flickered open.

It took him a moment to focus. It occurred to Johanna that this was certainly the longest their eyes had ever held. When she saw recognition in his, she bent to brush his cheek with hers.

"Good morning," she said, keeping her voice carefully neutral. "You gave us a scare."

"Johanna." He took her hand, surprising her. He'd never been quite so alone or quite so weak. "What have they told you?"

Why, he's frightened, she thought, and felt a stirring of sympathy. It had never occurred to her that he could be frightened. "That you're a fortunate man," she said briskly. "And that if you're sensible the world will still see quite a number of Carl W. Patterson Productions."

It was exactly the right thing to say. She hadn't realized she'd known him so well. "Damned inconvenient time for my body to set booby traps for me." He glanced around the room, and the moment of closeness vanished.

"The hospital's contacting Toni," Johanna told him. "I'm sure she'll be here soon."

Satisfied, Carl looked back at his daughter. "They say they intend to keep me strapped down here another day."

"Yes. More if you make a fuss."

"I've work to do that can't be done from a hospital bed."

"Fine. I'll tell them to release you. You might be able to edit *Fields of Fire* before you keel over again."

His expression changed from impatience to astonishment, then to something she'd rarely seen directed at her—amusement. "I suppose I could spare a few days. But I don't want that ham-handed Whitfield to get his hands on it."

"I've sent for Loman." His expression tightened immediately, and he became the cool, disapproving man she'd lived with most of her life. "I'm sorry if I overstepped my bounds, but when I contacted Whitfield last night and saw how things were, I thought you'd prefer Loman."

"All right, all right." He waved away her apology. "I do prefer Loman. Whitfield has his place, but God knows it's not in an editing room. What about the press?"

He'd forgotten to be frightened. Johanna thought, and bit back a sigh. It was business as usual. "Under control. Your publicist issued a release this morning and will update it as becomes necessary."

"Good, good. I'll meet with Loman this afternoon. Set that up for me, Johanna."

"No."

The effort of making plans had already sapped his strength, and that only made him more furious. "No? What the hell do you mean, no?"

"It's out of the question." Her voice was calm, which pleased her. There had been a time he could have used that tone and made her quake. "It should be all right in a day or two, once you're in a private room and stronger."

"I run my own life."

"No one's more aware of that than I."

"If you've got some idea about taking over while I'm down—"

The fury leaped into her eyes and stopped him cold. He'd never seen that look before, or the power behind it. Or, if it had been there, he'd never bothered to look. "I don't want anything from you. I did once, but I learned to live without it. Now, if you'll excuse me, I've got a show of my own to produce."

"Johanna." She started to whip the curtain aside. It was the tremor in his voice that stopped her.

"Yes?"

"I apologize."

Another first, she thought, and made herself turn back. "All right. The doctor told me not to stay long, and I've probably already overtired you."

"I almost died."

He said it like an old man, an old, frightened man. "You're going to be fine."

"I almost died," he repeated. "And though I can't say my life flashed in front of my eyes, I did screen a few clips." He closed his eyes. It infuriated him that he had to stop just to gather the strength to speak. "I remember getting in the back of the limo—on my way to the airport, I think. You were standing on the steps with that dog Max forced on me. You looked as though you wanted to call me back."

Johanna didn't remember that particular incident because there'd been so many of them. "If I had, would you have stayed?"

"No." He sighed, not with regret but with acknowledgement. "Work has always come first. I've never been able to put a marriage together the way I could a film. Your mother—"

"I don't want to talk about my mother."

Carl opened his eyes again. "She could have loved you more if she'd hated me less."

It hurt. Even having known it all these years, it hurt to hear it said aloud. "And you?"

"Work has always come first," he repeated. He was

tired, much too tired for regrets or apologies. "Will you come back?"

"Yes. I'll come back after the taping."

He was asleep before she drew the curtain aside.

Max Heddison's estate was as distinguished and well-tended as the man. Sam was ushered through the thirty-room house the actor had purchased a quarter of a century before. On the terrace were thickly padded chaises and half a dozen wicker chairs that invited company to spread out and be comfortable. An aging golden retriever was curled up in one, snoring.

In the sparkling L-shaped pool beyond the terrace, Max Heddison was doing laps. Across the sloping lawn, partially hidden by squared-off hedges, were tennis courts. To the east, identifiable only by a distant flag, was a putting green.

A houseboy in a spotless white jacket offered Sam his choice of chairs. Sun or shade. Sam chose the sun. As he watched, Sam counted ten laps, cleanly stroked and paced, and wondered idly how many Max had done before he'd arrived. The official bio said Max was seventy. It could have taken off fifteen years and still have been believable.

He accepted coffee and waited while Max hauled himself out of the pool.

"Good to see you again." Max dragged a towel over his hair before he shrugged into a robe.

"I appreciate you letting me drop by this way." Sam had risen automatically.

"Sit down, boy, you make me feel like a king about to be deposed. Had breakfast?"

"Yes, thanks."

The moment Max sat, the houseboy was back with a tray of fresh fruit and dry toast. "Thank you, Jose. Bring Mr. Weaver some juice. Straight from our own oranges," he told Sam. "I figure it only costs me about three dollars a glass." With a grin, he dug into his breakfast. "My wife's the health nut. No additives, no preservatives. Enough to drive a man to drink. She's at her morning class, which means I'll have time to sneak a cigarette before she gets back."

Sam's juice was served in cut crystal. He sipped, letting Max fall into a conversation about pruning and organic sprays.

"Well, I don't suppose you came here to discuss fertilizers." Max pushed his tray aside and reached in his pocket for a pack of unfiltered cigarettes. "What did you think of the script?"

"Who do I have to kill to get the part?"

Max chuckled and drew in smoke with great pleasure. "I'll hold that in reserve. You know, I don't care too much for today's moviemakers—money-makers, I should say. In the old days, men like Mayer might have been despots, but they knew how to make films. Today they're a bunch of damn accountants running around with ledgers and red pencils—more interested in profit than entertainment. But my gut tells me we might be able to give them both with this one."

"It made my palms sweat," Sam said simply.

"I know the feeling." Max settled back, regretting only that his cigarette was nearly done. "I've been making movies since before you were born. Over eighty of them, and only a handful ever made me feel that way."

"I want to thank you for thinking of me."

"No need for that. Ten pages into the script and your name popped into my head. It was still there when I finished." He crushed out his cigarette, sighing. "And, of course, I went straight to my consultant with it— my wife." He grinned, drank more coffee and thought it a pity his wife had ordered decaf. "I've relied on her opinion for over forty years."

It made Sam remember how important it had been for him to hear Johanna's opinion.

"She finished it, handed it back to me and said if I didn't do it I was crazy. Then she told me to get young Sam Weaver to play Michael. By the way, she admires your…build," Max said. "My sainted wife's an earthy woman."

The grin came quickly and lingered. "I'd love to meet her."

"We'll arrange it. Did I mention that Kincaid's been signed to direct?"

"No." Sam's interest was piqued again. "You don't get much better."

"Thought the same myself." Max watched Sam thoughtfully from under his bushy white brows. "Patterson's producing." He saw Sam's eyes sharpen and reached casually for more coffee. "Problem?"

"There might be." He wanted the part, more than he could remember wanting any other. But not at the cost of his still-too-tenuous relationship with Johanna.

"If you're concerned about Jo-Jo, I don't think it's necessary. The complete professional, our Jo-Jo. And she respects her father's work." He saw the dull anger in Sam's eyes and nodded. "So, it's gotten that far, has it? I wasn't sure Johanna would ever let anyone get that close."

"It wasn't so much a matter of choice as circumstance." He hadn't come just to talk about the script. When Sam had called to make the appointment, he'd already decided to dig for whatever Max might have buried. "I take it you haven't heard that Patterson had a heart attack last night."

"No." The concern came automatically. The friendship went back a quarter of a century. "I haven't so much as flicked the news on today. I go for days at a time without it. How bad?"

"Bad enough. As far as I know, he's stable. Johanna went back to the hospital this morning."

"He lives hard," Max mused. "Carl never seemed to be able to settle down long enough to enjoy what he was working for. I hope he still gets the chance." Max tipped back in his chair and looked out over the pool, the grounds. "You know, I have three children of my own. Five grandchildren now, and the first great-grandchild on the way. There were times I wasn't there for them, and I'll always regret it. Holding a family and a career together in this business is like juggling eggs. There's always some breakage."

"Some people juggle better than others."

"True enough. It takes a lot of effort and more than a few concessions to make it work."

"It seems to me that in Johanna's case she made all the concessions."

Max said nothing for a moment. He considered having another cigarette but decided his wife's sensitive nose would find him out. "I hate old men who poke into young people's business. Ought to be out playing checkers or feeding pigeons. But…just how serious are you about Jo-Jo?"

"We're going to get married," Sam heard himself say, to his own astonishment. "As soon as I talk her into it."

"Good luck. And that comes from the heart. I've always had a soft spot for that girl." Max poured another cup of coffee and knew he was a long way from ready to feed pigeons. "How much did she tell you?"

"Enough to make me understand I've got an uphill battle."

"And how much do you love her?"

"Enough to keep climbing."

Max decided to risk a second cigarette. If his wife came sniffing around, he could always blame it on Sam. He lit it slowly, savoring the taste. "I'm going to tell you things she wouldn't appreciate me saying. Whether it'll give you an edge or not I can't say. I can tell you I hope it does."

"I appreciate it."

With the smoke trailing lazily from between his fingers, Max looked back. A long way. "I knew her mother well. A beautiful woman. A glorious face. Bone structure always makes the difference. Johanna favors her physically, but it ends there. I can say I've never known anyone more completely her own woman than Johanna."

"Neither have I," Sam murmured. "It doesn't always make it easy."

"You're too young to want things easy," Max told him from the comfortable perspective of seven decades. "When something comes easy, you usually let it go the same way. That's my philosophy for the day.

Now, Glenna was selfish, driven by her own demons.
She married Carl after a brief and very torrid affair.
Affairs were just as torrid thirty years ago, only a bit
more discreet."

He drew in smoke and remembered a few of his
own. Though he'd let them go without regret upon his
marriage, he could still be grateful for the experience.

"They were a golden couple, the photographers' dar-
lings. Carl was dark, ruggedly handsome, broad shouldered. Glenna was almost waiflike, pale, fragile. They
threw incredible parties and incredible tantrums. To be
honest, I quite enjoyed both. You may have heard I was
a hellion in my youth."

"I heard you were a hellion," Sam agreed. "But I
didn't hear it was something in the past."

"We'll work well together," Max declared. He took
one last drag before crushing the second cigarette out.
"When Glenna was pregnant, she spent thousands dec-
orating the nursery. Then she started to lose her figure
and went on a rampage. She could sit for a photographer
like a Madonna, then toss back a Scotch and curse like
a sailor. Glenna had no middle ground."

"Johanna told me she was ill, a manic-depressive."

"Perhaps. I don't pretend to understand psychiatry.
I will say she was weak—not weak-minded, but weak-
spirited—and tormented by the fact that she was never
as successful as she needed to be. There was talent in
her, real talent, but she didn't have the drive or the grit
to stay on top. It became easy for her to blame Carl
for that, and the marriage. Then it became easier to
blame the child. After Johanna was born, Glenna went
through phases of being a devoted, loving mother. Then

she'd be almost obscenely neglectful. The marriage was crumbling. Carl had affairs, she had affairs, and neither of them ever considered putting the child first. Not in their nature, Sam," he added when he saw the fury flare. "That's not an excuse, of course, but it is a reason. Carl wouldn't have cared if Glenna had had one child or thirty. He'd had no more than a passing interest. When the break finally came, Glenna used the child as a weapon. I don't mean to make Carl a hero, but at least he never used Johanna. Unfortunately, she was never that important to him."

"How could two people like that ever have someone like Johanna?"

"Another question for the ages."

"Is Patterson her father?"

Max lifted both brows. "Why do you ask?"

It was a confidence he felt he had to break. Not for himself. Sam had already decided her parentage meant less than nothing to him, but the truth would be important to Johanna.

"Because when she was still a child, Johanna found a letter her mother had written to Patterson right after she'd gone back to England. She told him she'd never been sure if he was Johanna's father."

"Good God." Max ran a hand over his face. "I had no idea about that. It's a wonder it didn't destroy Johanna."

"No, she wasn't destroyed, but it did plenty of damage."

"Poor little Jo-Jo," Max murmured. "She was always such a lonely little girl. Spent more time with the gardener than anyone else. It might not have mattered if Carl had been different. I wish she'd come to me with this."

"I don't think she's told anyone about it until last night."

"You'd better not let her down."

"I don't intend to."

Max fell silent for a time, thinking. Johanna's parents had been his friends. He'd been able to accept them for what they were and for what they weren't, all the while regretting it for the child's sake.

"For what it's worth, I'd say the letter was pure spite and total nonsense. If another man had fathered Johanna, Glenna would have blurted it out long before the separation. She could never keep a secret for more than two hours. Make that two minutes if you added a drink. Carl knew that." His face clouded as he hunched over the table. "I'm sorry to say that if Carl had suspected Johanna wasn't his flesh and blood he never would have kept her under his roof. He'd have put her on a plane to her mother without a backward glance."

"That doesn't make him a saint."

"No, but it does make him Johanna's father."

"We have something special for our home audience," John Jay began, giving the camera a brilliant smile. "If you've been listening this week, you know that our Drive American contest is already underway. We at *Trivia Alert* are very excited about having the chance to show all of you at home how much we appreciate you. To win, all you have to do is watch and answer. Every day this week, sometime during the show, I'll be asking questions. Today it's time to tell you at home what you have a chance to win."

He paused, giving the announcer the time to describe the cars and eligibility requirements. As requested, the studio audience applauded and cheered.

"The week of Fourth of July," John Jay continued on cue, "one of you at home will win not one but both luxury cars. All you have to do is answer five questions in order. Send your answers to Trivia Alert, Drive American, Post Office Box 1776, Burbank, California 91501. Now for today's question."

There was a dramatic pause as he drew the sealed envelope from the slot. "Question number three. What is the name of Captain America's alter ego? Write down your answer and be sure to tune in tomorrow for the fourth question. All complete sets of correct answers will be part of a random drawing. Now, back to our game."

Johanna checked her watch and wondered how she could get through two more segments. They were already behind schedule due to a delay caused by an over-enthusiastic member of the studio audience who had called out answers during the speed round. They'd had to stop, reset, calm the contestant and begin again with a new batch of questions. Usually she took that sort of thing in stride, but somewhere along the way her stride had broken. For the past few hours, Johanna had been struggling to find her pace again.

When the segment ended, she nearly groaned with relief. She had fifteen minutes before they would begin again. "Beth, I have to make a call. I'll be in the office if a crisis comes up."

Without waiting for a response, she hurried off the set. At the end of the corridor a small room was set up with the essentials. A phone, a desk and a chair. Making use of all three, Johanna called the hospital. She still had ten minutes left when she learned that Carl had been downgraded from critical to serious condition. She was rubbing her eyes and thinking about another cup of coffee when the door opened.

"Beth, if it isn't a matter of life and death, put it on hold."

"It might be."

She straightened immediately at the sound of Sam's voice. "Oh, hello. I didn't expect you."

"You don't expect me nearly often enough." He closed the door behind him. "How are you doing?"

"Not bad."

"Your father?"

"Better. They think he can be moved out of CCU tomorrow."

"That's good." He came over to the desk and sat on the edge before giving her a long, critical study. "You're dead on your feet, Johanna. Let me take you home."

"We haven't finished, and I promised to stop by the hospital after the taping."

"Okay, I'll go with you."

"No, please. It's not necessary, and I'd be lousy company tonight."

He looked down at her hands. They were linked together tightly. Deliberately he took them in his own and separated them. "Are you trying to pull back, Johanna?"

"No. I don't know." She took a long breath, and her hands relaxed in his. "Sam, I appreciate what you did for me last night more than I can ever tell you—the way you listened and didn't judge. You were there when I needed you, and I'll never forget it."

"Sounds like a kiss-off," he murmured.

"No, of course it isn't. But you should understand now why I feel so strongly about being involved with you. Why it won't work."

"I must be pretty stupid, because I don't. I do understand why you're scared. Johanna, we have to talk."

"I have to get back. There's only a few more minutes."

"Sit down," he told her as she started to rise. She might have ignored the order, but the look in his eyes had her sitting again. "I'll try to make it quick. Time's either a blessing or a curse now, anyway. I've got to fly East the day after tomorrow to start filming."

"Oh." She dug deep for a smile. "Well, that's good. I know you've been anxious to start."

"I'll be gone three weeks, probably more. It isn't possible for me to put this off."

"Of course not. I hope—well, I hope you let me know how it's going."

"Johanna, I want you to come with me."

"What?"

"I said I want you to come with me."

"I—I can't. How could I? I have my job, and—"

"I'm not asking you to make a choice between your job and us. Any more than I'd expect you to ask me to make one between mine and the way I feel about you."

"No, of course I wouldn't."

"I'd like to think you meant that." He paused a moment, searching her face. "The script that Max sent me—I want to do it."

"You should do it. It's perfect for you."

"Maybe, but I want to know if it's perfect for you. Your father's producing it, Johanna."

"Oh." She looked down at her hands a moment, hands that were still caught in his. "Well, then, you've got the best."

"I want to know how you feel about it, Johanna. How you really feel."

"It's more a matter of how you feel."

"Not this time. Don't make me use pliers."

"Sam, your professional choices have to be yours, but I'd say you'd be a fool not to grab a chance to work with Max and Patterson Productions. That script might have been written for you, and I'd be disappointed if I didn't see you in it."

"Always sensible."

"I hope so."

"Then be sensible about this. Take a few days off and come east with me." Before she could protest again, he was continuing. "You've got a tight crew, Johanna. I've seen them work firsthand. You know they could run things for a couple of weeks."

"I suppose, but not without any notice. Then there's my father..." She let her words trail off. There must have been dozens of reasons, but they seemed to slide away before she could get a grip on them.

"All right. Take a week to make sure your crew is on top of things and that your father's recovering. Then fly out and meet me."

"Why?"

"I wondered when you'd ask." He reached in his pocket to pull out a box. Through his life he'd done a great many things on impulse. This wasn't one of them. He'd thought it through carefully, and had kept coming up with one answer. He needed her. "Things like this usually speak for themselves." After opening the lid, he took her hand and set the box in her palm. "I want you to marry me."

She stared at the single flawless diamond. It was square-cut, very classic and simple. The kind of ring, Johanna thought, girls dreamed about when they thought of white chargers and castles in the sky.

"I can't."

"Can't what?"

"I can't marry you. You know I can't. I had no idea you'd started thinking like this."

"Neither had I, until today. When Marv called I knew I had two choices. I could go East and stew about it or I could take the step and let you stew about it." He touched her hair, just the tips. "I'm sure, Johanna."

"I'm sorry." She offered the box back to him. When he didn't take it, she set it on the desk. "I don't want to hurt you, you know I don't. That's why I can't."

"It's about time you unloaded some of the baggage you've been carrying around, Johanna." Rising, he drew her up with him. "We both know what we've got doesn't come along every day. You might think you're doing me a favor by turning me down, but you're wrong. Dead wrong."

His fingers tangled in her hair as he kissed her. Unable to deny him—or herself—she curled her arms up his back until she gripped his shoulders. She held on to him even while her mind whirled with dozens of questions.

"Do you believe me when I tell you I love you?" he demanded.

"Yes." She held him tighter, burying her face against his shoulder to absorb his scent. "Sam, I don't want you to go. I know you have to, and I know how much I'll miss you, but I can't give you what you want. If I could…if I could you're the only one I'd give it to."

He hadn't expected to hear even that much. Another man might have been discouraged, but he'd run into too many walls in his life to be put off by one more. Particularly since he had every intention of tearing this one down, brick by brick.

He pressed a kiss to her temple. "I already know what I need and what I want." He drew her away until their eyes met. "You'd better start thinking about yourself, Johanna. About what you want, what you need. Just you. I figure you're smart enough to come up with an answer before too long." He kissed her again until she was breathless. "Keep in touch."

She didn't have the strength to do anything but sink into the chair when he left her. The show was starting, but she continued to sit, staring at the ring he'd left behind.

CHAPTER TWELVE

The man was playing games. Johanna knew it, and though she tried not to nibble at the bait, she was already being reeled in. He'd been gone two weeks, and she hadn't gotten a single phone call.

But there had been flowers.

They'd arrived every evening. Black-eyed Susans one day, white orchids another. She couldn't walk into any room of her house without thinking of him. After the first week they'd begun to arrive at her office—a small clutch of violets, a huge bouquet of tea roses. She couldn't even escape from him there.

The man was definitely playing, and he wasn't playing fair.

Of course, she wasn't going to marry him. That was absurd. She didn't believe people could love, honor and cherish for a lifetime. She'd told him so, and she'd been sorry, but she had no intention of changing her mind.

She might carry the ring with her—for safekeeping, that is—but she hadn't taken it out of its box. At least not more than two or three times.

She was grateful that her work load had intensified so that she was unceasingly busy. It didn't leave much time to mope around missing him. Unless you counted the long, solitary nights when she kept listening for the phone.

He'd told her to keep in touch, but he hadn't told her where he'd be staying. If she'd wanted to, she could have found out easily enough. It did happen that a few discreet inquiries had put the name and address of his hotel in her hands, but that didn't mean she would call him. If she called, he'd know she'd gone to some trouble—damn it, a great deal of trouble—to find out where he was.

Then he would know she'd not only nibbled at the bait but swallowed it whole.

By the end of the second week, she was furious with him. He'd pushed her into a corner where she didn't want to be, wedged her in and then strolled off, leaving her trapped. A man didn't ask a woman to marry him, drop a ring in her hand, then waltz off.

Once she'd considered putting the ring in the mail and shipping it off to him. That had been at three o'clock in the morning on the fifteenth day. Johanna had rolled over, slammed the pillow a few satisfactory times and vowed to do just that the minute the post office opened in the morning.

She would have, too, if she hadn't been running a few minutes late. Then she'd been tied up at lunchtime and unable to get five free minutes until after six. She decided against mailing it, thinking it would be more civil and courteous to throw it in his face when he got back into town.

It was just her bad luck he'd chosen to send forget-me-nots that day. They happened to be one of her particular favorites.

As the third week approached, she was a wreck. Johanna knew she deserved the wary glances of her staff. She pushed through Monday's taping, growling at every interruption. Her excuse was that she'd agreed to take duplicates to her father that evening.

He wasn't particularly interested in the show, she knew, but his recuperation wasn't sitting well with him. He wanted to live badly enough to follow his doctor's orders, but that didn't mean he couldn't review everything Patterson Productions had a part in. Johanna waited impatiently for the copies, pacing the set and toying with the ring box in her pocket.

"Here you go." Bethany put on an exaggerated smile. "Try not to gnaw on them on the way home."

Johanna dumped them in her bag. "I'll need you here by nine. We can work until it's time to set up for taping."

"Whatever you say."

Johanna narrowed her eyes at the overbright tone. "Have you got a problem?"

"Me?" All innocence, Bethany opened her eyes wide. "No, not me. Well, there is my back."

"Your back? What's wrong with it?"

"It's nothing really. It always aches a bit when I've been flogged."

Johanna opened her mouth, then shut it again on a puff of air. "I'm sorry. I guess I've been a little edgy."

"Just a tad. Funny, if someone had been sending me flowers every day for weeks I'd be a bit more cheerful."

"He thinks that's all it takes to twist me around his finger."

"There are worse positions to be in. Forget I said it," Bethany said immediately, holding up a hand. "There's nothing more diabolical than sending a basket of tiger lilies. The man's obviously slime."

For the first time in days, Johanna smiled. "He's wonderful."

The smile confirmed what Johanna's scowls had already told her. "You miss him?"

"Yes, I miss him. Just like he knew I would."

Bethany looked at romance in the most straightforward of terms. If you cared, you showed it, then put all your energy into making it work. Her solution for Johanna was just as simple. "You know, Johanna, it's the same distance from the West to the East Coast as it is from East to West."

She'd already thought of going. Not that she'd *considered* it, but she had thought of it. "No, I can't." She fingered the box in her pocket. "It wouldn't be fair to him."

"Because?"

"Because I won't…can't…" On impulse she pulled the box out and opened it. "Because of this."

"Oh, my." Bethany couldn't help the long-drawn-out sigh. "My, oh, my," she managed, already smelling orange blossoms. "Congratulations, best wishes and bon voyage. Where's a bottle of champagne when you need it?"

"No, I didn't accept it. I'm not going to. I told him no."

"Then why do you still have it?"

Because the question was so reasonable, Johanna could only frown and stare at the diamond while it winked at her. "He just dropped it in my hand and walked off."

"Romantic devil, isn't he?"

"Well, it wasn't exactly— That's close enough," she decided. "It was more of an ultimatum than a proposal, but either way, I told him no."

It sounded wonderfully romantic to Bethany. She stuck her tongue in her cheek. "So you just decided to walk around with it in your pocket for a few days."

"No, I..." There had to be a reasonable excuse. "I wanted to have it handy so I could give it back to him."

Bethany thought that over, then tilted her head. "I think that's the first lie I've ever heard you tell."

"I don't know why I've still got it." Johanna closed the box with a snap, then pushed it into her pocket. "It's not important."

"No, I've never thought proposals of marriage or gorgeous engagement rings were anything to get excited about." She put a hand on Johanna's shoulder. "What you need is some fresh air."

"I don't believe in marriage."

"That's like not believing in Santa Claus." At Johanna's lifted brow, Bethany shook her head. "Johanna, don't tell me you don't believe in him, either? He might be something of a fantasy, but he's been around a while, and he's going to stay around."

It was hard to argue with that kind of logic. Johanna decided she was too tired to try. "We'll talk about the logic of that some other time. I have to drop off these tapes." With Bethany beside her, she started out. "I'd like you to keep this to yourself."

"It goes with me to the grave."

"You're good for me," Johanna said with a laugh. "I'm going to be sorry to lose you."

"Am I fired?"

"Sooner or later you're going to fire me. You won't be content to be anyone's assistant for long." Outside, Johanna took a deep breath. So much had changed since she'd walked with Bethany from the studio weeks before. "Leaving Santa Claus out of it, do you believe in marriage, Beth?"

"I'm just an old-fashioned girl with strong feminist underpinnings. Yeah, I believe in marriage as long as two people are willing to give it their best shot."

"You know what the odds are of a marriage making it in this town?"

"Lousy. But strikeout or home run, you've got to step up to bat. See you tomorrow."

"Good night, Beth."

She did a great deal of thinking as she drove to Beverly Hills. Not all of it was clear, but every thought circled back to Sam. Johanna was coming to realize that her thoughts would, whether she was with or without him.

The gates were locked, as they always were. Reaching out, she pressed the button on the intercom and waited for her father's housekeeper to ask her name. In moments the gates opened soundlessly.

The drive toward the house didn't stir any childish memories. She saw the estate as an adult. Perhaps she always had. It was stunning—the white columns, the terraces and balconies. The exterior had changed little from her earliest recollections.

Inside, it had gone through major overhauls, depending on its mistress. Her mother had preferred the feminine and delicate look of *Louis Quinze*. Darlene had chosen art nouveau, right down to the light fixtures. Its last mistress had gone for the opulently elegant. Johanna didn't think it would take Toni long to put her stamp on it.

The door was opened for her by the gray-uniformed maid before she'd reached the top of the wide, curved steps.

"Good evening, Miss Patterson."

"Good evening. Is Mr. Patterson expecting me?"

"He and Miss DuMonde are in the sitting room."

"Thank you."

Johanna crossed the glossy tiles, skirting the fish pond her father's last wife had installed. She found her father looking well, and impatient, in a dark blue smoking jacket. Toni sprawled lazily on the sofa across from him, sipping wine and flipping through a magazine. Johanna nearly smiled when she saw that it was one on home fashion and decoration.

"I expected you an hour ago," Carl said without preamble.

"We ran late." She took the tapes from her bag to set them on the table beside him. "You're looking well."

"There's nothing wrong with me."

"Carl's a bit bored." Toni stretched herself into a sitting position. She wore silk lounging pajamas the color of ripe peaches. The pout she wore went with them beautifully. "Perhaps you can entertain him better than I." Rising, she stalked gracefully out of the room.

Johanna lifted a brow. "Have I come at a bad time?"

"No." Carl pushed himself up and headed for the bar. Johanna bit back a protest and was relieved when he poured club soda. "Do you want anything?"

"No, thank you. I can't stay."

Carl halfheartedly added a twist of lime. "I assumed you'd stay until I'd previewed the tapes."

"You don't need me for that." He wanted company, she realized. Because she remembered how old and alone he'd looked in the hospital, she relented. "I could put them in for you, answer whatever questions you might have about the first segment or two."

"I've seen the show before, Johanna. I doubt I'd have any questions about my own show."

"No." She picked up the bag she'd just set down. "Then I'll leave you to it."

"Johanna." He cleared his throat and he turned back, then took his seat again. "You've done a good job with it."

This time both brows rose. "Thank you." She set her bag down again and checked her watch.

"If you've got some damn appointment, go on, then."

"No, actually, I was just marking the time. Since it's

the first time in my life you've ever complimented me on anything, I want to remember when it happened."

"There's no need to be sarcastic."

"Maybe not." She crossed the room to sit but stayed on the edge of her chair. She'd never been comfortable in this house. "I'm glad you're doing so well. If you're interested, I can see that you get dupes of tomorrow's taping for the evening shows. We're giving away a trip for two to Puerto Vallarta during the speed round."

He only grunted at that. Johanna folded her hands and continued. "If a contestant reaches the winner's circle and can answer all of the questions himself, without deferring to his partner, he'll win a car. We're using a sedan this week. Four-door."

"I'm not interested in the prizes."

"I thought not, but you might prefer a different angle or see a flaw when you preview. I'm sure you know that you can accomplish as much here as most men can in an office."

"I won't be sitting here forever."

"There's no question of that." No, he would be back, full steam, very soon. Maybe this was the time, the only time. "Before I go, I'd like to ask you something."

"If it has to do with the new pilot, I've already seen it and approved it."

"No, it's personal."

He sat, cradling his glass. He didn't mind giving up liquor half so much as doing without his cigars. Rather than answer, he simply nodded for her to go on.

"Why do you want to marry Toni DuMonde?"

As far as Carl was concerned, the question had come out of left field. No one questioned his motives or his reasons. "I'd say that was between Toni and myself. If you're uncomfortable with the age difference—"

"It would hardly matter to me if there was twice as much difference as there already is," Johanna said. "I'm just curious."

"I'm marrying her because I want to."

Johanna sat for a minute, studying him. Maybe it was just that simple with Carl. I want, I do. I covet, I take. "Do you plan to stay married to her?"

"As long as it suits both of us."

She smiled a little and nodded. That, at least, was the unvarnished truth. "Why did you marry my mother?"

If her first question had surprised him, this one left him speechless. Staring at Johanna, he saw the resemblance he'd always ignored. But there was more character in this face. More courage. "Why are you bringing this up now? You never asked about her before."

"Maybe I should have. We began to talk about her when you were in the hospital, but I suppose I wasn't ready. Now I have a decision of my own to make, and I can't do it until I understand a little better. Did you love her?"

"Of course. She was beautiful, fascinating. We were both building our careers. There wasn't a man who met Glenna in those days who didn't love her."

She didn't find reasons for love and fidelity in those answers. "But you're the only one who married her. And the only one who divorced her."

"The marriage was a mistake," he said, abruptly uncomfortable. "We both realized it before the first year was out. Not that we weren't attracted to each other. As I said, she was beautiful, very delicate. You favor her."

His glass paused halfway to his lips when he saw her expression. Perhaps he'd never been a loving father, but he'd always been an astute man. "If you're concerned about her health, don't be. Glenna was always erratic. Drinking made her more so, but I've never seen any part of that in you. Believe me, I've watched for it."

"Have you?" Johanna murmured.

"You've never been one for extremes," he went on. "Apparently you inherited enough from me to offset the rest."

"Did I?" This time her voice was firm and her eyes level. "I've always wondered what, if anything, I inherited from you."

His look was so blank that she couldn't believe he feigned it. "You're a producer, aren't you? And a good one. That should say something. The Pattersons have always been strong, practical people. Ambitious. I'd say, now that I think of it, that you take after my grandmother. She was strong minded, never one to sit around and let the world go by. Got the hair from her, too," he decided, looking thoroughly at his daughter for the first time in years.

A little dazed, Johanna reached up to touch her hair. "*Your* grandmother?"

"Didn't get it from your mother," he said with a sour laugh. "Got hers from her hairdresser. That was one of her most prized secrets. Hers was brown, mousy brown. God knows you didn't get your drive from her. That's the Patterson in you." He didn't say it with pride, just stated it as fact.

So this was her father after all. Johanna sat, waiting for a flood of feeling. When none came, she sighed.

Nothing had really changed. Then her lips curved. Then again, maybe everything had.

"I'd like to hear about her sometime. Your grandmother." She rose, taking a look at her watch in earnest. "I really have to go. I'm going to be out of town. Everything should run smoothly enough without me for a few days."

"Out of town? When?"

"Tonight."

Johanna caught the last plane out. She'd had just enough time before final boarding to call Bethany and give her quick and not completely coherent instructions about the next day's business and the care and feeding of her cat. Bethany had been awakened out of a sound sleep, but she could be depended on.

Strapped in, Johanna watched L.A., and the resolutions she'd lived with all of her life, slip away. She'd taken a step, the largest one of her life, without even being sure she would land on solid ground.

Somewhere over Nevada she dozed, then woke over New Mexico in a kind of blind panic. What in God's name was she doing, traveling thousands of miles without so much as a toothbrush? It wasn't like her not to plan or make lists. They were taping the next day. Who would handle the details, check the staff? Who would deal with John Jay?

Someone else, she told herself. For once it would just have to be someone else.

She traveled from one coast to the other, sleeping in fits and starts and wondering if she'd lost her mind. In Houston she nearly lost her nerve, as well. But she changed planes and strapped in a second time, determined to see it through.

Perhaps she wasn't being smart or responsible, but everyone was entitled to do something on impulse once. Even if they lived to regret it.

Almost certain she would, she arrived in Baltimore just after dawn. The terminal was deserted except for a few napping passengers waiting for connections. The air was cool in Maryland, and she was grateful for her suit jacket. The same jacket, Johanna remembered, that she'd put on that morning when she'd still been sane. The sky, full of pewter clouds, promised rain as she climbed into a cab and gave the driver the name of Sam's hotel.

This was it, she told herself. It helped a little to close her eyes and ignore the unfamiliar landscape. If she didn't watch it, she wouldn't think too much about being on the other side of the country. In L.A. people were rolling over in bed, snuggling into pillows with morning still hours away. Here they were waking up, preparing to face the day.

So was she.

She paid off the driver and tried not to think. The rain began as she walked into the lobby.

Suite 621. At least she knew the number, so she'd be spared the embarrassment of going to the desk and convincing the clerk she wasn't a fan. Clutching the strap of her bag, she rode to the sixth floor. It was easy enough to step from the elevator. She even managed to walk down the hall to his door.

Then she stared at it.

What if he didn't want her there? What if he wasn't

alone? After all, she had no claim on him, had made no promises. She'd refused to accept, even to listen to, his promises. He was free to…to do whatever he wanted, with whomever he wanted.

Certain she couldn't go through with it, she turned away and took two steps back from the door.

It was absurd, she told herself. She'd just spent hours in a plane, traveled thousands of miles, and now she couldn't even get up the nerve to knock on a door.

With her shoulders straight and her chin up, she knocked. When her stomach rolled, she reached in her pocket automatically for her antacids. Her fingers closed over the small velvet box. She drummed up her courage and knocked again.

He woke swearing. They'd worked until after two, and he'd barely had the energy to strip before tumbling into bed. Now the damn assistant director was banging on the door. Any idiot knew they couldn't film any of the scheduled outside shots in the rain.

Groggy and full of the desire for vengeance, Sam dragged the top sheet from the bed and wrapped it around him. He tripped over the hem, cursed again, then yanked open the door.

"Goddamn it—" His mouth dried up. He had to be dreaming. Johanna was a continent away, snuggled under the covers. Then he saw her lips curve before she began to stumble out an apology.

"I'm sorry I woke you. I should have…waited. Called." *Stayed away,* she thought desperately.

Then she didn't think at all, because he was dragging her inside. The door slammed and she was pressed back against it, her mouth captive.

"Don't say a word," he ordered when she sucked in her breath. "Not a word. Not yet."

It would have been impossible to speak. Even as he pulled her through the sitting room, he was peeling off her jacket, fighting the buttons on her blouse. With a throaty laugh, she tugged at the sheet. It was left behind in a stream of white as they worked their way to the bedroom.

Her skirt slid down to her hips, and he lifted her out of it. While his hands played over her, she stepped out of one shoe. They were nearly at the bedroom door before she managed to rid herself of the other.

He wasn't even awake. Sam clung to the drowsy fingers of sleep as they fell onto the bed.

She was here. Dream or reality, she was here. Her skin was just as soft under his hands, just as fragrant. Her lips as they parted for his had the same unique flavor he'd craved since he'd tasted them last. At her sigh, as her arms locked around him, he heard everything he needed to hear.

Delighted with each other, they rolled over the already rumpled bed as the rain grew heavy and streaked the windows.

She'd been right to come. Whatever had happened before, whatever happened after, she'd been right to take this moment. And to give this time to him. There would be no questions, no need for explanations or excuses, just gladness that was racing harder and faster toward dazzling pleasure.

In tune, body and mind, they came together, taking that pleasure to its pinnacle.

The thunder started as he gathered her against him again. Or perhaps it had been there all along but they hadn't heard it. Now, as the storm rattled over the city, they were together and alone and in love. Sometimes that really was all that mattered.

She kept her hand on his heart and her head on his shoulder as they floated down to solid ground. The gloom kept the room dim, but for Johanna there had never been a more beautiful morning.

"Were you just passing through?" Sam murmured.

She spread her fingers over his chest, watching the movement. "I had urgent and unexpected business on the East Coast."

"I see." He hoped he did, but he could afford to wait. "You on a contestant search?"

"Not exactly." The nerves began leaking back. "I take it you don't have an early call today."

"If the rain keeps up, please God, I won't have one at all." Slowly, like a man who had all the time in the world, he stretched. "We were scheduled to shoot down at the Inner Harbor. Terrific place. Best crab I've ever eaten." He was already imagining showing it to her himself. "Once that's wrapped, we'll be finished here."

A pout, something she never allowed herself, formed on her lips. "You've run a little over your three weeks."

He certainly hoped it was annoyance he detected in her voice. "A little."

"I guess you've been too busy to call and let me know how things were going."

"No."

"No?" She propped herself on her elbow to frown at him.

"No, I haven't been too busy to call. I didn't call."

"Oh, I see." She started to push herself up and found herself flat on her back again with Sam leaning over her.

"I hope you don't think you're getting out of this room."

"I told you I have business."

"So you did. Is it a coincidence that you have business in Baltimore and just happen to be staying at the same hotel—apparently in my room?"

"I'm not staying."

"Guess again." He nipped her gently on the jaw. "Why did you come, Johanna?"

"I'd rather not discuss it. I'd like my clothes," she said stiffly.

"Sure. Let me get them for you." He strolled out, leaving Johanna with the dubious cover of a pillow. She started to rise when he came back in with her suit bundled in his arms. Then she could only gape, open-mouthed, as he opened the window and tossed them out.

"What in the hell are you doing?" She forgot the pillow as she leaped up and ran to the window. "You threw out my clothes." Dumbfounded, she could only stare at him. "You threw them out the window."

"Sure looks that way."

"Are you out of your mind? I flew out here with the shirt on my back, and now it's six floors down and soaked. I don't have anything to wear out of here but my shoes."

"I was counting on that. Seemed like the best way to guarantee your staying put."

"You *are* out of your mind." She started to crane out of the window, remembered she was naked, then dropped on the bed. "What am I supposed to do now?"

"Borrow another of my shirts, I guess. Help yourself." He gestured toward the closet. "You might toss me a pair of jeans while you're at it. It's hard for me to talk to you reasonably when we're not wearing anything but smiles."

"I'm not smiling," she told him between her teeth as she heaved jeans in his direction. "That was one of my best suits, and I—" Her fingers froze on the buttons of the shirt she'd pulled on. "Oh, God. Oh, my God, in the jacket. I had it in the jacket." With the shirt still half buttoned she jumped for the door. Sam was just quick enough to slam it closed before she ran out.

"I don't think you're dressed for a stroll, Johanna. Not that you don't look terrific. In fact, you look so terrific I think I'd like you to give me my shirt back."

"Will you stop being an idiot?" She tried to shove him aside but met with solid resistance. "You threw it out the window. I can't believe what a complete fool you are. You threw my ring out the window."

"Whose ring?"

"My ring, the one you gave me. Oh, for God's sake." She ducked under his arm to run to the window again. "Someone's going to take it."

"Your suit?"

"No, I don't care about the suit. The hell with the suit. I want my ring."

"All right. Here." Sam drew it off his pinky and offered it. "The box must have dropped out of your pocket when—when I said hello." Johanna had given a cry of relief and grabbed for it before she realized she'd been taken.

"Damn it, Sam, you had it all the time and you let me think it was gone."

"It was nice to know it was important to you." He held it between them. "Are you going to let me put it on you?"

"You can take it and—"

"I'm open to suggestions." Then he smiled at her in a way she found completely unfair. Even her temper failed her.

"I'd like to sit down a minute." She did, sinking into the bed. The relief was gone, and the anger. She'd come for a purpose. and it was time to see it through. "I came to see you."

"No? Really?"

"Don't make fun of me."

"All right." He sat beside her, draping an arm over her shoulders. "Then I guess I can tell you that if you hadn't come, or called within the next twenty-four hours, I was heading back, movie or no movie."

"You didn't call me."

"No, I didn't, because I think we both knew you had to make the next move. And I hope you suffered as much as I did." He pressed his lips to her hair. "So what's it going to be?"

"I want to tell you that I spoke with my father last night." She tilted her head so that she could look at him. "He is my father."

Gently he brushed her hair back from her face. "Is everything all right?"

"It's not like a story where everything turns out beautifully at the end, but it's all right. I don't suppose we'll ever be close, and I can accept that now. I'm not like him, nor like my mother, either. It's taken me all this time to figure out that that's okay. I'm okay."

He kissed her hair again, enjoying the fragrance as much as the familiarity. "I could have told you that, if you'd listened."

"I can listen now, now that I've told myself." With a

long breath, she took his hands in hers. "I need to ask you something, Sam. You could almost say it was the championship question."

"I work best under pressure."

But her eyes didn't smile. "Why do you want to marry me?"

"That's it?" His brows rose, and then he was laughing and holding her close. "I thought you were going to ask me a tough one. I want to marry you because I love you and I need you in my life. It changed when you walked into it."

"And tomorrow?"

"A two-part question," he murmured. "I could promise you anything." He drew her away to kiss her cheek, then her brow, then her lips. "I wish there were guarantees, but there aren't. I can only tell you that when I think about tomorrow, when I think about ten years from tomorrow, I think about you. I think about us."

He couldn't have said it better, she thought as she touched his face. No, there weren't any guarantees, but they had a chance. A good one.

"Can I ask you one more thing?"

"As long as I'm going to get an answer eventually."

"Do you believe in Santa Claus?"

What made it perfect, even more than perfect, was that he didn't even hesitate. "Sure. Doesn't everyone?"

Now she smiled, completely. "I love you, Sam."

"That's the answer I wanted."

"Looks like you win." She held out her hand so that he could slip the ring on her finger. It felt as though it belonged, and so did she. "Looks like we both do."

* * * * *